T0197911

HEAVY
HITTER

ALSO BY KATIE COTUGNO

Hemlock House

Meet the Benedettos

Liar's Beach

Birds of California

You Say It First

Rules for Being a Girl

9 Days and 9 Nights

Top Ten

Fireworks

99 Days

How to Love

HEAVY HITTER

A Novel

KATIE COTUGNO

HARPER PERENNIAL

NEW YORK • LONDON • TORONTO • SYDNEY • NEW DELHI • AUCKLAND

HARPER ● PERENNIAL

HarperCollins books may be purchased for educational, business, or sales promotional use. For information, please email the Special Markets Department at SPsales@harpercollins.com.

FIRST EDITION

Designed by Jamie Lynn Kerner
Microphone image © by Visual Generation/stock.adobe.com
Baseball image © by DELstudio/stock.adobe.com

Library of Congress Cataloging-in-Publication Data

Names: Cotugno, Katie, author.
Title: Heavy hitter: a novel / Katie Cotugno.
Description: First edition. | New York, NY: HarperPerennial, 2024. |
Identifiers: LCCN 2024011423 (print) | LCCN 2024011424 (ebook) | ISBN 9780063393950 (paperback) | ISBN 9780063393967 (ebook)
Subjects: LCGFT: Romance fiction. | Novels.
Classification: LCC PS3603.O873 H43 2024 (print) | LCC PS3603.O873 (ebook) | DDC 813/.6—dc23/eng/20230414
LC record available at https://lccn.loc.gov/2024011423
LC ebook record available at https://lccn.loc.gov/2024011424

ISBN 978-0-06-339395-0 (pbk.)
ISBN 978-0-06-341938-4 (library edition)

24 25 26 27 28 LBC 5 4 3 2 1

For you, this time. Thanks for sticking around.

CHAPTER ONE

LACEY

LACEY IS SUPPOSED TO HAVE TWO GLORIOUSLY UNSCHEDULED days in New York after MetLife Stadium, only then her mom flies into JFK unannounced with the idea that they should get dinner at Balthazar and go see *Moulin Rouge* on Broadway, which means Lacey actually has *one* gloriously unscheduled day in New York after MetLife Stadium. Still, she thinks, snapping a picture for Instagram out the window of her hotel suite, the city already humming fifty floors beneath her: It's better than nothing.

"You want me to set anything up for today?" Claire asks, once she's settled Lacey's mom in the car to the airport and come back upstairs for their morning meeting. Claire has been Lacey's assistant for six years and four albums, an erstwhile engineering major with a septum piercing and a mind like a Swiss watch. "Reservations or anything?"

Lacey hesitates. What she really wants to do while she's in town is sneak into Henrietta Lang's gig at Irving Plaza, to close her eyes and throw her arms in the air and lose herself in the weird, moody folk-rock she's had in her headphones on obsessive repeat the last few months. She could tell Claire that, obviously, and Claire would arrange it in roughly two and a half seconds. But Lacey knows if she does it the whole night is automatically going to be about her and not about Henrietta Lang, and whether she's pulling focus from a less-established artist, and how corny it is the way she's always trying to make New York into her whole personality, and does everyone remember how she started talking about how much she loved experimental jazz all the time right after she started dating Toby? Suddenly Lacey feels overwhelmed by the Discourse, even though it's only eight a.m.

Also, she isn't really cool enough to just drop into a Henrietta Lang show. She doesn't know exactly what she'd wear.

In the end she sends flowers and a good-luck card to the venue and spends most of the day in the cloistered quiet of the spa downstairs at the Mandarin, listening to pan flute renditions of eighties love themes while her bodyguard Javi waits patiently outside. "I'm so sorry," the masseuse says, once Lacey has put her bra back on and stepped into her terry cloth slippers. "I could lose my job for this, but I'm such an enormous fan. Would you mind—?"

"Oh!" Lacey says, hitching the sash of her robe a little tighter around her waist and leaning in for a selfie. "Um, of course."

Matilda texts as she's heading back upstairs in the elevator. *How was your Big New York Day?* she asks, alongside a flood of apple and taxicab emojis. *Still on for a late dinner?*

Yes! Lacey writes back, although even an early dinner for Matilda is like ten p.m. and Lacey generally tries not to eat after seven thirty. Still: she did say she was going to have a Big New York Day, which at the very least probably means she ought to leave the hotel. *Definitely.*

She texts Claire, who sends over hair and makeup. The whole

floor is sealed, just Lacey's people, though the dancers had sixty hours off and will meet her tomorrow afternoon in Toronto. Back downstairs Lacey blinks in the flashing lights of the cameras as she waves to the scrum of fans clustered behind the barriers outside the building. "Have you guys been out here all day?" she asks as disbelievingly as possible, though of course she knows they have been. They've been here since she arrived in the city nearly a week ago; they've been here, more or less, for ten years. A few of them have started bringing their own daughters, little girls with pigtails and SECOND-GEN LACEY LEAGUE T-shirts. "I'm going to order you some pizzas."

Matilda is waiting at Via Carota, her curly blond hair sticking up in every direction and her wire-rimmed glasses huge on her heart-shaped face. "There you are, you absolute vision!" she crows, flashing a nasty look at anyone who dares to glance over at them. Matilda just called it off with the guy she was seeing, an impishly unwashed Irish singer who plays the bodhran, so now she hates every man indiscriminately and most women for good measure. Lacey knows from experience that this will endure for roughly as long as it takes for some mustachioed Icelandic playwright to catch her eye from across a crowded room.

They debrief the breakup over grilled artichokes and cacio e pepe, a green salad with a sharp, bracing vinaigrette. Matilda is talking animatedly about the weird sex stuff Eoghan was into when Lacey's phone starts to buzz on the table—her mom back in Cincinnati. Lacey bites her lip. She tries to pick up whenever her mom calls, but they literally just saw each other this morning; her mom slept over in her hotel room last night, the wine-and-perfume scent of her familiar and a little bit suffocating. Lacey tossed and turned until the light turned gray in the gap between the blackout curtains, some animal instinct deep inside her vigilantly attuned to the possibility of a threat.

"What about you, dove?" Matilda asks now, peering at her curiously across the table. Matilda is from England so everything she says sounds sophisticated and a little imperious. "Have you talked to your Saturday Night Bastard?"

Lacey clears her throat. "To Toby?" she asks, taking a sip of her water and tucking her phone facedown underneath her thigh, where it continues to buzz like a coin-operated bed. "I have not."

Matilda tuts. "The baby looks like a tiny goblin, doesn't it."

"You're terrible," Lacey chides through a laugh, though she has privately, in her lowest moments, thought basically the same thing. "The baby looks like a baby. None of this is the *baby's* fault."

"You should send them an extremely fucked-up little gift," Matilda advises, reaching for her wine. "A crocheted jumper embroidered with your likeness. Or a note saying how flattered you are by the offer to be its godmother, and how delighted you are to accept."

Lacey laughs again, but she's relieved when the waiter comes over to see how they're enjoying everything. She doesn't want to talk about this anymore. There isn't really that much to say. She lived with Toby for almost two years, and then it turned out he had both a secret cocaine addiction and a secret relationship, and also that his secret girlfriend was pregnant with his secret baby, and now Lacey is on an international tour singing a bunch of wildly popular love songs she wrote as she lay in their bed beside him.

So: nothing that unusual, really. Just, like, normal girl stuff.

"Tell me about work," she says to Matilda, once they're alone again. "When does filming start back up?"

Matilda claps her manicured hands together, launching into a convoluted story about two of her castmates who can no longer be in the same room together following an undisclosed incident at a SAG dinner in West Hollywood. Lacey lets her mind wander. She feels restless all of a sudden, a panicky Sunday-night kind of feeling, even though it's the middle of the week. It was just a short break, but she wanted to accomplish something with it, to do something memorable or independent or creatively inspiring, and instead she had an Ayurvedic scalp treatment and watched 4 New York in bed. She's not complaining, obviously—one thing about Lacey is that she knows better than to ever, ever complain—but she's disappointed in herself, in her own lack of bravery. She could have figured out something to wear.

She's startled out of her thoughts by the insistent buzz of her phone underneath her. Lacey reaches down and flips it over, glancing quickly at the screen. *Where are you?* her mom wants to know. *Call me.*

Then, a moment later: *It's an emergency.*

Lacey feels the iron pulse of her own heart at the back of her mouth. "Hold that thought," she tells Matilda, smiling as calmly as possible and hurrying off to the bathroom, already dialing. "Mom," she says, once she's shut herself inside and locked the door, "are you okay?"

"There you are," her mom says pleasantly. "Are you out?"

Lacey shuts her eyes, just briefly, leaning back against the sink in irritation and relief. "I'm at dinner," she says. "What's the emergency?"

"What?"

"You said there was an emergency, Mom."

"Oh," her mom says. "Did I? No, I just got back to the house and I hate all my furniture. Do you still have the name of the decorator who did your place in Nashville?"

Lacey grits her teeth so hard she feels it in her neck. "Sure," she says. "I'll text you her contact info in the morning."

"Who are you with?"

"Just Matilda."

"Oh, I love Matilda!" her mom exclaims, though they've never actually met each other. Lacey finds it's best to spend time with her mom one-on-one. "Tell her I said hello."

Back at the table Matilda is taking video of the bustling restaurant, brow furrowed in concentration like Martin Scorsese with an iPhone Pro. "One more drink?" she asks. "There's a place near Hudson Yards that's supposed to be fun."

Lacey hesitates. She's got a flight out first thing tomorrow morning, the first of six shows over two weekends in Toronto tomorrow night. She should go back to the hotel, do her hour of potions, chug her dutiful liter of water, and go to sleep with the white noise machine humming on the nightstand beside her.

"One more drink," she agrees, and tucks her phone back into her purse.

Outside the restaurant a small crowd has gathered: a few photographers she recognizes and a trio of girls in TEAM LACEY T-shirts, plus some curious tourists lured by the promise of a celebrity sighting. Lacey glances up over their heads at the tops of the buildings and thinks of Henrietta Lang stepping onstage a few blocks from here, her red hair long and wild and her voice like a flamethrower in the darkness. The night isn't over yet, Lacey decides, feeling suddenly impetuous. There's still time for something to happen.

"A spinning wheel," she announces, raising her voice so Matilda can hear her over the sounds of the screaming, flashbulbs still exploding all around them. "That's what I'm going to send."

CHAPTER TWO
JIMMY

THEY GET THEIR ASSES HANDED TO THEM AT YANKEE STADIUM IN a truly spectacular fashion, and by the time they get back to the hotel after the game all Jimmy wants is a burger from room service and never to talk to anyone again for the rest of his natural life, but Tuck catches him in the lobby and reminds him that Rose is in town with some friends tonight. "Come on, man," Tuck says when Jimmy tries to beg off. "It makes her think I'm cool and popular when I get the whole team to come out."

"You are unequivocally neither one of those things," Jimmy promises, tapping his key card as they step into the elevator. Then he looks at Tuck's hopeful face and sighs. "Text me when you pick a place."

In the end it's almost half the team piling into a motorcade of Ubers headed downtown: Tuck and Jonesy and a bunch of the guys from the outfield, plus a couple of the new call-ups whose names Jimmy keeps forgetting, kids so young they still have acne dotted all along their greasy hairlines. He swears they look more like babies every single year. "That's because you're a bag of fuckin' bones, you grizzled bastard," Tuck says whenever he mentions it. Jimmy guesses he's got a point.

The bar—club, whatever—is on the top floor of a fancy hotel, high ceilings and an enormous roof deck that looks out over the water, a view of the Hudson River that might make a certain kind of person feel sentimental about New York. Jimmy's drinking a beer and listening idly as Jonesy and Tito insult each other's mothers when suddenly Tuck elbows him in the ribs.

"Shit," Tuck says, motioning toward the corner. "Isn't that—"

Jimmy follows his gaze to a cordoned-off VIP area—the team is *also* in a VIP area, allegedly, but all at once Jimmy understands that theirs isn't the real one, that there's another area *within* the VIP area that's for actual celebrities. There's a curtain, lush green and thick-looking, but it isn't quite closed all the way.

"Oh, fuck me," Ray says, popping up in his seat like a prairie dog. "Is that Lacey Logan?"

It is in fact Lacey Logan, Jimmy sees now, seated on a low couch with her long legs crossed demurely at the ankles. She's with the other girl she's with all the time, the actress from the survivalist thing on HBO, the one with the face that's kind of mean. "Stars," Jimmy concedes, taking a swig of his beer. "They're just like us."

"They are *nothing* like us," Tuck corrects, gazing longingly in the post-apocalyptic pirate queen's direction.

"Isn't your literal fiancée supposed to be meeting us here any minute?" Jimmy asks him. Tuck scratches his eyebrow with his middle finger instead of answering.

Jimmy smirks, glancing over at the curtain one more time before turning his attention back to the guys, pulling Tito into a different conversation before things with Jonesy get too heated and they all wind up getting their asses kicked out onto Tenth Avenue.

Rose arrives with a gaggle of her girlfriends, tufted and patterned and boring as a suite of expensive furniture, and they order another round of drinks. They went to dinner in the Meatpacking District before they got here, but pretty soon Jimmy is hungry again; he wonders if there's a food menu at this place, though he already knows that if there is it's going to be full of raw fish and various gourmet foams. He's about to order buffalo chicken sliders to his hotel room and call a car to take him back uptown when Ray gets unsteadily to his feet. "I'm going to go say hello," he announces.

Jimmy looks up at him, confused. "To who?" Then, as it dawns on him: "To *Lacey Logan*? Oh, buddy." Jimmy shakes his head. "Please don't."

"Why not?" Ray asks, looking wounded. Ray is twenty-one, maybe twenty-two at the outside, dressed in jeans and an oversized polo shirt; he was wearing an Orioles cap when they got here, but the bouncer downstairs made him take it off before they got in the elevator, and his hair is a little bit matted. "We're both Very Important Persons, right?"

"The opacity of that curtain suggests otherwise," Tuck points out.

Ray ignores him. "She's from the Midwest," he goes on, with the authority of a seasoned Wikipedian. "I'm also from the Midwest." Then, like he's trying to convince them: "She's on the *rebound*, my dudes."

Jimmy thinks he heard something about that, actually: Lacey Logan breaking up with some skinny nice-guy comedian from *SNL* his ex-wife Rachel used to like. The guy was on coke, or the guy was cheating? Maybe both. Jimmy is about to ask Ray for the details, if only to try and distract him into sitting back down and drinking a glass of water until his blood alcohol level dips beneath the legal limit, but the kid is already trotting off across the club like Tom Cruise gunning it down the runway in an F-14, all aviators and flight jacket. Jimmy can practically hear the theme music playing in his head.

"Well?" Tuck says expectantly.

Jimmy looks back. "Well what?"

"You're his captain, Jimmy. As far as that young man is concerned, you are his *father*. You need to go and save him from himself before he winds up in jail."

"You get him," Jimmy counters stubbornly. He didn't want to come out tonight in the first place, and this is why. Well, not *this*, specifically, he didn't portend this exact clusterfuck, but he's over the late nights and the paparazzi, the whole who's-fucking-who scene of it. He's too old.

"They're going to send him to Rikers Island, Jimmy. You ever read about Rikers Island?"

"They're not gonna—" he starts, but Tuck just keeps on looking at him, and finally Jimmy rolls his eyes and gets up off the couch, his knees cracking loudly in protest. He jams his hands into his pockets and ambles over to the curtain, where by some miracle Ray has not yet been forcibly removed by a bouncer twice his size and tossed out the window onto a passing trash barge. "Ray, buddy," he says, swinging an arm around the kid's skinny shoulders, "your team needs you. For, uh. Top secret sports stuff." He nods at the women on the sofa, holding up one conciliatory hand. "Ladies."

The blonde nods back, but the brunette—and the brunette, make no mistake, is Lacey Logan—narrows her eyes in his direction, pointing with one short vermilion fingernail. "Jimmy Hodges, right?"

"Uh." That startles him. "Yeah."

She nods, unfolding herself from the sofa and offering a hand. "Lacey Logan."

Jimmy clears his throat. "Nice to meet you."

"You too." She's got a firm handshake, businesslike. She's taller than he would have thought she was—not as tall as him, but close to it—and slightly gawky-looking, like a very lovely ostrich. Her hair is twisted into a long, complicated-looking ponytail over one shoulder. "This is my friend Matilda."

Jimmy nods, patting the kid on the back. "This is Ray."

"Oh, now," Matilda says Britishly, sounding like Dame Maggie Smith in that show about the rich people in the castle. It occurs to Jimmy to wonder if her accent is even real. "Ray, we have met."

"Yeah," Jimmy says, feeling bad for the kid, a little defensive on his behalf. He only got called up from the minors last week. "Well. We were just—"

"You guys got killed tonight, huh?" Lacey says.

That surprises him, both the fact that she's got that knowledge as well as what a less confident guy might call the rudeness of her deploying it quite so baldly. "You could say that," he admits, rubbing a hand over his beard. She's wearing a fringy dress and a pair of red platform stilettos. Her legs are, like, ten miles long. "You watch a lot of baseball?"

"No," she says with a smile. "But I like to put the local news on in my hotel room."

Jimmy nods. "I usually watch the Food Network, myself."

"Also pleasantly numbing," she agrees. "You cook?"

"Quesadillas, mostly," he confesses. "The odd bag of frozen vegetables. I can grill a steak."

"Yeah, that tracks."

"That's the vibe I give off, huh?" Jimmy asks wryly. "Red meat and freezer-burned green beans?"

"All-American," she says. "Like a Kraft Single."

Jimmy lets out a low whistle. "Like a *Kraft Single*," he repeats slowly. "I gotta tell you, pal, that's gonna fester. That one smarts."

Lacey's red mouth drops open. "It's a compliment!"

"Is it?" Jimmy is very dubious.

"It is!" she insists seriously. "Kraft Singles are the superior melting cheese."

"Uh-huh." He shakes his head. "I'll take your word for it."

Neither one of them says anything for a second too long, both of them still looking at each other. It's only when Matilda abruptly announces her intention to use the loo that Jimmy realizes Ray has also drifted mournfully off, so it's just the two of them now, him and Lacey Logan, and he means to say his goodbyes but instead he just keeps standing there, waiting for her to send him on his way. "You're on tour right now, yeah?" he asks, shaking out his aching hands for a second before tucking them back into his pockets. "Where you headed after New York?"

"Canada tomorrow," she reports. "This was the end of the US leg. And Europe after that, but not 'til after the holidays." She nods back in the direction of the team, none of whom are even pretending not to be watching. "What about you guys?"

Jimmy thinks for a minute, trying to imagine the calendar in his mind. "Minneapolis," he tells her. "So, like, basically the same."

Lacey laughs at that—a real laugh, loud and open-mouthed. Jimmy grins at her; he can't help it. If he didn't know better—and he *does* know better, obviously, he's a thirty-seven-year-old has-been catcher with knees like hamburger and twenty extra pounds in the gut—he would almost think she was—

What he means to say is—

It sort of feels like Lacey Logan is *flirting* with him.

As soon as Jimmy thinks it he feels deeply and profoundly ridiculous, heat creeping up the back of his neck in a way that makes him grateful the club is so fucking dark. He's delusional. It's like thinking a stripper really likes you. She's arguably the most famous person in America, in the middle of a stadium tour that's on track to gross billions of dollars. Also, she's young. Jimmy tries to remember how young, exactly: Twenty-five? Twenty-six? It's not that he's never dated that young, but it's not a great look at this point. He tries to avoid it.

Not that he's planning on dating Lacey Logan.

Not that it's even on the table.

"One more game here tomorrow, though," he hears himself tell her, "so who knows. Maybe we'll redeem ourselves before we leave town."

"I hope so," Lacey says. "For your sake."

"Thank you for that vote of confidence."

She grins. "You're welcome."

She's drunk, maybe? Jimmy guesses it's conceivable she's flirting with him if she's drunk.

"Can I ask you something?" he blurts. "Are you drunk?"

Lacey looks at him a little strangely. "Uh," she says, "nope."

That's right, Jimmy remembers. She doesn't drink. It's a part of her good-girl, *Mickey Mouse Club* image, how there's never been a picture of her spilling messily out of a restaurant or a video of her losing her temper and yelling at a photographer. Lacey Logan never fucks up.

"Are *you* drunk?" she asks curiously.

Jimmy shakes his head. "No, actually," he says. "Although I understand why you might think that."

"Yeah," she agrees, but she's smiling at him again, nodding at the space on the couch lately vacated by her mean friend Matilda. "You wanna sit?"

So. Jimmy sits.

She's strangely easy to talk to, Lacey Logan, about the folly of trying to get anywhere by car in New York City and the Joan Didion essays she's been reading in between tour stops and how Ray spent all day trying to convince the rest of them to go on the Circle Line. She's funnier than he was expecting. She seems smart. She's—not *normal*, certainly, but normal *enough* that Jimmy is still sitting there almost an hour later, trying to act like a person who would not be more comfortable in a chair with better lumbar support, when he glances across the club and realizes that at some point Tuck did him the favor of quietly collecting the rest of the team and taking off.

Not that Jimmy needs the privacy, obviously. Not that there's anything for anyone to see.

"Are you hungry?" he asks her, looking around for a waitress. He'll eat the sushi at this point. He doesn't give a fuck. "I would, like, kill a man for a mozzarella stick right now."

"If you order mozzarella sticks I will one hundred percent go in on them with you," she promises, and she sounds sincere enough that Jimmy laughs.

"I don't think they have mozzarella sticks here."

"They'd get them for me," Lacey says, then has the good manners to look abashed. "Sorry. I'm sure that sounded very—" She wrinkles her tidy nose.

"No, no," Jimmy says, holding a hand up. "Honestly, it just

makes you sound like a good person to know. In, like, the deep-fried appetizer space."

Lacey smiles. "I like to think so." She pulls her phone out then, scrolling through what looks like an endless stream of notifications. Jimmy is about to take it as his cue to say good night when all at once she lifts her sharp face from the screen. "We could go somewhere else," she announces.

Jimmy snorts. "Okay."

"What?" Lacey looks at him blankly. "For mozzarella sticks, or whatever. Why is that funny?"

He opens his mouth, then closes it again. "Be serious."

"I am," Lacey insists. "And also, you're the one who came over here to talk to me to begin with, so I don't know why you're now acting like it's so ridiculous that I might actually want to—"

"I came *over* here to—"

"To what, exactly?" Lacey raises one perfect eyebrow.

Jimmy gapes at her for a moment, the silence stretching out like taffy between them. "What do you want me to say?" he asks finally, feeling caught out and a little embarrassed. "Like, am I attracted to you? Of course I'm attracted to you. Do you even—I mean, everybody is attracted to you."

He's trying to couch it in the broadest, most general terms possible, but Lacey's smile, when it comes, feels decidedly specific. "Okay," she agrees, like she's pleased they concur on the terms of the arrangement. "I'm attracted to you, too."

Jimmy feels a trapdoor open deep inside him, the unmistakable sensation of something tumbling right the hell through. "Okay," he echoes slowly.

"So, like I was saying," she continues, folding her hands neatly in her lap, "let's go somewhere."

CHAPTER THREE

LACEY

JIMMY DOESN'T SAY ANYTHING FOR A FULL THIRTY SECONDS AF-ter she suggests it. Lacey watches as a thousand different expressions skitter across his face: amusement, curiosity, deep and abiding skepticism. A warm flicker, quick but unmistakable, of desire.

"What . . . would even be the procedure for something like that?" he asks finally, rubbing a speculative hand over his beard. "For you to, like, leave a location? Do you need to call someone?"

"Like who?"

Jimmy shrugs. "I don't know," he says. "The Secret Service? Whoever you call."

"The Secret—" Lacey snorts. "You're insane."

"*I'm* insane?" Jimmy laughs, low and rumbling. "You're the international superstar who wants to leave this very nice bar with me, some fat fuck you just met."

"First of all, don't say it like that."

"Like what?"

"You know like what." She pitches her voice low and dopey. "*International superstar.*"

Jimmy smirks. "What, am I embarrassing you?"

"No, of course not, I just—"

"Because I gotta tell you, you're pretty successful. It's a little late for polite modesty about your career."

Lacey huffs a breath. "Okay," she says, shaking her head, angling her body away from him. This was a wild hair, that's all. She was being silly for a minute. "You know what? If you don't actually want to do this, then—"

"Hold on a second," he cuts her off, holding a finger up. "I definitely never said I didn't want to."

"Really?" she counters. "Because I wouldn't say you sound particularly enthusiastic about the idea."

Jimmy fixes her with a look then, long and leveling. "Lacey," he says, so quietly she almost doesn't hear him. "Come on."

Lacey breathes in, the sound of him saying her name briefly but violently rearranging all her organs. She knew who he was before he came over here. Of course she knew who he was, Jimmy Hodges with his beard and his big shoulders and his unfashionable button-down. He was Rookie of the Year back when she was in high school, all shaggy hair and sulky mouth and a million ingenue girlfriends. Lacey had his milk ad taped to the wall above her bed. He's thirty-seven or thirty-eight now, she calculates, five or six years older than she is. She clocked him as soon as he walked in.

"Wait here," she instructs, then gets up to go find Javi.

There *is* a procedure, obviously. The procedure is that she tells Claire where she wants to go and Claire handles it, calling ahead to let them know Lacey's coming and coordinating with Javi and the rest of the security team. At least, that's how it used to work. She stopped going to so many places when she was dating Toby, on account of how moody and jealous he always got whenever they went out.

Fuck Toby, Lacey thinks with surprising ferocity. And fuck Claire! Well, no, not *fuck Claire*, Lacey loves Claire. Claire is arguably the person she is closest to in the entire world, but fuck the *procedure*. The *procedure* is how she wound up with Toby in the first place, the two of them set up on a lunch date by their managers in LA three years ago. The *procedure* feels abruptly absurd.

Javi is standing near the emergency exit, crisp as nine a.m. in his tailored blue suit even though it's well after midnight. "I want to get out of here," she tells him. "And I want to travel light."

Javi nods, his gaze flicking over her shoulder for a fraction of a second. *Travel light* means one bodyguard and a driver. "All right."

She finds Jimmy right where she left him, tall and broad and barrel-chested, incongruous in the floral print and neon of the club. "Come on," she says, and she can hear that she sounds a little breathless. "Let's go."

Jimmy considers her for another moment, like he's gauging something. "Okay," he agrees finally. "Let's go."

They leave through the service elevator, same as the one she came up through. Christopher is waiting in the garage. Jimmy puts a hand on her lower back—just lightly, just the very tips of his fingers—as she boosts herself up into the SUV.

"Are you okay to drive around the neighborhood for a bit?" she asks Chris, leaning forward a little as Javi buckles himself into the passenger seat. "I'll tell you when to stop." She sits back, the edge of her thigh brushing Jimmy's. She hopes she sounds more confident than she feels.

She does not, evidently: "You got a destination in mind?" Jimmy asks her as they turn the corner onto West 14th, the lights from the bars and clubs and restaurants winking across his face through the window. Lacey only knows the fancy places.

"No, actually," she admits. "I'm kind of flying by the seat of my pants here."

"Fair enough," Jimmy says easily, settling the bulk of his body back against the seat. "I guess I just didn't think that was your style."

"It's not."

Lacey peers out the window as the SUV creeps along the narrow street, everything too bright or too trendy or too public, until all at once she spots it: a deeply unremarkable tavern a little ways from the corner, its tall front windows flung open to the balmy night. "What about that one?" she asks, looking first to Jimmy and then to Javi. "That one could be good."

Chris pulls over in front of a hydrant. "Wait here," Javi instructs.

The car is quiet for a moment, all of them breathing. When Lacey glances over at Jimmy she sees he's gazing frankly back. She shifts her weight in the seat, her whole body warm and humming. She doesn't know what her deal is tonight: she's never into guys like this, the kind who look like they could fling you over their shoulder and carry you back to a cave somewhere to have their way with you. Toby could have fit in her jeans with room to spare.

"It's fine," Javi reports a moment later, Chris rolling down the passenger-side window as he strides back across the sidewalk. "We're good."

"They're not kicking people out, are they?" Lacey asks nervously. "I don't want to, like—"

But Javi shakes his head. "There's hardly anyone in there."

He's right: the place is mostly empty, just a couple of middle-aged drinkers at a table in the corner. An old Marc Cohn song is playing on the speakers overhead. It's not a dive, exactly; instead it's just deeply anonymous, with brick walls and black wooden barstools, Edison bulbs in little wire cages hanging in a row above the bar. They could be anywhere. They could be any*body*.

"This is perfect," Lacey announces.

Jimmy looks at her a little oddly. Lacey feels herself blush, all at once exquisitely aware of the lunacy of having ghosted her most gossipy friend to go sit at a weird bar with this stranger while her head of security sips a bottle of water across the room. She and Toby had been together three months before they were ever even photographed in the same zip code. This is emphatically not the kind of thing she does.

Well, she thinks, as Jimmy settles himself onto a stool and orders a Brooklyn Summer, she's in it now. Nothing to do at this point but soldier through.

"So," she says, once she's asked the bartender for a club soda and cranberry, "what's your favorite thing about living in Baltimore?"

Jimmy blinks, probably because it sounds very much like she's interviewing him for a profile in *Chesapeake Bay Magazine*. "My favorite thing?"

"Yeah." Lacey shrugs, determined. "You've stayed there your whole career, right? You must love it, to have been there so long."

"That's not . . . totally how it works."

"No, I know that." Lacey winces. "I mean, of course I know that. I just—"

"I do, though," he interrupts, apparently having decided at the last possible second to bail her out after all. "Love it, that is. The people, mostly. They're scrappy." He takes a sip of his beer. "Also, the crab cakes are lights out."

Lacey feels her shoulders drop in gratitude. "I have heard the crab cakes are special."

"You've never had the crab cakes?"

She shakes her head. "I've been a vegetarian since I was twelve."

"Yeah, well." Jimmy shrugs, like *What can you do?* "Nobody's perfect."

Lacey grins. "I'm close, though, right?"

Jimmy barks out a laugh, rowdy and surprised, but then it vanishes into the air halfway through—and oh, the way he's *looking* at her, like he can't quite believe she's happening to him. Like he doesn't quite believe she's real. "I think," he says slowly, "that is probably true."

Neither one of them says anything for a minute. Finally, Lacey clears her throat. "How's your season going?" she asks, reaching for her drink and fussing with the straw for a moment. Her hands aren't shaking, but it's a near thing.

Jimmy smirks. Just like that he's himself again, a veteran ballplayer, unflappable and wry. "Well, as you may have seen on the local news, Lacey, we got killed by the Yankees today."

"I did catch that, yes."

"So." He tips the beer bottle in her direction. "Like that, basically."

She shrugs. "It's still early."

"Not that early," he counters. "Almost the end of the summer. We're not making the playoffs, that's for sure."

"Next year, then."

"For the rest of the guys, maybe." Jimmy shakes his head. "But I'm done at the end of the season."

That stops her. "What, like—" Lacey sets her drink back onto the bar. "Done for good?"

"Yeah, cupcake, done for good." He grins, his eyes crinkling up around the edges. They're a pretty shade of hazel, warm with flecks of gold in the irises. "I'm retiring."

"Why?"

Jimmy shrugs. "It's time, that's all. Lots of reasons." He runs his thumb over the mouth of his beer bottle, not quite meeting her gaze. "Bad back. Bad knees, bunch of other boring shit. It's just time."

"I didn't know."

"I haven't told anybody." He tips his head to the side. "Until now, I guess."

"Well," she says. "I'm a vault."

Jimmy nods like he doesn't doubt it. "What about you?" he asks. "How's your tour going?"

Lacey considers that. He told her a secret just now, Jimmy Hodges. She could tell him one back, probably—how lonely she is, how bored of herself, how trapped she feels sometimes—and for a moment she almost does, but in the end she just shakes her head. "You know," she says, smiling her most brilliant international-superstar smile, "it's been really, really great."

Something in Jimmy's expression shorts out briefly, like he suspects she's full of shit and finds it vaguely disappointing, but he doesn't know her well enough to call her on it. "Well, I'm glad to hear that," is all he says, getting to his feet and nodding in the direction of the restrooms. "I'll be right back."

Lacey sits at the bar for another moment once he's gone, sipping her drink and wondering why she feels so sad all of a sudden.

Something about the idea of him retiring is faintly heartbreaking—she's going to *miss* him, she realizes with a sharp flash of clarity, which is a deeply deranged emotion to be having, since they only met an hour ago and he's in the bathroom of this bar at this very moment—but that isn't the only reason. It's that she had the chance to be brave just now, same as she did with the Henrietta Lang show, and she whiffed it. It's that she could have said or done something to surprise herself, and instead she wasted her chance.

Lacey glances over at Javi, who's pretending to watch ESPN on the TV mounted in the corner.

Then she slips off her barstool as casually as she can.

The bathrooms are in a dim little hallway lined with fake Art Deco posters of European travel destinations. Lacey leans back against the wall to wait, tucking her hands neatly behind her back and squinting at a crude rendering of the Eiffel Tower. Toby did a couple of dates in Paris last year, after his tour through England and Ireland, but the jokes didn't really translate and he was in a bad mood the entire ti—

The door opens. Jimmy steps out, then stops short when he sees her, his eyes widening. "Hi."

"Hi."

He jerks his thumb back toward the bathroom. "Are you—?"

"No."

"Then what—"

"What do you think?"

She watches as Jimmy processes that, his gaze turning a full shade darker. "Okay." He takes a step closer, then another, crowding her a little, his body huge in the tiny hallway. Lacey needs to lift her chin to look him in the eye. "You realize this isn't going to do a single fuckin' thing for your career," he warns her softly, his face so close their lips are almost touching. He smells like restaurant-supply hand soap and underneath that like cologne.

Lacey shakes her head. "Fuck you," she tells him primly, then grabs the front of his shirt with both hands and slams her mouth up against his.

CHAPTER FOUR

JIMMY

JIMMY LETS OUT A QUIET *OOF* AS HE CATCHES HER WEIGHT, STUM-
bling backward into the tiny bathroom and kicking the door shut
behind them. Lacey fists her hands in his hair. She's an entirely
different kind of kisser than he would have thought, nipping at his
bottom lip and sliding her clever tongue into his mouth, her strong
arms muscled tight around his neck. She tastes like cranberries
and lime.

"Okay, hang on, hang on," she gasps at last, wriggling until he
sets her down on the tile. "Didn't you literally just say your back is
messed up? I'm going to hurt you."

"You're definitely not," he tells her calmly, grinning against
her brightly painted mouth. "Anyway, fuck my back. I'm retiring."

"You're retiring," Lacey agrees solemnly, and kisses him again.

Jimmy works his knee between her thighs as he presses her
up against the door, taking quick stock of his surroundings. The
bathroom is a single-shooter, decently clean, with a tiny votive
candle flickering on the edge of the sink next to the EMPLOYEES
MUST WASH sign; still, it is very much a public toilet, and even if

she is the one who picked the venue, he's definitely not about to consummate this thing in the john of a drinking establishment so pathologically nondescript it might as well be called *Bar*.

Not that he thinks they're *going* to consummate—

At least, he's definitely not *expecting*—

Jimmy growls, a sharp zip of pain at the crook of his neck startling him out of his head. "Did you just *bite* me?" he asks incredulously.

"Um," she says, lifting her head and looking at him a little sheepishly. Fuck, but she's a beautiful girl. Jimmy knew that, obviously, but there's something different about noticing it in the specific and not the generic way he knows most famous women are beautiful. Her mouth is a little too wide for her face. "No?"

Jimmy grins. "Lacey Logan," he mutters—biting her back, just gently, all along the elegant cliff of her jaw. "Who fuckin' knew."

It goes on like that for a while, Jimmy cupping her ass and Lacey hitching a leg up like she's trying to climb him, her fingertips sliding down into the collar of his undershirt. Jimmy palms a breast through her dress. He wants to do more than that, wants to peel down the cups of her bra and lick her nipples, wants to *see* her, but the dress is expensive and tight, the fabric thick and a little bit shiny with no give to it at all. Jimmy doesn't know who designed this dress, but they can go screw themselves, truly. It's got, like, three layers and a corset. It sucks. "What the *fuck*," he mutters finally, still fumbling for a zipper and not finding one. Lacey throws her head back and laughs.

"Shh," he chides quietly, giving up and dropping to his knees on the extremely questionable tile. Lacey's eyes go gratifyingly wide.

"I'm wearing Spanx right now," she warns him. "I mean, I don't know what you're planning to—but—"

Jimmy nods seriously. "Please believe me when I tell you from the bottom of my heart that I do not give a shit," he promises, and slides the palms of his hands up her thighs.

In the end he does actually give a little bit of a shit, but only because the thing is *also* so difficult to get off, the high waist of it covering her stomach and rib cage. Jimmy peels it carefully down her body, rucking up her skirt and rubbing his face against the lower part of her belly. She smells private, like baby powder and a little bit like sweat. "Isn't that so fucking uncomfortable?" he asks, using his index finger to trace the angry red line the seam of it left against her hip.

Lacey peers down at him, fixing him with an arch expression. "Actually, I love it," she deadpans pleasantly. "I sleep in it now."

Jimmy winces. "Point taken." He ducks his head, then hesitates at the last possible second, glancing back up at her in the dim light of the bathroom. "Is this—?" he asks. It feels important to get affirmative consent. "I mean, do you want me to—?"

"*Yes*," she hisses. "Of course I—I followed you to the *bathroom*, James." She makes a face. "Do people call you that, even?"

Jimmy shakes his head. "No," he says with a smile. "Nobody."

"I'm going to," she decides.

"Uh-huh," he mutters, grabbing one smooth knee and slinging it over his shoulder, reaching up to cup her with one hand. "You can do whatever you want."

Lacey grins again, that same luminous smile that momentarily undid him when they were sitting out there at the bar. "I know."

It's the quietest sex he's ever had. Lacey hums softly, gripping the edge of the sink and tilting her hips against him, letting out the occasional sigh. Jimmy shifts his weight on the tile, trying to ignore the sharp twinge in his knees. He has no idea if it isn't working for her or she's like this all the time or she's going over her tour choreography, but at the very least he wants to make sure he has her undivided attention, so he slides two fingers inside her and curls them, pressing with the heel of his hand.

Lacey almost kicks his face clean off. "Oh," she gasps, her shocked gaze finding his in the half dark. "*Oh* my god."

Well, thank fuck. "There you are," he says, trying not to sound too openly relieved. "Hi."

"You told me to be quiet!"

Jimmy grins into the crease of her thigh. "So be quiet."

"So don't do everything you can possibly think of to make me—" Lacey starts, but then he twists his fingers one more time and all of a sudden she's arching sharply against him, her chin dropping back again to expose the long, graceful line of her throat. Jimmy hums his quiet encouragement into her skin.

"Oh my god," she repeats a long moment later, clutching at his shoulders. Her legs are shaking a little as he sets her foot back down on the tile, unsteady in her ridiculous red shoes. "Oh my god, okay, come up here."

Jimmy gets to his feet, trying not to wince too visibly at the way his knees are singing. Lacey stamps another kiss against his mouth. "That was—"

"Uh-huh."

Lacey laughs a little hysterically. "I never do this," she mutters, dropping her head and burying her face in his chest for a moment. "I *never* do this."

"Mm-hmm." He smooths a hand over her hair, squeezing the

back of her neck a little. Her skin is burning hot against his palm. "Me either."

"Fuck you."

"You know, I gotta say, you've got a real trash mouth for such a pristine individual," he scolds, thinking they're still playing, but when she pulls back to look at him, her eyes are huge and panicky.

"I mean it," she says, stepping backward so quickly she bumps into the sink. "I'm serious, this can't—"

Right away, Jimmy puts his hands up. "Okay," he says, "yeah. Sorry, I didn't—"

"No, it's just, I've never—" She breaks off. Her hair is frizzing up a bit, just around her hairline. Her cheeks are flushed bright red. "I don't—"

"What?" Jimmy scans her face, searching. He has no idea what just happened here. "Are you a virgin?"

Lacey huffs. "Fuck you," she says again, snatching her titanium underwear up off the edge of the sink and stepping nimbly back into them. "I'm thirty-two years old."

Jimmy blinks. "Really?"

"Yeah," she says, pausing to look up at him. "Why, is that a problem?"

"No," he says, shaking his head quickly. "No, that's *great*, actually, I was—"

"I'm not a virgin," she interrupts. "But I'm also not like you."

Jimmy scowls, surprised by how stung he feels by that particular assessment. "What am I like, exactly?" he asks, though it's not like he doesn't know what she's getting at. And sure, there was a time before he was married—and, okay, also after he got divorced—that he had a little bit of a reputation for sleeping around, but—

"You can't tell anyone about this," Lacey says instead of answering. "I mean it. And I meant it when I said I don't do this kind of thing. You can't—what I'm trying to say is—"

"Who do you imagine I'm going to be falling all over myself to tell?" he snaps, then immediately feels like a dick about it. On the one hand he's insulted, to be so brutally appraised by a pop singer who undoubtedly owns a small and annoying dog and captions her Instagram photos with phrases like *all the feels*. But on the other, she looks so worked up about it. She looks . . . *afraid*. "Lacey," he says gently. "I get it. I'm not going to tell anyone. All right?"

Lacey nods. "Okay." She looks like she believes him, then like she doesn't, then like she does again. "Thank you." She produces a slim tube of bright red lipstick from a tiny bag he didn't notice until right this moment, slicking it onto her mouth so fast and so expertly he's not even sure he sees her do it at all. "Do you want to go out first, or should I?"

Jimmy thinks about that for a moment. He guesses it doesn't really matter, at this point. He guesses it would be dumb to think it did. "Go ahead," he tells her, nudging her toward the exit, then stands there with his hands in his pockets as the door snicks shut behind her.

CHAPTER FIVE

LACEY

SHE WAKES UP WITH A GASP AT SIX THIRTY, HER HEART POUNDING.
Lacey gropes for her phone on the nightstand, fumbling it with clumsy hands and dropping it with a thud on the hotel carpet. Holy shit, what was she *thinking?* Anyone could have taken pictures. Anyone could have seen. Lacey hasn't been that careless in years. She's *never* been that careless, if she's being honest with herself; on her grave, it will probably say, *Here Lies Lacey Logan! She cared A LOT.* Is this what drunk people feel like the morning after a bender? Does her mom feel like this all the time?

Lacey fishes the phone off the floor and forces herself to search *Lacey Logan + Jimmy Hodges*, her whole body going soft with relief when the only thing that comes up is a photo of her singing the national anthem at an Orioles game seven years ago. Lacey flops back onto the mattress, waiting for her breathing to slow before reaching up for her water bottle. She didn't drink the whole thing before bed and she can feel it now, the stale, recycled dryness of the hotel in her skin and her sinuses. The insides of her thighs feel raw underneath her pajama shorts, and it takes her a second to realize it's from the scrape of Jimmy's beard.

Lacey opens a new search window. *Jimmy Hodges + girlfriends*, she types, then clicks on a slideshow from *Entertainment Tonight*. It's old stuff, mostly, from before he was married: three moderately famous actresses, one singer who died a few years later in a car accident. Two Victoria's Secret models. One Olympic gymnast. They probably had very athletic sex, Lacey thinks with a bizarre, inappropriate stab of jealousy, then sucks down the rest of her water even though it makes her feel a little sloshy.

His ex-wife wasn't famous, she notes. His ex-wife was a schoolteacher from Aberdeen. Lacey doesn't know why that's interesting to her, but it is.

Her phone dings just as she's about to try and find something more recent, and Lacey startles, dropping it onto the mattress one more time. *Morning!* Claire's texted from her room next door, just like she does every day at precisely seven a.m. *Let me know when you're ready for coffee.*

I'm up! Lacey texts back, then chews her bottom lip for a moment. *Also, would you mind setting up a call with Maddie for sometime this morning?*

The typing bubble appears, then disappears, then appears again. Lacey knows Claire wants to ask what the call is for, and also knows that she isn't going to. *ofc!* Claire assures her. *Will do.*

Lacey showers and pulls on a tank and leggings, slips a light-weight hoodie on overtop. When she looks in the mirror she can see that her mouth is still a little bit swollen from last night, smudged around the edges; she touches her lips with her finger-tips, just gently, shivering at the memory of Jimmy's warm tongue rasping against hers. She's embarrassed by the way she ran out of the bar—she was flustered enough when she came back from the bathroom that Javi asked, just once and very quietly, if everything was okay—and a little guilty about the things she said to Jimmy as she was leaving, even if the *Entertainment Tonight* slideshow does seem to confirm her general impression of him as a person who probably messes around with women in public places every day of the week. She was rattled by her own desire, the sudden, starving intensity of it. She was rattled by how badly she didn't want to stop.

It doesn't matter, Lacey tells herself as Claire knocks on the door that separates her suite from Lacey's. It's not like she's ever going to see him again. It's a thing that happened, that's all; she'll talk to Maddie, they'll address it, and then everyone will move on. Lacey knows how to control a story. Lacey is, and has always been, the one in charge.

"How was your night?" Claire asks, handing her the latte and pulling up the schedule on her iPad.

"Good," Lacey promises, and settles in to hear about her day.

They have to be at Teterboro at nine for the flight to Toronto, and Maddie FaceTimes from LA while they're still in the tunnel, the connection a little stuttery and slow. "Hey there!" Maddie says, immaculately dressed and seated in her office even though it's barely five a.m. in California. Maddie took Lacey with her when she started her own PR firm eleven years ago, back before either one of them was nearly this successful. Lacey likes to think it paid off for them both. "How was New York?"

"It was great," Lacey says automatically, and they do another few minutes of what Lacey always thinks of as *gals-in-business chit-chat* before finally she takes a deep breath, tucking one leg underneath her. "So, this definitely isn't a big deal," she begins, "but I did want to get out in front of it just in case."

"Sure thing," Maddie says brightly, though Lacey catches the flicker of trepidation on her face in the moment before she can school it coolly away. None of them ever like to let Lacey see them lose their composure. "Hit me."

Lacey explains it as casually as she can—making a jokey, madcap adventure of it, playing up the goofiness of the thing with the mozzarella sticks. If Javi, sitting quietly next to Chris in the front seat of the SUV, has anything to contribute by way of clarifying details, Lacey knows he would never volunteer them in a million years. "Anyway," she finishes breezily, "if you hear something in the next couple of days about me and Jimmy Hodges from the Orioles going to some random bar in the West Village, that's why."

"What bar?" Maddie asks, making a note.

"I have no idea," Lacey says honestly, which leads to ten excruciating minutes of Claire pulling up the websites of various places until finally Maddie tells her not to worry about it and sets her pen down on her desk.

"Okay," she says, her voice perfectly even. "Did anything happen between you guys I need to know about?"

Lacey hesitates for the barest fraction of a second. She knows, she *knows* Maddie can only do her job if Lacey is 100 percent honest with her. Maddie was Lacey's first call when she found out about Toby and the coke, her first call when she found out about Toby and Audriana; Maddie is one of exactly four people on Lacey's payroll who know the whole truth about Lacey's mom. Lacey trusts Maddie completely, and she's fully aware that the correct thing to do is to come clean, or at least clean-ish, to say she and Jimmy kissed or whatever and have Claire call the lawyers about drawing up an NDA.

But then she thinks of the way he rubbed along her hip bone

with the thumb of his free hand while she worked through her long, shuddering orgasm. She thinks of his giant shoulders. She thinks of the sound of his laugh. Maybe Jimmy does that kind of thing all the time, with all kinds of people, but Lacey doesn't. And it's something she doesn't want to share.

"Nope," she promises Maddie brightly. "Nothing you need to know about."

He's not going to say anything, Lacey tells herself, collapsing into her seat on the plane with her noise-canceling headphones and a cashmere blanket twenty minutes later. He's not the type.

At least, she doesn't *think* he's the type.

She fucking hopes not.

The rest of the day goes exactly as Claire outlined it for her over breakfast this morning: They get settled into the hotel in Toronto. Lacey eats a double protein salad and takes a nap. They head over to the Rogers Centre in the late afternoon to do the sound check, then down into the labyrinthine bowels of the stadium; Lacey sits in hair and makeup, watching the local news in her dressing room while forty thousand fans shuffle in above her, and all she can think about the whole time any of it is happening is the thickness of Jimmy's fingers inside her. The curve of his smile against her ear.

"You're not getting sick, are you?" Claire asks, handing her a water bottle. It's twenty minutes to places; Lacey can hear the thrilled, thunderous roar of the crowd overhead. "I feel like you've been quiet today."

"I'm great," Lacey promises, trying to ignore the way the insides of her thighs are still stinging pleasantly within her three layers of dance tights. "Ready to roll." Then, a moment later: "Sorry I didn't get a chance to fill you in ahead of time," she says quietly, "about, you know. The whole Jimmy Hodges thing." She caught it on Claire's canny, foxlike face as she was telling the story to Maddie—a flash of surprise, what might or might not have been hurt at the lack of a heads-up before the call. It's not like Lacey doesn't get it: normally she doesn't so much as take a Midol without giving Claire both full advance warning and a detailed postmortem. "I guess I *have* been a little out of it."

It's thin, as far as excuses go, but Claire just shakes her head. "No worries," she chirps. "Sounds like a nonissue, right?"

"Absolutely," Lacey agrees gratefully. "Total nonissue."

Just before she needs to go on she picks up her phone and googles it, *Yankees vs. Orioles*, scanning the results from this afternoon's game in the Bronx. *Orioles 5–4*, she reads, a slow smile spreading over her face. Jimmy Hodges homered in the eighth to break a tie.

Lacey laughs loudly enough that Claire looks up quizzically from her iPad, hit with a rush of gratified pleasure that's almost embarrassing for how strong and sentimental it is. So he had a good day at the office, she scolds herself as the five-minute warning sounds over the loudspeakers. It has nothing to do with Lacey herself.

Still, though. Still.

She doesn't have his phone number. She could ask Claire to find it, which is what she has done every other time she's wanted to get in touch with someone in the last six years, but she doesn't want Claire to know about this, so she waits for Claire to go back to whatever she's looking at and pulls up Instagram instead. He doesn't follow her, Lacey notices, trying not to feel stupidly disappointed by that. After all, it's not like she follows him, either. She doesn't follow anyone anymore, not since three albums ago when she deleted her account and started over again six months later to coincide with the release of a single called "Phoenix," briefly crashing the app in the process. She sent lunch to the corporate offices by way of apology.

Just saying, she types now, once she's clicked the icon to send jimmyhodges14 a private message, *it seems to have done something for *somebody's* career.*

"Lacey?" There's the PA at the door to her dressing room, a serious-looking Canadian in stage blacks and a headset. "It's time."

Lacey takes a deep breath, then locks her phone and hands it to Claire for safekeeping. Heads upstairs to the stage.

CHAPTER SIX

JIMMY

ALONE IN HIS KING-SIZE BED AT THE WESTIN IN MINNEAPOLIS, Jimmy stares at his phone for a long, silent moment. Then he swears under his breath and tosses the thing onto the sheets.

He's not going to reply, obviously. What would even be the point of replying? What exactly does he think he's trying to accomplish here? She's a little bit nuts, or that's what people say about her. She's the benevolent dictator of a densely populated nation comprised entirely of screaming girls. Jimmy's been with famous women before, has gamely held their purses while they walked red carpets and struggled to keep his composure while cameras strobed six inches from his eyeballs. He promised himself a long time ago he was never getting anywhere near any of that Hollywood bullshit ever again.

Also, not for nothing, he stood alone in that bathroom for four full minutes waiting for his fucking erection to go down.

He picks his phone up off the mattress. The time stamp on her message is 7:52 p.m., a little over two and a half hours ago. She must have sent it before she went onstage, assuming she had a concert tonight. *Did* she have a concert tonight? Jimmy's not about to fucking check. He makes himself do a hundred push-ups instead of considering the possibilities. Then he makes himself do seventy-five more.

Finally he gets up off the carpet and reads her note one more time, rubbing a contemplative hand over his beard. He thinks of the pleased, slightly mischievous way she looked at him as the elevator whooshed down to the parking garage at the hotel last night, like the two of them were in cahoots about something. He thinks of the sounds she made as she came.

Oh yeah? he types—and already, *already* he knows he's going to live to regret this. *What happened, you get some good coverage in* CosmoGirl?

Jimmy puts his phone down, for real this time. Then he grabs it again, locks it in the hotel safe, and marches himself down to the bar to get a beer.

A couple of the guys are already down there, Ray and a few of the other call-ups slouched with their skinny legs spread on the red leather armchairs in the lounge. They spent the entire afternoon in the dugout giving Jimmy shit about last night, about where he might or might not have gone after the rest of them left the club. "Back to my hotel room to jerk off," he told them truthfully, yanking his ballcap down over his forehead and shoving his sunglasses onto his face. "Just like the rest of you fucking clowns." He thinks he may have hit the homer mostly just to shut them up.

Still: "Yo," Tuck said quietly, sliding into the seat beside him on the bus to the airport after the game. "Between you and me. Did you really not—?"

"I really did not," Jimmy said firmly. "Nice girl, though."

"Yeah," Tuck agreed, glancing over at him for what may or may not have been an extra, bullshit-smelling second. "Nice girl."

In any event, Jimmy's not about to surrender himself for further questioning, so he flips the rest of them a friendly bird and takes his beer back upstairs to his room, where he drinks it, plus another one from the minibar, while staring out the plate glass window and thinking, resolutely, about nothing at all. He takes a shower, soaping himself up with hotel-issue body wash that purports to smell like green tea and bergamot. He watches half an hour of *SportsCenter*. He ices his swollen knees.

Just after midnight, he takes the phone out of the safe.

Sure as shit: two new messages from Instagram user laceylogan, 254M followers. The little green circle, the one that means the person has the app open at this very moment, glows like a beacon right next to her name.

First of all, she's written, *that's a sexist comment.*

Second of all, no. I was talking about you. Nice game today.

Jimmy sits down on the edge of the mattress. She said she was going to Canada, which means the local news wouldn't have carried Yankees/Orioles baseball, which means she actively sought that information through alternate channels. He concentrates for a moment on not feeling any particular kind of way about that, and mostly fails.

Thanks, he types, then: *Sorry. For being sexist.*

Joke's on you, she fires back, so quickly it startles him a little. CosmoGirl *folded like twenty years ago.*

Jimmy gets another beer from the minibar, though that's three, which is more than he tries to have the night before a game now, the way hangovers hit quicker and harder on this side of thirty-five. It's a bold move, adding an elective headache to his long list of bodily grievances. *Explains why my subscription hasn't been arriving, I guess.*

The little red heart appears, the one that means she liked it. *I'm sorry too,* she writes. It's weird how fast she's replying, though Jimmy supposes one doesn't have to worry about looking thirsty in one's direct messages if one is Lacey Logan, Queen of the Glitter Universe. *For running out like that. And, you know. For slut-shaming you, I guess.*

For slut-shaming—oh, for fuck's sake. Jimmy types and discards three different responses, all boasting slightly different ratios of humorous to douchey, before finally settling on: *No big deal. I get it.*

The typing bubble appears, then disappears and stays gone for so long Jimmy wonders if maybe that's the end of the conversation. That could have been all she wanted to say, he guesses. Closure, or whatever. He could leave it like that—*should* leave it like that, probably, should file this strange interlude away with the end of his marriage and the weekend he spent in Ibiza drinking mezcal flights with John Mayer under *Experiences It's Probably Best Not to Dwell On* and move the hell on with his life.

So, he types instead, *how's the Great White North?*

Pretty good so far, Lacey reports immediately. *They made me the mayor for a couple of days.*

Oh yeah? Jimmy flops back onto the pillows. *What are your duties?*

I have no idea, she confesses. *I should probably ask for a briefing. Couldn't hurt.*

They riff back and forth on executive orders for a while, then on Canada in general, then on celebrities who seem Canadian but aren't, then on Michael Bublé. When Jimmy finally glances at the clock on the nightstand he realizes they've been at this for almost an hour, like how he used to talk to girls on Instant Messenger back in middle school. His arm is a little bit numb from holding the phone.

Fuck it, he decides suddenly. After all: she messaged him first. *Hey,* he types, hitting send before he can talk himself out of it, *what's your number?*

A pause then, maybe twenty or thirty seconds. Jimmy can feel his pulse ticking. He's got the mostly empty Heineken balanced on his chest, one hand holding it loosely, and the thud of his heart makes the beer slosh a little inside.

Like, my phone number? she finally asks.

Jimmy lets a breath out. *No, your body count,* he types, then deletes it letter by careful letter. *Yes, princess,* he replies instead. *Your phone number.*

Are you going to call me?

Well, I don't usually send nudes until the third date, he tells her, *but just this once, I guess. Since you asked so nicely.*

Oh, you're hilarious, Lacey says, which is neither a yes nor a no, but a moment later a number comes through, an area code Jimmy doesn't recognize.

That your burner? he asks, only half kidding.

Google Voice, baby.

Is it really?

No, she admits. *It's my real number, which means I'm trusting you not to fuck me.* Then, before Jimmy can even begin to decide how to respond to *that* particular declaration, she continues: *I can't actually talk tonight, though. I've got three shows in a row every weekend on this tour, so I do strict vocal rest those days.*

Same, he tells her, then closes out of the Instagram app and texts her number instead. *There,* he says. *Now you've got me too.*

Another heart, quick and decisive. *Now I've got you*, Lacey agrees.

\\\\\\\

THEY WIN THEIR FIRST GAME AGAINST THE TWINS ON FRIDAY, the Minnesota night cool and green-smelling, a breeze in the air that tempts fall. This is Jimmy's favorite time of the whole season, the middle-end of August, the team broken in like a well-oiled mitt and the playoffs still far enough away that he can ignore the faint sound of his own mortality tapping softly at the window of his hotel room. It's—not *easy*, exactly; it's professional fucking sports, it's not supposed to be easy—but easier than it's been feeling lately. It's nice.

Then his alarm goes off on Saturday morning, and he can't bend either one of his knees.

Jimmy swears out loud, wincing with every step as he eases himself out of bed and hobbles slowly to the bathroom. This happens a decent amount now, him waking up in the body of a person twice his age, every single one of his joints on white-hot fire. He needs cortisone shots, probably. He needs a peaceful retirement surrounded by fruit trees and beautiful women, but cortisone shots will get him through his fucking game.

He calls over to the clubhouse and spends the better part of the afternoon with one of the team doctors, a middle-aged orthopedist named Moira with a scratchy voice and the bedside manner of Attila the Hun. "Pain level?" she asks, rolling her stool back a few inches to peer at him curiously, her red-brown hair frizzy around her face.

It's a nine in his back, easily. A seven in his hands and knees. "Two?" he tries with a shrug. "Three? I dunno. I'm fine to play."

"Uh-huh." Moira does not look impressed. The average catcher in the major leagues has a career that lasts a little over five seasons. Jimmy has stuck it out for more than twice that, and his body has kept the dutiful score: tendinitis in both knees and nerve damage in his catching hand, a wonky shoulder left over from six years ago when a runner from the Marlins took a flying leap directly into his left side and tore his labrum basically in half. His lower back aches so much and so constantly he barely even notices it anymore, which is all to say: it's manageable, just like he told her. It's fine.

In the end Moira gives him the shots and writes him a prescription for a different kind of anti-inflammatory, telling him to text her if he has any weird side effects. "What kind of side effects?" Jimmy asks, a little suspicious, but Moira is already out of the room.

He makes it through all nine innings, if barely, collapsing onto his bed back at the Westin later that night and fishing his phone out of his jeans. Lacey had texted him again this morning, a picture of the embossed certificate they gave her to commemorate her brief foray into Canadian politics.

Congrats, he replied. *Planning to issue any proclamations?*

Thinking about it, she told him. *Open to ideas.*

Oh, I've got ideas, he typed back, then deleted it and suggested National Old Fucking Catchers Day instead. Considering he's already had his mouth between her legs, Jimmy finds he's weirdly afraid to come on too strong with her, to be caught wanting anything in particular from these little chats. It feels not-impossible he's misreading whatever the fuck is happening here. She's texting so much because she's bored and got nothing better to do, in all likelihood. She's stuck in a hotel room. She's literally not allowed to talk.

Well, he realizes now, still lying prone on his own hotel mattress late Saturday night: she *couldn't* talk. Three shows at a time, she said, and if the third one was tonight then conceivably *now* she—

Jimmy taps her name in his contacts before he can talk himself out of it. It's a lark, that's all, he tells himself, listening to the crackle of the line as it connects. She's probably out drinking fountain Cokes with her dancers or driving around in a red convertible wearing a sash and crown. It's not like she's going to pick up.

"Hi."

Jesus Christ, on the second ring. "Uh," Jimmy says, clearing his throat and feeling distinctly like she just called his bluff. "Hi yourself."

"How was your game?" she asks. "Did you win?"

"We did," he admits, warmly pleased in spite of himself. Just for a moment, his knees don't hurt at all.

"Did you hit a home run?"

"Did I—no," he says, laughing, a little taken aback. "That's not really something that happens every time."

Lacey *hmm*s. "I think if I was a baseball player I would try to hit a home run at every game."

"That's . . . solid strategy," Jimmy agrees. "I'll be sure to mention it to the rest of the team."

"Thank you."

He rubs at his beard for a moment, feeling the curve of his own smile under his palm. "What about you?" he asks—shoving a pillow behind his back, trying to get comfortable. "How was your night?"

"It was good," she reports. "Well, mostly good. My dancing was a little stupid on the bridge during 'Fameland'—that's one of my songs that I do, I don't know if you—?"

Jimmy laughs out loud. "It's one of your songs that you do, huh?" "Fameland" was the number one record in the US for, like, thirty-three consecutive weeks last year. "You know, I think I've heard of it."

"Okay, well!" Lacey laughs, too, huffing a little. He can picture the exasperated face she's making on the other end of the phone. "I'm just, like, contextualizing. I don't know what you listen to."

"Sea shanties, mostly. The occasional German opera."

"I can't tell if you're being sarcastic or not."

"Not at all."

"Love that for you," Lacey says. "Anyway, there's this one turn that I can only ever nail, like, eighty percent of time, and tonight wasn't one of them, so I'll just, you know. Be here perseverating on that nonstop until next Thursday night."

Jimmy knows better than to tell her that probably nobody noticed. "Yeah," he says instead. "I know how that goes."

"I get too in my head sometimes."

"I hear that." He reaches for another pillow, trying not to groan with the effort. He took some high-test Motrin earlier, but it isn't doing much. "So you're off for a few days now, right? What'll you do?"

"I'm flying back to LA first thing tomorrow," she says, rustling around a little. He wonders if she's getting ready for bed, what she sleeps in. What she'd look like in his T-shirt and nothing else. "I'll see some friends, take care of some admin stuff. Water my plants."

"You water your own plants?"

"I do, as a matter of fact," she informs him a little haughtily. "When I'm home."

"Me too."

"You have a lot of plants?"

"I have a farm, actually."

"Wait." That stops her. "Do you really?"

"Small one," Jimmy admits. "Fourteen acres, up in Baltimore County."

"What do you farm?"

"I don't know," he says, faintly embarrassed all of a sudden. The guys love to tell him how corny he is, how he's Old Mac-Donald. On his birthday they got him overalls and a straw hat. "Regular farm shit. Vegetables, mostly. I've got a little orchard."

"Animals?"

"Horses," he says. "Some chickens. Coupla dogs."

"Wow."

"Yeah, well." Jimmy shrugs into the pillows. "I needed a project after my divorce. And I'm not really that into cars, so."

"Yeah," Lacey says. It sounds like she's smiling. "I'm not really that into cars, either."

"What *are* you into?" he asks, then realizes a beat too late that it sounds like . . . whatever it sounds like. He thinks again of her mouth, her cold hands skating over his chest and his stomach. She left a not-insignificant hickey on his collarbone, and he's had to hide it from his team all weekend long. "Uh. When you're not working, I mean."

"I'm always working," she says immediately, then seems to reconsider. "That sounds bleak."

"Nah," Jimmy lies. "I mean, I get it."

"I guess I don't actually have a lot of . . . like . . . hobbies?" she confesses, her voice quiet on the other end of the line. "I used to. I went through a knitting phase. I knit scarves for all my bus drivers on the last tour. I did sourdough during COVID. My starter was

named Carole King. And I used to really like to go hear other mu-
sicians, to go to concerts and stuff."

"Used to?" Jimmy asks.

"Well, yeah," she says. "It can get kind of complicated, now
that I'm—" She breaks off. "It can kind of be, like, thunder-
stealing, you know? If I go. The attention is automatically all on
me, which people are understandably not always crazy about."

"Even if you're low-key about it?" he asks. "Sit in the back,
wear one of those glasses-and-funny-nose situations?"

"*Low-key* isn't really a thing in my life," Lacey admits. "I
mean, it's not a big deal. But after a while my fans started figuring
out what shows I was most likely to be at and coming by to say hi."

Coming by to say hi sounds like a euphemism for some real
stalker-level shit if ever Jimmy has heard one, but he doesn't say
that out loud. "All your fans are in the Illuminati," he teases instead. "They all think you're trying to send them secret messages
via the outfits you're wearing on TikTok."

"I mean, to be fair, I often *am* trying to send them secret messages via the outfits I'm wearing on TikTok."

"Are you really?" Jimmy blinks. "Like, the . . . what do you
call it, the numerology and shit? The hidden pictures?" Ana-
grams, too. He read about this, alone in bed in his hotel room the
other night after the bar in New York, when he tried and failed not
to careen down the Lacey Logan Internet Rabbit Hole. He thought
there was no way it was a real thing, the idea that her social media
feeds and album notes are all teeming with various winks and hints
and puzzles, the solving of which purportedly opens the door to a
deeper and more profound understanding of the life and times of
one Lacey Elaine Logan: her love affairs and blood vendettas, the

secretmost chambers of her heart and mind. This woman has 254 million amateur cryptologists following her on Instagram. The CIA should recruit them to break enemy code.

"Yeah," Lacey confesses now, sounding a little sheepish. "It's different, with my fans. It's not—I mean, they're special. It's a game we're playing together, that's all. We have a whole little thing that we do."

"Okay."

"I'm serious!"

"I can tell."

"Yeah, and you think it's totally fucking creepy."

Jimmy considers that for a moment, trying to come up with an answer besides *Yup! I totally fuckin' do.* "I think you're objectively the most successful person I've ever met," he tells her finally, which has the benefit of being the truth in addition to being a compliment, "so whatever you're doing is working for you, and if you're cool with it then it's not really my business to judge it either way."

Lacey grumbles quietly. "Good answer," she admits grudgingly.

"Was it?" he asks. His back still hurts, so he gets up and walks around the room for a minute, trying to stretch it without making any embarrassing grunting noises. It's dark in here, the TV flickering on mute and the AC humming quietly. It's been a long time since he talked to anyone on the phone like this. "I'm trying."

"I appreciate that," Lacey says. "Also, my friend, let's not forget that you're literally a professional athlete. You're going to sit there and tell me you don't have any weird shit you do for your career?"

"I mean, yeah, I sit in a recycling bin full of ice for half an hour every morning and average, like, two surgeries a year."

"Now that's what I'm talking about!" She laughs, full-throated and charming. "Tell me more about the ice."

They stay on the line for a while longer, comparing their respective workout routines and the questionable diets they've attempted, the supplements and the juices and the shakes. Jimmy doesn't mention his little *March of Progress* episode from this morning, how it took him the better part of an archaeological age to even stand upright. *A bunch of other boring shit,* he told her when she asked why he was retiring. No reason to advertise the gory details.

Finally Lacey lets out a quiet yawn—quick and ladylike, sure, but Jimmy pictures it before he can stop himself: her mouth open, the wet pink flash of her tongue. He wants to ask her if she's in bed, if she's lying down, how she touches herself when she's alone in the darkness. He wants to get on a plane to Canada and finish what he started last Wednesday night. "All right, you," he says instead, glancing at the alarm clock one more time and realizing it's after two. "I've gotta go. I've got a game in eleven hours."

"Try to hit a home run," she advises.

"I will," he promises. "If I manage it you'll know it's just for you, how about."

"Mm-hmm," Lacey agrees before yawning one more time, the sound of it like a secret thing between them. "I'll know."

\\\\\\\\\\

HE HITS ONE, ACTUALLY.

He thinks about her as soon as the bat connects, her dark hair and soft neck and quick, brilliant smile. He knows the ball is gone before he even starts to run. Jimmy hauls ass anyway, the adrenaline coursing through him, his whole body quick and sleek and painless and the din of the crowd echoing in his head; when he finally slides home, covered in dust and sweat and bruises, for a moment the glare of the sun makes it too bright to see.

CHAPTER SEVEN

LACEY

WHEN LACEY WAKES UP ON SUNDAY MORNING, THERE'S A BLIND item about Jimmy and her on the landing page of the Sinclair.

HALL OF FAME, reads the headline on the hot pink gossip site. *Which uberfamous pop princess was spotted enjoying America's Favorite Pastime at a downtown NYC club earlier this week? Sources say the chart-topping songstress and not-*quite-*World-Series-winning MLB catcher were seen looking awfully cozy before leaving together through a side exit—presumably to, shall we say, round the ol' bases?*

Lacey grits her teeth, one single firework of panic exploding deep inside her chest before she manages to douse it. It's not a big deal, she reminds herself firmly. She knew this would probably happen, and she planned accordingly. She's in control of her narrative; she teaches her fans how to read her. She is, and always has been, her own Rosetta Stone.

She texts Maddie to give her the heads-up, then hesitates for a moment before scrolling to Matilda's name in her contacts. *Hey,* she types. *You didn't happen to say anything to anybody about me and Jimmy Hodges, did you?*

Matilda texts back right away: *Of course not!* she says, complete with the zipped lips emoji. *I would never.*

Then, a moment later: *Why, was there something to say?*

Lacey gets back to LA just after ten a.m. Pacific, putting Henrietta Lang on the stereo and walking around the house for a while, getting reacclimated. Her place—her compound, technically, though that word makes her sound like the leader of a fundamentalist sex cult and she doesn't like to use it—is in Malibu: four outbuildings, a recording studio, and a full gym, plus a cantilevered living room in the main house with a huge wall of windows that juts out over the ocean. The glass is tinted so nobody can see in—they were worried about people coming by in boats, which is in fact a thing that happens sometimes—but still Lacey finds herself avoiding that room altogether if she can help it. Something about being in there makes her feel like she's always onstage.

She's standing at the kitchen island dumping some flaxseed into a cup of yogurt when her phone dings with a text. Lacey looks at it hopefully, but it's just Claire wanting to know if the house was ready and whether she got settled okay. *Yes!* Lacey reassures her. Claire has the next few days off, but she coordinated with the West Coast team so Lacey's fridge was stocked and the blinds were open, the thermostat set to 69.5 degrees just how she likes. The housekeeper will be by in the morning. The chef left three days' worth of meals. *Now go enjoy your break!*

Will do, Claire replies. *Talk to you Wednesday!*

Lacey nods, satisfied. She has a reputation as a generous employer, openhanded with time off and bonuses, and she likes to think that she deserves it; still, she can't help but feel a little bit bereft at the thought of Claire turning off her work phone and going back to her actual life. She told Jimmy she was going to spend time with friends while she's here, which was technically true—she's having lunch with a hip female movie director tomorrow, and she always sees Maddie when she's in town—but the truth is that for an undeniably famous and arguably beloved public figure, Lacey has never been exactly what one might call . . . popular. With actual people. In her actual life.

Well, she amends reflexively, even though there's nobody here to spin the PR for, *that's not entirely true.* In her twenties she did the whole girl-gang thing, a high-profile best friendship with a model named Cora that ended in a spectacular inferno when Cora's boyfriend came on to Lacey at a party, Lacey admittedly did not rebuff him *quite* as quickly as she might have, and Cora leaked a bunch of Lacey's texts to the Sinclair in retaliation. Lacey sold 2.5 million albums about it, then swore off public-facing friendships altogether, which was actually less lonely than it sounds, since she was dating Toby by then and he didn't particularly like to share her. Still, once that relationship imploded it occurred to Lacey that maybe she should have tried a little harder to find a pal who wanted to get a casual cup of coffee from time to time, since when it comes to people who aren't her mother and who don't work for her who she talks to with any regularity, there's, like . . . Matilda. There are a couple of girls from her performing arts high school back in Cincinnati, one who does Hallmark movies in Vancouver ten months out of the year and one who lives in Akron and has four daughters in competitive dance. And—well.

There's Jimmy Hodges, now.

Maybe.

Lacey pulls up the Orioles' regular-season schedule on her phone, even though she already did that earlier this morning, and yesterday also. They're playing an afternoon game today, then leaving from Target Field to head home to Baltimore. She googles *Jimmy Hodges + People magazine*, scrolling a "50 Most Beautiful" photo shoot from a couple of years ago that she has *also* already perused on more than one occasion. She googles the flight time from Minnesota to BWI.

"Enough," she mumbles finally, setting her phone down on the counter. She pulls out her notebook instead to distract herself, flopping down on the sofa in the den with the same kind of Five Star wide-ruled spiral situation she's been using since she was thirteen. She's been writing like crazy the last few days, the lyrics falling out of her brain almost faster than she can get her hand to move. She knows what people say, obviously—*Lacey Logan can't bump into a guy in line at a Starbucks without making a double album about it*, or whatever—but she hadn't written anything since she and Toby split and it feels nice to tap into that part of herself again, to put pen to paper, to hum the melodies under her breath. She feels most like herself when she's writing, though she doesn't think anyone would necessarily believe it. She knows she's always been a spectacle first.

She's plucking experimentally at the strings on her guitar when her mom calls. "Who's Jenny Haines?" she asks, when Lacey answers.

"The designer," Lacey reminds her, getting up off the sofa and padding back into the kitchen for some water. Her fingers are a little crampy from gripping the pen. She remembers Jimmy periodically shaking his hands out back in New York City, wonders how much pain he's actually in at any given moment. Wonders if he'd trust her enough to tell her, if she asked. "You told me to send you her info, remember? For the house?"

"What?" Her mom sounds annoyed. "I didn't do that."

"You did," Lacey says patiently. This happens sometimes:

whole conversations her mom has no recollection of having, lost to a haze of alcohol and her own distraction. Lacey tries not to tell her anything particularly salient after two thirty p.m.

"I didn't," her mother insists now. "She's the one who did your Nashville place, isn't she? That isn't actually my favorite of yours, to be honest. I don't think I'd want to use her myself."

"Okay," Lacey agrees now, which is generally the easiest way to handle it if she doesn't want to have an argument. "Maybe I was wrong."

"Well, you've got a lot on your mind," her mom says magnanimously. "How was the weekend?"

Lacey fills her in on the first three Toronto shows, on the mistake she made last night during "Fameland." "You know," her mom says thoughtfully, "now that you mention it, I've always thought there was an extra step in that choreography."

"There is?" Lacey blinks. Her mom was a college cheerleading coach when Lacey was small, taking her team to Nationals seven years running before she quit to start bringing Lacey to auditions full time. She wasn't a stage mom—Lacey is always careful to clarify this point in interviews—but she was exacting. She expected a lot. "Where?"

"Right where you're talking about," her mom says impatiently. "Trying to execute three full turns in that break before the bridge is asking for trouble. You're showboating, that's all. Lose one and it'll give you an extra beat to hit your mark."

"Huh." Lacey thinks about that for a moment, though as soon as the words are out she knows her mom is right. Frankly she's annoyed at herself for not seeing it first. "I didn't even know you were still paying attention to my choreography."

"Of course I'm still paying attention to your choreography."

Her mother sounds unperturbed. "Are you kidding me? I could probably *do* your choreography. Any of your dancers goes out on disability, you could slot me right in."

Lacey laughs before she can stop herself, only the laugh turns into something else on the way out and Lacey has to swallow it again like a too-big shard of tortilla chip, scraping her throat on the way down. It's disorienting, sometimes, when her mom acts like the person Lacey remembers from when she was younger: the two of them eating Tuna Helper for dinner in the apartment they moved into after Lacey's dad left, watching music videos on VH1. In some ways, it almost feels worse than when she's too drunk to stand. "Okay. Well. Thank you."

By the time they hang up Lacey feels itchy and restless and sad for no reason, pacing the empty house looking for something she can't quite name. She's going to get a new place after the tour, she decides suddenly: some weird bungalow in the Hollywood Hills, maybe, something full of crystals where she can invite Stevie Nicks over for jam sessions. Beaded curtains in the doorway. Lots of pink. Michelle Pfeiffer's apartment in *Batman Returns*, basically, only expensive. Something Toby would absolutely hate.

She heats up some grilled chicken and vegetables in the microwave. She scrolls through her social media tags. Finally she picks up her phone. It's a little past ten on the East Coast, and as soon as Lacey flicks to Jimmy's name in her contacts she realizes she's been waiting to do this all day—that, even if she didn't explicitly admit it to herself, she's been planning it since the moment they hung up last night. Hell, there's a part of her that's been planning it since she saw him across the room in New York. *You've never in your life come into a human interaction without an endgame*, Toby told her once, and while she knows he probably didn't mean it as a compliment, in Lacey's opinion that kind of strategy is just good sense and self-preservation. There's nothing she hates more than being surprised.

"Hey," Jimmy says when he answers. "I was hoping you'd call."

"Really?" Lacey winces at the sound of it, a full click too eager. God, sometimes she is so acutely aware that there's a universe in which she never got famous at all and is instead a children's librarian wearing whimsical dresses printed with cats riding bicycles, trying unsuccessfully to connect with guys on Bumble. "I mean. You were?"

"Yeah," he says easily, sounding completely unselfconscious about it. She likes his phone voice, how it's low and a little bit grumbly, how he always sort of sounds like he just woke up. "You back in LA?"

"I am," she admits, hoping it doesn't occur to him to wonder why she isn't out doing something fabulous. "What about you—home to tend to your goats?"

"I'm in the city tonight, actually," he says with a laugh. "I've got a condo in Fells Point."

"That's cool," Lacey says, as if this is new information to her, which it is not. She searched a couple of days ago to see if he'd done a house tour anywhere, but didn't come up with anything useful. She wanted to be able to imagine him in context, to picture his giant body filling the space. "How was the flight?"

They talk for a long time, Lacey heading upstairs and putting him on speaker while she does her going-to-bed routine. Jimmy tells her about his teammates and a poker game they've had going on and off since 2016, about his plans for his day off tomorrow, which include a visit to the acupuncturist and breakfast at his usual spot. "What about you?" he asks. "Glad to have a break?"

"Oh, yeah!" she says brightly, then can't quite maintain it. "I mean, kind of."

"Only kind of?"

"I don't know," Lacey admits, leaning close to the mirror and inspecting her skin for various spots and imperfections. "I guess sometimes I look forward to the time off, but then when I have it I don't always know how to fill it."

"Could always take up knitting again."

"Careful," she warns him. "You'll wind up with an ugly scarf."

"Come to think of it, my neck has been a little cold."

Lacey laughs, but then he doesn't say anything else, and even though she knows the trick of staying quiet so the other person will talk more and likes to think it doesn't work on her, all of a sudden she's telling him about Cora and her text leak and how empty her cavernous house feels, how lonely it is in LA. "I'm not one of those girls that doesn't like other girls," she says, flipping her head down and brushing her hair out. It feels important that he understands this. "I love girls! In fact, I love girls so much that there's a significant faction of the internet that thinks I secretly date them. But I haven't had a real best friend—like, an active-duty best friend—in years."

"Active-duty friend," Jimmy repeats. "I like that. What about whatshername, though? The one you were with in New York?"

"Matilda?" Lacey says, righting herself again and heading into the bedroom to change into her pajamas. "I mean, Matilda is great. Matilda is wonderful, in a King George III sort of way." Matilda is, Lacey is nearly 100 percent certain, the source of this morning's blind item on the Sinclair, but she doesn't want to say that out loud and scare Jimmy off. After all, the gossip could have come from anywhere. It could have been about *anyone*, and even if Lacey knows, of course, that it is emphatically not, well, there's no point in drawing unnecessary attention at this time to the reality of what it's like to be linked to her in any remotely romantic context. "You just kind of have to assume that anything you say to her is public property, you know what I mean?"

"Sure," Jimmy says. "I can see that."

"I'm not complaining," she says quickly. It feels important that he understand this, too. "It's just kind of like—what am I supposed to do, you know? Go join a pickleball league for single women in their thirties?"

"You could," Jimmy tells her. "Pickleball is the fastest-growing sport in America."

"My schedule kind of precludes activities," she reminds him. "I'm also not very good at sports. So then I'm just that weird girl on the pickleball team with sporadic attendance and a paparazzi presence who nobody likes."

"I don't think that's what would happen."

"You don't?"

"Nah," he says. "You're likable."

Oh, that makes her smile. "I am?"

"I like you."

"I like you, too," Lacey admits, then clears her throat. She wants to ask him if he keeps thinking about it the same way she does, the other night in the bathroom of the bar in New York City. She wants to ask if he shivers every time he remembers what they did. "Anyway," she says, curling up on the velvet chaise in the corner of her bedroom and pulling a faux-fur throw blanket into her lap, "this makes me sound like a sad sack. Let's talk about you instead. Do you have family in Baltimore?"

"Not really," Jimmy tells her. "My folks are in Utica, where I grew up. And my brother passed away a while back, so."

"Yeah." This isn't new information, either, though Lacey couldn't find anything online where he talked about it publicly. She knows he gives a portion of his salary to a sober-housing nonprofit every year. "I'm sorry," she says quietly. "That really sucks."

"It does," Jimmy agrees. "But anyway, it's just me here."

"In your bach pad?" she teases. "Where everything is made of marble and stainless steel?"

"And concrete, yeah."

"Even the bed?"

"Nah," he says, and it's not so much that he misses a beat as it is that his voice changes ever so slightly, getting kind of low and private and wry. "Bed's regular."

"That where you are now?"

"Not yet," he says. "Getting there." He does pause then, just for a second, like he's deciding something. "You?"

"Not yet." She gets up off the chaise and pads across the room, flipping the covers back and sitting down on the edge of the mattress. "There," she tells him, aiming for flirtatious and not quite hitting it. "*Now* I'm in bed."

"You are, huh."

"I am."

"All right," he says. There's some rustling, what might or might not be the whoosh of fabric. "Me too."

"How about that," she says as she wriggles down underneath the covers. She feels the same way she felt as she walked across the bar the other night, half thrilled and half telling herself she isn't actually doing anything. "Is this the part where you ask me what I'm wearing?"

Jimmy isn't laughing. "Do you want me to ask what you're wearing?"

"I mean." Lacey puts a palm on her sternum, stroking a thumb along her collarbone. It isn't lost on her, how cautious he's being. The way he's letting her be the one to come to him. It's not what she might have expected from a person who touched her with such confidence, though to be fair she did insult him and run out of the bar immediately after he did it, so she guesses she can't exactly blame him for not being sure how she's going to react. *Yes*, she thinks as hard as she can, hoping he'll hear it in the ether. *I want you to.* "You can try."

Jimmy swallows; Lacey can hear his throat click. "What are you wearing?" he asks.

"Pajamas," she tells him honestly. She slides her hand down the center of her rib cage to her stomach, rucking her shirt up and dipping a thumb into her navel. She can feel her heart slamming away inside her ribs. "Joggers and a tank top."

"What color?"

"Black." Lacey slips her fingertips under the waistband of the sweatpants, tracing along the jut of her hip bone. She's never had phone sex before; it feels like a relic from the distant past, like key parties or porn theaters. Not that they're *about* to have phone sex, necessarily. Or, more accurately, not that Lacey wants to be the only one who is hoping that's what might be about to occur. "Um. What are you wearing?"

"Boxers," he says. "They're black, too."

"Is that it?"

"That is it."

Lacey frowns. "Wait, like, actual boxer shorts, or—"

"They're boxer briefs, Lacey, Jesus."

"Well, I'm just asking!" she all but shrieks, struggling upright. "Fuck me for trying to get the full picture, I guess."

Jimmy laughs, but not meanly. "Is that what you're trying to do?"

"*Yeah*," she confesses. This is happening, then, the two of them on this phone call; all at once it feels silly to try to act like it's not. "I am."

"Yeah." Jimmy blows out a breath. "I've been thinking about you," he tells her quietly. "Ever since the other night. I can't stop thinking about you."

"Same," Lacey gasps. Oh, it's such an enormous relief to hear him say it. "Like. Constantly. All the time."

"What do you think about?"

"Your hands," she says immediately. "Your arms." She swallows. "How I wanted to take you back to my hotel room."

"And then what?"

"You know what."

"I do," he agrees, "but I want to hear you say it."

"Say what, exactly?" Lacey fires back before she can stop herself, feeling brave and wild alone here in the dark. "That I wanted you to fuck me?"

"I—" Jimmy makes a low sound, not quite a cough. "Yeah, sweetheart," he admits. "That's about it."

"Well," she says, pleased with herself. Her whole body feels like it's on fire. "That's what I wanted."

"That's what I wanted, too."

"Do you still want to?"

"Of course I do."

"How bad?"

"Bad."

"Good." Lacey forces herself to breathe normally. She never talked to Toby like this. Or maybe, like, once in all the time they were together, on his birthday or something. But he's got an unshakable quality to him, Jimmy Hodges, a fundamental unshockability that makes her want to take him by surprise. It's the same reason she suggested the two of them leave the club the other night: because she knew he wasn't expecting her to do it in a million years, and she wanted to see the look on his face when she asked him.

"Are you—I mean," Lacey says, then tries again. "Like, right now, are you—"

"Yeah," Jimmy confesses. It sounds like he's forcing himself to breathe normally, too. "I am."

Right away she pictures it: his bare chest and the trail of dark hair underneath his navel, his hand wrapped tight around himself. Lacey has never in her entire life been able to fathom why a person would ever want to receive a picture of a guy's junk via text message, but she sort of understands it right this second. Not enough to ask for one, to be clear. But, like. Just for a second, she can imagine the appeal. "Okay," she says, sliding her hand down inside her underwear, her own skin smooth and warm beneath her palm. "Me too."

Jimmy groans. "How?"

Lacey squeezes her eyes shut. "However you tell me to."

"Oh, fuck." He laughs again, disbelieving. He sounds so sincere. "Really?"

"Yeah."

There's a pause, then: "Okay, sweetheart," he says softly. "Here's what you're going to do."

He's specific, Jimmy Hodges. He takes his time. It's a trip, the thrill of following his directions as scrupulously as she can: slipping out of her clothes until she's naked under the covers, cupping her breasts with both hands. "How's that?" he asks as she reaches between her legs and rubs with two fingers, his voice all grit and gravel three thousand miles away. "That working for you over there?"

"It's working," Lacey gasps—bucking up into her own touch, chasing the build of it. "It's good."

"Good," Jimmy echoes. "I think the real thing would be better, but we'll make do."

"Tell me," Lacey manages, "what the real thing would be like."

That surprises him; she can hear it. "You are something else, you know that?" he asks quietly, but then he tells her that, too: how he'd lay her out on his mattress and lick her all over, all the ways he'd fuck her until she came. She's worried he's going to expect her to return the favor—she feels shy suddenly, same as she felt the other night in the bathroom, how she can't quite believe the things he makes her want to do—but all at once Jimmy sucks in a breath on the other end of the phone. "Lacey, honey," he says, and his voice is so urgent. "Are you close?"

Lacey slides her fingers inside herself, curling them the same way he did the other night in the bathroom. "Yeah," she manages, her hips coming clean up off the bed. "I'm close."

"That's a girl," he says. "You gonna let me hear you?"

And—yes, actually. She is. Lacey keens as the feeling of it bursts inside her, waves and waves of warm, syrupy pleasure radiating out all over her body. Jimmy growls into her ear, low and vulnerable; *fuck*, but Lacey wants to see his face.

"Was that—" she asks when she can talk again. "I mean, did you just—"

"Yeah," he says with a sheepish-sounding laugh. "*Yeah*. You?"

"Yeah." Lacey collapses back against the pillows. She's exhausted all of a sudden, satisfied and wrung-out and sleepy. She wishes she could curl up next to him, that she could tuck herself close against his chest. That was another thing she kept thinking about after the night they met: the size and the sturdiness of him, like here was a person she wouldn't need to make herself smaller in order to be with. Like here was a person who could handle the bigness of who she is. "Stay on the phone?" she asks, tucking it between her face and the pillow even though she knows that's a one-way ticket to Breakoutville and she's going to regret it in the morning. "Just for a couple of minutes, I mean."

She's embarrassed as soon as she asks it—it feels needy somehow, too forward, even though they literally just got each other off—but Jimmy only hums his assent. "Sure," he tells her, like maybe he's here in her bed beside her and not clear on the other side of the country. "I'll stay for as long as you want."

CHAPTER EIGHT

JIMMY

Two weeks pass like that, August seeping slowly into September. Jimmy works out. He plays baseball. And on the nights Lacey Logan is allowed to talk on the telephone, he lies in his bed in whatever anonymous four-star Bonvoy property he's currently calling home and tells her, in precise, exacting detail, all the things he would like to do to her, given the time and opportunity. He tells her all the things he wants her to do to herself.

It's not all filthy. They talk about other stuff, too: their Sweetgreen orders and Bruce Springsteen's best albums and what Bruce Springsteen's Sweetgreen order might be, if he has one. The games they liked to play when they were kids. One night they watch *Bull Durham* on cable together in mostly complete silence in their separate hotel rooms, the hiss of her sheets faintly audible on the other end of the line. It's Jimmy's favorite part of the day, talking to her. He's dated plenty of women, but he hasn't liked just shooting the shit with somebody so much since Rachel. He's never been so interested in what a person might *say*.

"So here's a question," Lacey posits, late at night on the Monday of Labor Day weekend. "What's the deal with your ex-wife?"

"What's the deal with her?" Jimmy repeats, laughing a little nervously. He's lying in bed watching a *Friends* rerun on mute, the picked-over remains of a room service club sandwich on a tray on the dresser across the room. They played a one o'clock against the White Sox and won. "What do you mean?"

"You know what I mean." He can hear her rustling around in her hotel room, the going-to-bed noises he's started to recognize the last couple of weeks. "Like, why did you get divorced?"

Jimmy snorts; he can't help it. It's interesting, how blunt she is. He would have thought she was the kind of girl who would beat endlessly around the bush, who would obfuscate indefinitely, but instead she is generally, disarmingly, direct. "A lot of reasons."

"Was one of them that you were a bad husband?"

"That was the main one, yes."

"Did you cheat on her?"

"I did not," he says truthfully, "but I got pretty close a few times."

"Gross."

"Yeah, well." Jimmy shrugs into the pillows. "I was gross. We were fighting a lot by that point, not that I'm making excuses."

"Fighting about what?"

"All kinds of stuff," he hedges, which is true, though the big one was what Rachel described to the therapist as *Jimmy's continued refusal to pursue emotional availability or grapple in any real way with his grief over what happened to his brother.* "About my schedule, about kids—"

"She didn't want them, or you didn't want them?"

She didn't. "Neither one of us should have been having them at that point anyway," Jimmy says instead of answering. "And it's a good thing we didn't, in the end, because I failed with great aplomb at couples therapy and we split inside a year."

"Do you still talk?"

"Nah." Jimmy clears his throat, swallowing down a stale-coffee mouthful of guilt. "Not for a long time." It's not that he doesn't want to. It's not that he hasn't tried. He did Al-Anon a few years ago—or started it, anyway, stalling out spectacularly somewhere around the fourth step and deciding the whole thing wasn't actually for him after all. He needed to reach out to Rachel, he knew— needed to tell her she'd always deserved better, that he was sorry for how it went—but he never quite managed to pick up the phone and do it. He keeps telling himself he's going to. He keeps telling himself he still could.

"What about you?" he asks now, shaking out his aching hands before tucking one arm back behind his head. "You still talk to your many famous exes?"

"Uh-uh. Hang on a second there, buddy," Lacey says. "If anything, you've got more famous exes than me."

"Did you go looking?" The thought of it makes him smile.

"Of course I went looking," she tells him, sounding utterly unselfconscious. "I needed to make sure you hadn't been with any- one I truly hate."

"Have I?" Jimmy asks, not uninterested in her answer.

"Wouldn't you like to know," Lacey shoots back. "And any- way, no. Generally I don't talk to any of my exes anymore."

"You write songs about them instead."

He's still joking around, but Lacey doesn't laugh. "Wow," she deadpans instead, "what a groundbreaking take on my extremely successful career as a multiplatinum performer. You should consider a second act as a music critic for *CosmoGirl*."

Jimmy considers that for a moment, surprised by the sudden heat in her voice. "You know what?" he says. "Fair enough."

"You know who else wrote a lot about his own life without anyone giving him shit about it?" she continues as if he hasn't spoken. "Ernest Hemingway."

"Point taken," Jimmy agrees easily. "His pop songs are truly spectacular."

"Shut up," Lacey tells him, but he can hear that she's smiling again, that she's forgiven him. "Anyway, you're just salty 'cause I haven't written one about you yet."

"Is that something I should anticipate for the future?"

"Maybe," she says, in a voice that he happens to know means she's about to wriggle out of her pajamas on the other end of the phone. "If you're lucky."

"Oh," Jimmy promises, "I think we both know I'm lucky."

\\\\\\\\

HE SEEMS TO BE, ACTUALLY—ON THE FIELD, AT LEAST. JIMMY wouldn't say their season has *turned around*, exactly, but it's objectively looking a hell of a lot better than it was a couple of weeks ago. "It isn't luck, fuckheads," he reminds the guys over and over, standing up on the bench for his pregame captain sermons while Hugo scratches his balls through his uniform and Jonesy shoves more nicotine gum into his cheek. "It's hard work and dedication and grit, and we've got it. We always have."

Whatever it is, all at once the Birds are hitting more baseballs than they have all year long, a string of tidy wins lined up one after another like freshwater pearls on a church lady's necklace. "That's seven in a row," Tuck points out when they beat the Pirates 8–5 a few days later, the two of them ambling back down the tunnel toward the locker room. The air smells like grass and sweat and popcorn. The hum of the crowd is still audible from the stands.

"Is it really?" Jimmy asks. That surprises him, not because he hasn't noticed they've been winning but because he hasn't let himself think of it as a streak until right this moment. Streaks, after all, are made to be broken. "Huh. Okay," he says, answering his own question. "I guess it is."

Tuck snorts. "What are you—don't act like you're so fucking cool, you piece of shit," he says, shoving Jimmy not-that-gently in the shoulder. "Do *you* remember the last time we won seven in a row?"

"Nope," Jimmy lies. He does, actually; it was six years ago, the first and only time they ever made it to the Series. "I do not."

"Well then," Tuck says, glancing at Jimmy sidelong. "Whatever you're doing, keep on doing it."

Jimmy ignores him, peeling off at the door to the locker room to go hit the showers. He hasn't told anyone, obviously. What would he even say? *I'm having a middle school phone call situation with the most famous woman on the planet, and it turns out she's got the dirtiest mouth I've ever heard?* It sounds insane. Jimmy has no idea what she's after with him: If it's an ego thing for her, the need to be perpetually admired. If maybe she's just killing time. He could ask, he guesses—he *would* ask, if it was any other woman he liked as much as he finds himself liking her—but again: she's Lacey Logan. And he is, for all his famous girlfriends, a leather sack full of grass stains and spit. It seems wiser, in Jimmy's estimation, not to draw any more attention to that than is absolutely necessary. It seems smarter to play it cool.

Also—and not that he's ever going to say this out loud in a million years—he can't be 100 percent certain that whatever he's got going on with Lacey *isn't* part of why he's playing so well all of a sudden. Jimmy doesn't like to think of himself as superstitious, but he's been in this game long enough to know that at the end of the day, most of it is mental. And a person doesn't spend almost a decade and a half in the major leagues without getting a little funny about his good luck charms.

It's fine, Jimmy tells himself when they win their eighth game in a row the following evening. Whatever. He's not complaining.

Ike takes the train down from New York to see him, and they go to lunch at the Capital Grille. Ike has been Jimmy's agent since Jimmy first got called up, a deeply unflashy Bronx native with a Peter Falk haircut and a face like a jack-o'-lantern two weeks after Halloween. "You still thinking you're done after this season?" Ike asks, as they're eating their steaks.

"Yep," Jimmy says immediately, then thinks of what Tuck said the other night in Pittsburgh. Eight games in a row isn't anything to get a hard-on about, but it isn't nothing, either. It felt easier to be sure he was done back when they sucked. "I don't know. I mean. Yeah, probably. Yes."

Ike raises his bushy eyebrows. "So you don't want to announce yet, I take it."

"I don't know," Jimmy says again. "No. Not yet, I guess."

"Well, since you seem to feel so strongly about it," Ike says mildly, shaking a truly eye-popping amount of salt onto his mashed potatoes. "Look, Jimmy, can I ask you something? And first of all, you know I'm saying this as a person who would be delighted for you to stay out there on that field until the day you keel over in the middle of extra innings and we have to shoot you in your head like a used-up racehorse—"

"Thanks for that."

"—but. Is it possible your, ah, reluctance to call it has anything to do with how it all went in Miami?"

Right away, Jimmy shakes his head. "What?" he says, reaching up reflexively to rub at his throbbing shoulder. "No. No, of course not. That was six years ago, Ike. I'm not losing sleep over that shit anymore."

"You sure?" Ike presses. "Because I could understand not wanting to be definitively done without getting another shot at it. Nobody's going to fault you for that."

"Maybe not," Jimmy says, trying not to think of the night sky in Florida in October. Trying not to remember the sear of muscle torn from bone. "But that's not what this is."

Ike looks at him for a long time. "Okay," he agrees, shrugging at Jimmy across the table. "Eat your steak."

〜〜〜〜

JIMMY SPENDS THAT NIGHT PACING THE CONDO, RESTLESS IN A way he can't quite name—a feeling like he's missing something, a feeling like there's something important he was supposed to do that he forgot. It's the retirement thing, he guesses: he's known he was running out of road for years, but now that he's about to reach the cliff he can feel himself slamming the brakes, wanting to stretch it out for a little while longer, wanting just a little more time. He always figured he'd know what he wanted to do next by the time he was finished playing baseball. He always figured at some point he'd manage to win a ring.

Still could, he reminds himself, then immediately feels like a boner for letting himself think it. Embarrassed, even though there's nobody here to know. Wanting that kind of shit, telling yourself you have a shot at it, is exactly how a person gets his heart broken. Better to just keep your head down and call one pitch at a time.

They've got a home game against Kansas City the following night. In the locker room at Camden he gets changed into his kit and stretches for a while, doing his best to warm his quads and his screaming hamstrings and trying to shrug off the weird uneasiness that's been dogging him for a full twenty-four hours now, an edginess he can't manage to shake. After all, Jimmy reasons, it's not like he's retiring right this second. After all, it's not like the season is already done. And after all, it's not like he thinks they've been winning all these baseball games all of a sudden because he's been playing *you hang up first* with Lacey Logan before he crouches behind the plate every night.

At least, he doesn't *really* think that.

In any case, she's got her first run of shows in Montreal this weekend, so he shoots her a good luck text as the crowds fill the stadium up above him; his phone dings with her reply a few minutes later, just before he needs to head out onto the field. At least, Jimmy *thinks* it's going to be a reply from Lacey, but when he digs his phone out of his gym bag he sees it's actually a message from his mom, which is unusual. *Hi, sweetheart,* she's written. *Just thinking of you today. Went to the cemetery this morning to lay some flowers. The weather was beautiful.*

"Oh, fuck," Jimmy mutters before he can stop himself. It's Matty's birthday, he realizes suddenly, the horror swooping deep and sickening inside him. He completely fucking forgot. He's been so distracted with—what, exactly? Dicking around on the telephone? The end of his middling career? He didn't even text his mother on what would have been the forty-second birthday of her dead fucking son.

"What?" Jonesy asks, looking at Jimmy askance from the other side of the locker room. "You all right?"

"I—yeah," Jimmy lies, clearing his throat a little, dropping his phone back into his gym bag. He can feel the panic sweat breaking out on the back of his neck. "Yeah, I'm good."

"You forget to take your arthritis medication or something?"

"Fuck you." His voice is almost normal. He rakes a hand through his tangle of hair, jamming his cap down over his eyes and turning back to his locker. Trying to remember what he came over here to do. Trying not to think about his brother, who died of a heroin overdose alone in the bathroom of his shitty apartment three weeks before Jimmy got called up to the majors and is buried in the cemetery at Saint Monica's in Utica, the same church where both of them were baptized as babies. Jimmy hasn't been to see him in years.

"Yo," Tuck calls now, making him jump; when Jimmy turns around to look at him, he realizes the locker room is mostly empty. "You planning to play any baseball this fine evening, or do you have a prior engagement you forgot to tell us about?"

Jimmy hesitates. For one insane second he imagines saying it: *It's Matty's birthday, and I forgot like a piece of shit*, before immediately dismissing the idea. He loves Tuck like family, but he doesn't want to talk to Tuck about this. He doesn't want to talk to his mom, either, to be confronted with the enormous hole in her heart and her life he knows he's not big enough to fill, no matter how many baseballs he sends flying into the stands.

If he's being honest with himself, the person he actually wants to talk to is—

"I'm coming," Jimmy announces, zipping the bag shut and tossing the whole thing into his locker. He shouldn't have been looking at his fucking phone in the first place. He needs to get his head in the game. What does he even think he's going to say to her, anyway? *I know you're busy single-handedly improving the value of the toonie, but I'm feeling sad and vulnerable about my dead brother?* That's not what they're doing, him and Lacey Logan. That's not even remotely what this is. "Let's go."

They squeak it out against the Royals, 3–2 in extra innings. It doesn't feel like much of a victory at all.

CHAPTER NINE
LACEY

SHE WAKES UP IN MONTREAL WITH A SNIFFLE, AND RIGHT AWAY she knows she's getting sick.

"Shit," Lacey whispers, rolling over in her hotel bed and taking careful inventory of her symptoms. She's achy. Her throat hurts. Her head feels like it's been stuffed with gauze. She texts Claire, who sets her up with a vitamin infusion, a gallon of electrolyte water, and a venti black tea with honey and lemon, which she drinks before pulling the shades down and going back to sleep for three hours.

"You good?" Claire asks when she wakes up again.

"I'm good!" Lacey promises, which is a lie, but there's nothing to be done about it. It's opening weekend for fifty thousand Quebecers, hundreds more already camped outside the venue hoping to scalp a last-minute ticket. She's not about to let them down because she has a sniffle.

She picks up her phone and texts Jimmy as she shuffles off into the shower: *Sorry I missed your text last night*, she tells him; she meant to message him back as soon as her encore was over, but she wound up passing out in the car back to the hotel instead, waking up in the parking garage with a slick of drool all down her chin. *I think I'm coming down with something.*

No worries, he replies a moment later. *Kind of a weird night anyway.*

Weird how? she types—or starts to, at least. Before she can hit the button to send, another message comes through: *We're chill, right? We're low-key?*

Lacey frowns. What the fuck does *that* mean? Is that weird? It *sounds* weird, but sometimes it's hard to tell over text. Toby always used to say she was imagining that he was mad at her, reading stuff into his tone that wasn't there: *You take the stereotype of oversensitive girl musician to the extreme,* he told her once, and while mostly Lacey thinks that Toby can go fuck himself, she wonders sometimes. She knows she can be too emotional, too navel-gazey, too *everything at once all the time,* and as much as what she liked about Jimmy to begin with was how unfazed he seemed by the very colossus of her, she doesn't want to scare him off. After all, they haven't even put a name to whatever it is they're doing. They haven't even talked about *seeing* each other again.

Yeah, dork, she texts him back, hoping she sounds careless and breezy. *We're low-key.*

\\\\\\\\

SHE DOESN'T *FEEL* PARTICULARLY CHILL, THOUGH, IF SHE'S BEING honest. She's tired and worn out and a little bit grouchy; her whole face feels puffy and clogged. Her fans deserve better, Lacey thinks, dragging herself to sound check later that afternoon. She doesn't want to let anyone down.

Claire's waiting for her when she steps off the stage, handing her a water bottle and two Tylenol gelcaps. "So, hey," she says carefully, once Lacey has swallowed the pills and scooped her fever-sweaty hair off her neck, pressing the chilly plastic against her skin, "I've got something you should take a look at."

Claire holds her phone out so that Lacey can see the screen, which is open to Audriana LaSalle's Instagram profile. Lacey doesn't follow Audriana LaSalle on social media, obviously—Lacey didn't follow Audriana LaSalle on social media even before she found out Audriana LaSalle was secretly pregnant by Lacey's live-in boyfriend—and it actually takes Lacey half a second to recognize her. She looks terrible, frankly: exhausted and gaunt, her face scrubbed clean of makeup and dark rings blooming under her eyes. The baby, less goblin-like now but still very much pale and bald, sucks a pacifier on her hip. *I was never expecting to be a single mother at twenty-six*, the caption begins.

Just for a second, Lacey forgets she's not supposed to be talking about anything that isn't strictly performance related. "Oh," she says, not quietly. "Fuck me."

She reads the rest of the post twice, taking the phone from Claire's outstretched hand and sitting down on a black equipment box at stage left. The split . . . does not seem to have been mutual. They're taking time apart to focus on their careers, Audriana reports—or Toby is taking that time, anyway. Audriana will, presumably, be home alone changing diapers for the foreseeable future, unless she's already found a nanny to do that for her.

"Okay," Lacey says at last, standing so abruptly she gets a little dizzy and handing the phone back to Claire. She's not going to be smug about this. She *feels* a little bit smug, sure, but it's not like she wants that poor child to grow up without a father. Then again, his father is Toby, so conceivably he might be better off only seeing him on weekends and holidays. Lacey can't say for sure. "Well. I mean. Good to know."

"Yeah," Claire agrees, in a way Lacey knows is meant to be reassuring but is not committal enough for Lacey's personal taste. "Maddie wants to do a call."

"Okay," Lacey says slowly. They've got time tomorrow morning, conceivably. She feels restless and jangly all of a sudden, like there's someone she ought to call or otherwise notify. She kind of wants to tell—well, she kind of wants to tell Jimmy, actually, because he's the person she's been telling all her news to lately, the person to whom she reports things in order to make them feel real. But it would be weird to talk to him about this, to bring him dumb gossip about her old relationship like he's Cora or Matilda. For a person who has been with his fair share of famous women, the Perez Hilton of it all doesn't really seem like his speed. "When was she thinking?"

"I think, like." Claire isn't quite making eye contact. "Now?"

They FaceTime while Lacey sits in hair and makeup, Claire holding the iPad while the girls busy themselves with brush selection, mixing various concealers on the backs of their hands. "Hi, honey," Maddie says. "I know you're not supposed to be talking, so I won't waste your time, but I did just want to get a read from you in person about how you want to handle the rumors."

Lacey frowns. "What rumors?" she asks—thinking immediately of the blind item on the Sinclair a couple of weeks ago, of Jimmy's mouth on her body in New York. She knew, she *knew* it was stupid to think she'd gotten away with it, and now they're going to have to handle a shitstorm of press before they ever even get a chance to—

"The—the Toby rumors," Maddie says, sounding surprised. "That you guys are getting back together."

"Me and *Toby*?" She whirls to look at Claire, whose gaze is studiously elsewhere. "And that's why he broke up with Audriana? Is that what people are saying?"

"I—yeah," Maddie says, her expression quizzical. "Wait, you really didn't know about this?"

Lacey winces. She's been so distracted with Jimmy lately that she hasn't been reading as much of her own press as she usually does—well, no, that's not true, she's been reading just as much of her own press as usual. It's the other stuff, the actually *important* stuff, she's been slacking on: the Reddit threads, the stuff on Tik-Tok, the old stalwarts still lurking on Tumblr. That's where the real information is, those are the venues in which she has always done her most meaningful diagnostic and strategic work, but it takes time to dig through it all, and the truth is she's been spending that time with her legs spread in various beds across the US and Canada, muffling her sounds with a pillow while Jimmy tells her to wait until he says it's okay to come.

Lacey clears her throat. "Well," she says, blushing a little bit at the thought of it, like Maddie's going to be able to tell from the sound of her voice. "That's insane. Has Toby *said* we're back together?"

"Not in so many words," Claire puts in, "but." She holds her phone out to display another Instagram account—Toby's this time, the most recent post on which is a picture of him in line at Katz's wearing a T-shirt from her first tour.

"Oh, for fuck's sake," Lacey says, louder than she means to. One of the makeup girls glances up in alarm.

"He's got an angle, probably," Maddie warns her. "I don't know what it is yet, but I'm working on it. In the meantime, do you want to shut it down?"

Lacey considers that for a moment—trying to wrestle her feverish brain into submission, to game out all the possibilities. She could call him out at the show tonight, she guesses. She could post something cheeky on Instagram, some assurance to her fans that they didn't spend all those weeks boycotting *SNL* for nothing. But her head hurts, truthfully, and her nose is still running; just for a second she feels too tired for PR gymnastics, to chase and scoop up all the various flyaway pages and arrange them in the order in which she wants them to be read. She doesn't *want* to manage spin on Toby's bullshit, she thinks crankily. She has to go be Michael Jordan and win the NBA Finals with the flu.

On top of which, Lacey reasons foggily, it might keep the heat off her and Jimmy a little longer if her fans think she's back with her ex.

It might—*huh.*

Lacey sits up a little straighter, shaking off a hairstylist as gently and politely as possible and looking from Claire to Maddie and back again. "You know what?" she says slowly, a plan starting to come together in her tired, fuzzy mind. Toby wants to use the idea of them getting back together for whatever the fuck kind of personal gain he wants to use it for? Fine. Lacey will see him and raise him. Lacey will call his fucking bluff. "No. I don't think we need to do anything about it yet."

"Really?" On the screen Maddie's lips are just slightly pursed, which is how Lacey knows she thinks it's a bad decision. "Are you sure you don't want to—"

"I'm sure."

Maddie hesitates, just for a moment. "Okay," she says at last. "You know your fans best, obviously."

Lacey nods, motioning for the stylist to come back over and finish turning her into the person everyone expects to see when she steps on the stage later this evening. "I do," she promises, and smiles.

\\\\\\\\\

FOUR HOURS LATER LACEY STANDS BENEATH THE STAGE AS THE crowd screams for an encore, a quick and uncharacteristic flicker of uncertainty zipping through her. She hasn't told anybody but her band what she's about to do here, not even Maddie. Not even Claire. It occurred to her to text Jimmy and give him a heads-up, but what would she even have said, exactly? *Just so you know, I'm conducting a quick and dirty psyop on my fans in an attempt to throw them off the scent of our sexy phone relationship?* It's not exactly a cool, un-creepy update to provide.

Maddie will get over it, Lacey tells herself. Claire will understand. And as for Jimmy: tomorrow's the last show of the weekend, with a four-day break in front of her. They'll talk; she'll ask him exactly what they're doing. She'll tell him she wants to see him again in real life.

And until then—they're chill, right? He literally just said it. They're low-key. It's not like he's going to be looking for secret messages in her set list. He follows the *New York Times*, other baseball players, and Alex Guarnaschelli on social media. This isn't something that's even going to remotely penetrate his world.

Lacey takes a deep breath as the lift whooshes her upward, thrusting her into the spotlight in the center of the stage. She wanted it simple, she told the lighting guys when she asked them to make the last-minute changes. Just her and her oldest guitar.

Lacey waits for the crowd to quiet and steps up to the mic, her nerves falling away like scales as she gazes out at the thousands of rapt faces in front of her. This is her favorite part of performing, knowing she has them. Knowing they're right in the palm of her hand. "I'm going to present this one without comment," she tells them coyly, then strums the opening chords of a song she hasn't played in ages and waits for the screams to begin.

CHAPTER TEN

JIMMY

THEY WIN THEIR GAME ON SATURDAY, WHICH MEANS THE STREAK is still alive when Jimmy comes into the locker room Sunday afternoon. Jonesy is sitting in a rolling chair with Hugo and a few of the other guys clustered around him, all of them snickering like middle schoolers waiting for their teacher to notice someone drew a cock and balls erupting on the dry-erase board.

"What's funny?" Jimmy asks, tossing his backpack into his locker and unbuttoning his shirt. They're looking at Jonesy's phone, their heads all ducked close together like pigeons going after a pretzel nugget in the waiting room at Penn Station. "I like to laugh, too."

"No no no, don't show him," Jonesy chides the rest of them immediately. "It's gonna hurt his feelings."

"Fuck you," Jimmy says with a roll of his eyes. "I don't have feelings."

"That's true!" Tuck calls from across the room, voice muffled as he rips a piece of KT off the roll with his teeth and sets about taping his ankles. "His ex-wife got 'em in the divorce."

Jimmy ignores him, hanging his shirt in his locker and holding his hand out for the phone. "Give me that fucking thing."

"Sorry, Cap," Hugo says, passing it over. On the screen is some hot pink web page—a gossip site, Jimmy sees on closer inspection, something called the Sinclair that he only vaguely recognizes. "But it looks like you're not going to be Lacey Logan's girlfriend after all."

It takes some effort, but Jimmy keeps his face very, very blank. "Oh yeah?" he asks. They mostly let that whole thing go after Minneapolis, distracted by Jonesy's feud with some fuckface on the Astros and a particularly disgusting rash on the back of Ray's calf that might or might not have been scabies. Jimmy figured they'd mostly moved on. "Why's that?"

"She's back with her man," Tito reports seriously. "The skinny dude, the comedian. He announced it on Instagram and she sang a song about it at her concert the other night."

Once, very early on in his career in the majors, Jimmy got hit in the head with a baseball so hard he briefly lost consciousness, coming to maybe thirty seconds later with no idea how much time had elapsed. He doesn't know why he's thinking about that right now. "Well," he manages eventually, aware of having paused for just a beat too long. It's not true, probably. And if it is true, it's not like he has any right to feel any kind of way about it. They were fooling around, that's all. Not even *actually* fooling around. Just, like . . . talking about it, or something. "My loss, I guess. I *was* awfully pretty for her."

"Yeah, I think she's a little taller than you, too."

She's not, Jimmy barely stops himself from shooting back. "Could be," he agrees gamely. "They say you start to shrink in your old age."

"Not your nose and ears," Hugo puts in helpfully. "Your nose and ears keep right on getting bigger and bigger until you die."

Jimmy nods. "Hot tip." He stands there for another moment, then abruptly *realizes* he's still standing there and heads back to his locker, managing by some miracle not to yank his phone out of his pocket and immediately start googling in front of God and the entire starting lineup. He clomps off to the bathroom instead, shutting himself in a stall and typing *Lacey Logan + Toby* into the search bar on his browser. He doesn't remember Toby's last name, but it turns out it doesn't fucking matter because here are a thousand fucking news articles about the two of them that no sane person needs to be reading; here are a million different slideshows ready to be pored over and perused. Jimmy thumbs the first result, a decently reputable news organization reduced to a gasping tabloid: *Tobcey Fans!* the headline proclaims. *We Are So Back!*

It's not . . . unconvincing, is the wildest part. Jimmy can see how, if one was the type to buy into a certain kind of deranged, tinfoil-hat logic, the clues are there: The sudden breakup. The T-shirt. And the smoking gun, Lacey's surprise encore at last night's show in Montreal, a deep cut called "Laugh Lines" widely known to be the first song she wrote back at the beginning of their relationship.

Jimmy scrubs a hand over his beard. He does not, as a general rule, make a habit of dabbling in conspiracy theories regarding the love lives of megacelebrities, but she said it herself, didn't she? *I am often trying to send secret messages.*

So. That's that, he guesses. Message received.

This is ridiculous, Jimmy thinks, remembering belatedly that he has a professional fucking baseball game to get ready for. He's thirty-seven years old. He's going to just call her. He scrolls to her name in his contacts, dialing before he can talk himself out of it.

She sends him directly to voicemail.

Jimmy grits his teeth, telling himself not to jump to any conclusions. He's going to be an adult about this. He's going to be a grown fucking man. *Hey*, he texts, hoping he sounds casual. *You got a minute to talk?*

I wish, she texts back a minute later. *In a car full of people headed to the airport. And I'm still super sick.* A frowny face here, and then the one with the mask. *There's some stuff I want to chat with you about, though. Call me when you get home later tonight?*

Aaaaaannd there it is. Jimmy doesn't slam his hand against the tile wall, but he thinks about it. He would certainly like to. He almost just asks her then—*Yo, real quick: Are you back together with your boyfriend? Just wondering, since if you guys are making another go of it I figure he's probably not going to like me telling you to lick your fingers and rub your nipples for me four nights of the fucking week*—but that makes him feel insane. That makes him feel like a girl, actually, and not just any girl but the kind of girl who might use the word *Tobcey* in casual conversation.

Sure, he texts back. *Will do.*

Okay, she replies—another emoji, the smiley face this time. *Have a good game.*

\\\\\\\\\

JIMMY DOES NOT HAVE A GOOD GAME.

The opposite, actually. It's a shitshow from the very first inning, sloppy and slow. Jimmy knows from the moment he crouches behind the plate that his head isn't in it, which is a thing that happened to him sometimes, back when he was breaking up with Rachel. Not that he's breaking up with Lacey—not that they were ever together; not that she owes him anything, an explanation included—but historically Jimmy's baseball has been better, by a not-insignificant margin, when he's been single. The last few weeks were a fluke—except they *weren't* actually a fluke, because again. He is single. He is unattached.

His game remains absolute shit.

Jimmy hates having a bad game as a catcher, because to casual fans it looks like the pitcher is the one fucking up. All game long Tuck pitches what Jimmy tells him to pitch, throwing a screwball when he calls for a screwball and a curve when he calls for a curve, and all game long he gets hit.

In the top of the sixth, Jimmy calls time and stalks up to the mound.

"I don't have it today," he admits, his glove over his mouth so the other team can't see him. "Just—do what you think you gotta do."

Tuck's eyes widen, and it's not like Jimmy blames him. The whole point of Jimmy is that he doesn't get rattled. That's the one thing he brings to the team. The other side could come out dressed in women's evening wear; a UFO could land in the outfield; and Jimmy could keep on calling for pitches, steady as a beating heart.

Except tonight, apparently.

By the time they take the loss and break the streak Jimmy's mood has blackened into something sticky and malignant. He's so deeply irritated at himself, at his own dumbass fallibility, at the fact that he's built this Little League non-relationship into some kind of idol in his head to the point that apparently he gets the fucking yips now if she's too busy to whisper sweet nothings in his ear every night. He doesn't deserve to be in the majors, if that's how he's going to act about it. He doesn't deserve to be the one behind the plate.

Jimmy doesn't say anything as they shuffle back down the ramp to the locker room. As their captain he's supposed to give the rest of the team a speech about how they'll get 'em next time, and he musters one up, sort of, but his heart isn't in it and he knows everybody can probably tell. It's not about Lacey, really. And it's not about his brother. It's about him.

He's done. He knows he's done. Fuck the streak; fuck the playoffs. He let himself get sentimental, a baseball diamond and a pretty girl and the idea that in spite of everything he might have one big win left in him after all. But Jimmy's known he was finished for a long time, is the cold hard truth of it. The last couple of weeks, he just let himself forget.

"You all right?" Tuck asks him as they're heading down to the garage.

Jimmy nods. "I'm fine," he says. After all, he thinks: it's not like he's never lost before. "I'm great." He *is* great. He's fine. He can lose a baseball game; Lacey Logan can get back with her boyfriend. He can go home for good at the end of the season having never won a World Series, and there will never be anybody less bothered about it than him. He is chill. He is low-key. Hell, he's ready to party.

"We should go out," he announces.

That gets Tuck's attention, a slow, brilliant smile spreading across his face. They haven't been out since New York. "Oh yeah?"

"Yeah," Jimmy decides. All at once it sounds like a truly excellent plan, the only logical thing to do. It's Sunday night; they've got tomorrow off before they need to be back at the clubhouse.

And what the fuck else is he going to do, go home and call Lacey so she can let him down easy? He'll pass, thanks. They can just as well have that conversation another day. "We should."

They round up a dozen guys and go to a dive bar on Miles Avenue: darts and a jukebox, the linoleum floor sticky underneath the soles of Jimmy's sneakers. "It was a good run," Jonesy says, raising his beer, and it takes Jimmy a minute to realize he's talking about the streak and not Jimmy himself.

"It was a good run," Jimmy agrees.

Ray trots off to try his luck with a couple of coeds playing the photo hunt game in the corner. Hugo feeds a twenty into the jukebox and programs it to play "Unwritten" by Natasha Bedingfield a dozen times in a row. Jonesy orders a round of shots, and then Tuck orders a round of shots, and then they all peel Ray away from the college girls and make him order a round of shots, too, even though he keeps crying poverty, and pretty soon Jimmy is filled with the kind of mellow, drunken well-being he associates with going to field parties in the summer outside Utica when he was in high school, the sky and the possibilities both endless overhead. He loves these guys, truly. He hasn't been paying enough attention to them.

"To the streak," Tuck toasts, standing up on a barstool.

"To Ray's maximum-strength antifungal medication," Tito volunteers.

"To Lacey Logan's inevitable sex tape," Hugo chimes in, "and the fact the rest of us will be able to enjoy it without Jimmy's hairy ass getting in the way of the shot."

That one really fucking tickles them, their hoots and laughter rowdy and good-natured. Jimmy laughs, too, but all at once he's not having fun anymore, swinging from good drunk to bad drunk in the time it takes the last shot of Fireball to burn sweetly through his chest. It feels like too much to hold all of a sudden, Lacey and the streak and the definitive end of everything. The polite, careful wording of the text from his mother. His brother, still relentlessly fucking dead.

He waits until enough time has gone by that he won't look like a whiny little pissant in front of the entire team, then digs a wad of cash out of his pocket and drops it onto the bar. "I'm out," he tells Tuck, who's trying to flag down the bartender for a bucket of Coronas. "I'll see you clowns on Tuesday. Don't take any wooden nickels, et cetera."

"Okay," Tuck says, eyeing Jimmy speculatively over the mouth of his beer bottle. "You sure you're all right?"

"Never better," Jimmy promises, then turns and weaves his way through the crowd and out onto the sidewalk, turning his face up for a moment to the cool, quiet Maryland night.

\\\\\\\\\

Lacey calls as he's letting himself into his condo. "Hey," she says when he answers, the noise of her TV faintly audible in the background. "There you are."

"Yeah, sorry." She texted him a couple of times while he was at the bar, *Still around for a phone call?* plus the eyes emoji. Jimmy didn't text her back. "I went out with the guys for a bit."

"Sounds fun," Lacey says, her voice a little congested-sounding. "How was your game?"

"It sucked, thanks."

There's a hesitation, just for a second. "That's too bad."

"Yeah, well." Jimmy sits down hard on the sofa, tries to soften his tone. "It happens that way sometimes."

"That's what I hear," she says. "Sorry I missed you earlier."

"It's fine," he says, tipping his head back. "You were busy."

"Not really," she counters. "I was just sitting next to my assistant in the back of a Chevy Suburban, so."

"Right."

Jimmy feels his eyebrows twitch. "That what's going on?"

Lacey huffs a quiet laugh. "Um, yeah," she says, sounding a little cautious. "Why?"

"No, nothing," he says, closing his eyes for a moment and wishing he'd gotten himself a glass of water before he sat down here. Already his head is starting to throb. "No reason."

"Are you okay?"

"I'm great."

"Okay," she says, "because you're kind of acting like a dick, so I'm just wondering if maybe you're tired and need to eat a banana—"

Jimmy opens his eyes again. "Okay," he echoes. "Well. Thanks for the advice."

"Seriously," she says, "what is up with you?" She pauses. "Look, is this about—"

"About what, exactly?" He cuts her off.

Lacey sighs. "I mean, you're going to think it's stupid, but I know there are rumors going around about me and Toby, and I don't know if that's something you care about or not, but for the record, there's nothing true about any of them. That's what I wanted to talk to you about."

"I—" Jimmy stops. "Okay." *Rumors*, he repeats to himself, embarrassed for a moment by how relieved he feels to hear it, only then instead of it calming him down it just feels like popping a particularly gross blister, like now the gunk is everywhere. Like he threw away a fucking ten-game streak on a piece of celebrity hearsay that wasn't even true. "Well. I don't really read the gossip rags, so."

"No, of course you don't," Lacey agrees, an edge in her voice. "You're too cool."

That irritates him. "Can I ask you something?" Jimmy says, and he knows, he *knows* he's being an asshole, but he can't seem to stop himself. It used to make Rachel insane when he did this, digging his heels in for no discernible reason like a little kid. "Just—in your estimation. What's the point of all this, exactly?"

Lacey is quiet for a moment. "The point of what?" she asks.

"This," Jimmy says. "The two of us. Just, like. Chitchatting on the phone."

"Is that what you'd call this?"

"What would you call it?"

"I mean, I think I probably would have called it something different twenty minutes ago, but now I'm not entirely sure, so by all means, you tell me."

"I don't know." Jimmy shakes his head, trying belatedly to clear it. He wants to tell her to come here so they can talk about this in person. He wants to tell her that he didn't realize he was lonely until they met. He wants to tell her he's scared of how much he likes her, that he's scared about the end of his career, but all of that feels like too much work for the drunken way the room is suddenly spinning, so he blows it all up instead. "A distraction, maybe."

"A distra—okay," Lacey says again. "That's good to know."

Right away, Jimmy knows that was the stupidest fucking thing he could possibly have said to her. Back when he and Rachel were in couples therapy the shrink was forever trying to get him to admit he was a person who sabotaged his relationships. "Lacey—" he starts, but this time she's the one who interrupts.

"No, you're right," she tells him tartly. Her consonants are very crisp. It's the diction of the person he thought she was before he spent all these hours talking to her, before he learned her ragged edges and her tells. "I think we've both been goofing off a little bit here, haven't we? Maybe it's better for us both to get back to work."

"Okay, hang on," he tries again. He feels panicky all of a sudden, sweaty with the queasy knowledge that once they hang up that's going to be it, it's going to be finished. He's going to have missed his chance. "That's not what I—"

"I gotta go," she announces. "This has been great. Loved talking to you, really."

"Lacey—"

"*What*, Jimmy?" She sounds so annoyed. "Because I gotta tell you, I'm a pretty busy person, so whenever you want to stop wasting my time would be super."

Jimmy opens his mouth, closes it again. "Fair enough," he says. "You take care."

\\\\\\\\

JIMMY HANGS UP AND STAGGERS AROUND THE APARTMENT FOR A while, collapsing into bed fully dressed and passing out on top of the covers only to startle awake two hours later with a blistering hangover, his mouth dry and sour with regret. He heaves himself up and forces himself to chug a bottle of water and pop a couple of painkillers, then kicks his jeans off and drags himself back into bed. He thinks about calling Lacey again, though it's three a.m. at this point and he suspects *I'm sorry, I'm drunk* is not an excuse that is going to particularly move her.

He gropes around until he finds his phone on the nightstand anyway, scrolling through his contacts until he gets to Ike's name. Ike isn't the kind of agent who answers texts late at night—in fact, he's not really the kind of agent who texts at all—but Jimmy feels like he needs to do this before he changes his mind.

Hey, he types, squeezing one eye shut so he'll quit seeing double. *Give me a call first thing, will you? Turns out I'm ready to announce after all.*

CHAPTER ELEVEN

LACEY

OH, FUCK HIM.

"Fuck him!" Lacey exclaims out loud, looking reflexively around her empty bedroom for—for what, exactly? She doesn't know. An audience, maybe. Someone to perform her anger to. She wants to go live on Instagram and tell all 254 million of her followers what a dick he is. She wants to send her fans to his house with pitchforks and meanly witty signs.

Ugh, she's so annoyed. She should have known this whole thing was too good to be true, whatever secret fantasy she's been indulging in the past few weeks as a balm for her own restless loneliness. The reality is that Jimmy Hodges is some grouchy, washed-up old athlete who probably doesn't even change his socks during the playoffs. He was never serious about this being a real thing.

She hates him. She hates him!

That's when Lacey starts to cry.

She lets herself indulge in it for a minute, sitting there alone on her enormous ship of a bed, feeling silly and snotty and sad. He is going to lift so neatly out of her life, she can already tell, because nobody but her knows he even was in it to begin with. He *wasn't* in it, really; he was just a disembodied voice she talked to sometimes, a blank screen on which to project all her hopes and fantasies and secret desires. He might as well have been her imaginary friend.

She wants to go for a long run alone and have nobody look at her. She wants to lie in her bed and sulk for a week. She wants to go have a casual fling and post about it on social media where Jimmy will be sure to see it and spend the rest of his life awash in shame and regret for letting her slip through his fingers. But none of those options are available to her, so instead she stuffs her resentment and heartache and all the other ugly, spoiled emotions she knows she isn't really entitled to feel back down where they belong, and she goes back to work.

She meets with Maddie first thing on Monday morning. "I guess I'm just a little concerned about the optics of it," Maddie says carefully, the two of them sitting on the couch in Lacey's den while Claire taps busily on her laptop in an armchair across the room. To say Maddie had questions about Lacey's decision to sing "Laugh Lines" the other night is . . . an understatement. "I mean, if you and Toby really *are* back together, then that's one thing, but—"

"We're not," Lacey interrupts.

"Right," Maddie agrees, "so then I'm just not sure about the benefit of letting people think he's abandoning the mother of his child in order to—"

"People can think whatever they want," Lacey points out sweetly. "I mean, it's not like we actually confirmed anything. I'm just a girl singing a song."

"Well." Maddie's lips twitch. "I think we both know that's not true."

Lacey frowns. It would have been easier just to tell them about Jimmy, obviously. It would have been smarter just to come clean. But now there *is* no Jimmy, and unfortunately the coverage of the Toby thing hasn't been terribly generous toward her, and Lacey can't quite quell the uncomfortable suspicion that she may have miscalculated this particular bit of guerrilla warfare. That she didn't think it all the way through. Still, she doesn't want Maddie to know that, so she takes a sip of water and smiles her calmest, most capable smile.

"Look," she says. "I don't know what Toby's game is, but I do know Toby, and he was one hundred percent going to keep pulling this petty shit unless he saw I was willing to pull it right back. Just watch. He's going to slink back into whatever dark, pee-smelling comedy club he crawled out of, and we're not going to hear from him again."

"Okay," Maddie says, though Lacey can't help but notice she doesn't look terribly sold on the idea. "You're the boss."

Lacey is expecting Claire to leave too once they've wrapped up with Maddie—technically today is her day off—but instead she hangs back for a moment, hesitating near the doorway to Lacey's mudroom. "Can I ask you something?" Claire asks. She's wearing a pair of black denim overalls and a rainbow-striped T-shirt, the tips of her short hair bleached bright white. "Is everything okay? Like, with you and me?"

"You and *me*?" Lacey asks, genuinely surprised. "Yeah, of course. Why do you ask?"

"No, no reason," Claire hedges. "I mean, it's entirely possible that I'm imagining—" She breaks off. "I guess I've just been getting the vibe that maybe there's something on your mind the last few weeks. And I'm not saying it's about Toby—"

"It's not," Lacey says, then winces at the heat in her voice and quickly amends: "I mean, there's nothing going on." Still, now that she's stopping to think it through, it's not like she doesn't understand why Claire is asking. Before New York they spent almost all their free time together, watching rom-coms on Netflix after Lacey's shows and ducking into boutiques on their off days. Paid assistant or not, she was the person Lacey was telling everything to, before she started telling everything to Jimmy instead.

Claire is still looking at her, her expression even, and for a moment Lacey almost just says it: *I'm worried my plan might have backfired a little bit. I'm terrified of letting everyone down. I let myself fall half in love with Jimmy Hodges over the telephone, and now it's over before it ever really began.*

"Everything's fine," she promises instead, and for a moment she's not entirely sure which one of them she's trying to convince here. "Go enjoy your time off."

\\\\\\\\

SHE'S BACK IN MONTREAL FOR THE SECOND WEEKEND OF SHOWS on Thursday, the crowd soaked and screaming in their branded ponchos and the stage so slick with rain she needs to be careful not to slip and break her neck. "You could cut it a little short and nobody would blame you," her tour manager urges, but instead Lacey leans in, playing extra songs for all three encores, spending the whole weekend eating, breathing, and sleeping this tour in a way she hasn't since New York City. Her fans report that these shows are the most energetic of the entire Canadian run, wondering if being back with Toby is giving her a sudden burst of inspiration. There's a picture of her on the cover of the *Montreal Gazette* with her arms raised as the storm comes down all around her, guitar slung over her shoulder: LACEY LOGAN CONTROLS THE WEATHER, the headline reads. She couldn't have asked for better coverage, truly. She couldn't have asked for better fans.

She's not having fun anymore, is the problem.

It's not that she *misses* him, Lacey tells herself, settling in beside Claire for a viewing of *10 Things I Hate About You* after her show on Friday night. It was just exciting, that's all—having a crush, the way it gave her days a kind of forward momentum. A reward at the end of the night. Not that the shows aren't a reward in themselves, obviously; not that the tour isn't enough to keep her busy and fulfilled. The performances are 180 minutes long, her set list covering forty songs from nine different albums. She's got sixteen costume changes, four different sets, pyrotechnics so impressive they scared her the first time she saw the demos. She trained by running on a treadmill singing the whole set list start to finish every day for five solid months. She *should* be giving it her full and undivided attention. Her fans deserve that much at least.

She'll recommit herself to her artistic calling, Lacey decides as the stage lights dim on Saturday evening, the screams of the crowd so loud and adoring she can feel them in her molars. She'll throw herself into her creative work. Forget the Catwoman house; she'll move to a yurt in the desert. Swear off men altogether and make ceremonial vows to herself.

Lacey Logan's North American tour ends the last Saturday in September with three sold-out shows in Calgary. She flies back to LA the following morning, then proceeds to spend four full days in bed, drinking smoothies and eating Chik'n Nuggets and watching the entirety of the run of *Riverdale* in one long, weird binge. As soon as it's over, she remembers absolutely nothing about it. It occurs to her to wonder if she might be depressed.

On the morning of Day 5, she's drinking her latte on the patio—*Look at me getting fresh air!* she texted Claire, who sent back the confetti emoji—when her phone dings with a news alert from ESPN, which Lacey signed up for when she was briefly considering becoming a sports person. *Orioles Catcher Jimmy Hodges Announces Retirement*, it proclaims.

Lacey gasps before she can quell the impulse. She clicks through and scans the article, then goes back and reads it more carefully:

Hodges informed the team late last week of his intention to hang up his cleats at the end of this season following a thirteen-year run with the Orioles, it reads, alongside a picture of Jimmy looking obnoxiously handsome in a clay-streaked jersey, his giant forearms tanned golden-brown. *In a statement, he expressed gratitude to his teammates and confidence that this season's O's have a chance to win the World Series—an honor that has to date eluded Hodges despite a storied career laden with awards and accolades.*

The article goes fawningly on, but Lacey isn't really registering anything it says. She's filled with the same weird, jangly longing she had that very first night at the bar—the panicky, sliding-doors certainty that the tether connecting her to Jimmy, the string connecting him back to her, is about to be snapped once and for all unless she does something to stop it.

She puts her phone down, then picks it up again.

Scrolls to his name.

There's no way he's going to text her back, Lacey warns herself even as she's typing. He's probably already sleeping with some twentysomething influencer with a show about flipping Airstreams on the Home Network's streaming platform. She knows this. Still, Lacey is the bigger person, isn't she? Lacey is fucking huge.

Saw your announcement, she tells him. *Congrats on a great career.*

That's sufficiently businesslike, right? There's plausible deniability there. Plausible deniability up the wazoo.

Her phone rings five seconds later, *Jimmy Hodges* appearing on the screen. Lacey is so startled she fumbles the thing altogether; it goes skittering under the patio table and she has to drop to her knees to fish it out again, wincing at the fresh new crack blooming across the front. She barely hits the button to answer in time.

"Hey," she says, a little out of breath, unable to keep the surprise—and, fine, the pleasure—out of her voice. "Everything okay?"

"Uh." Jimmy clears his throat, the sound of it a little thick. "Yeah, totally."

Right away Lacey frowns, sitting down on one of the lounge chairs beside the pool and tucking her legs up underneath her. "You sure?"

"No, actually. Sorry. I'm kind of, uh. I don't know. I'm fine. I hope it's okay I called, I know we—" He breaks off. "I guess I'm just kind of, like. Freaking out a little."

"About retiring?" she asks, and then it clicks. "Or about *announcing* retiring? Because now it's real?"

"Uh. The second thing, yeah." He sounds grateful not to have to explain it.

Lacey nods even though he can't see her. "I mean, of course you are."

"Of course I am?" That surprises him, she can tell.

"I mean, yeah," Lacey says, leaning back and making herself comfortable, settling in. "Did you actually think you'd be able to announce your retirement from the only thing you've done in your entire adult life and not feel any kind of way about it?"

"Uh." Jimmy clears his throat one more time. "That was the hope, basically."

"Wow," Lacey says calmly. "That's the stupidest fucking thing I've ever heard."

That makes him laugh, only then it turns into something else halfway out, a weird coughing sound. "My heart is racing right now," he admits quietly, sounding sincerely embarrassed about it. "It's been racing all morning. Ever since the statement went out, I just—I feel like I can't even breathe."

"Oh, buddy." Just like that, Lacey isn't really mad anymore. She knows she should be, probably—should make him apologize and grovel and prostrate himself before her. But she doesn't actually want to do that, she realizes. Mostly she's just glad he called. "Have you ever had a panic attack before?"

"No," Jimmy says immediately, then: "I don't know. Maybe. Is that what this is?"

"Sounds like it."

"Lucky me."

"Lucky you," Lacey agrees, "because I'm going to talk you through it."

"You are?"

"I am."

"This happen to you a lot?"

"Not nearly as much as it used to," she says truthfully. "Now listen."

She does the trick of making him name the things he can see and hear and smell all around him. She does the trick of making him do math problems in his head. She does the trick of telling him the entire plot of all three Fifty Shades movies, which to his credit Toby once did for her when she was in a bad way following a stupid online feud with a big-name YouTuber and sure her career was well and truly finished. She makes him go outside and breathe in the fresh September air. "How you feeling?" she finally asks.

Jimmy seems to consider that. "Better," he concedes. "Less like I need somebody to scrape me off the ceiling, at least."

"Well," Lacey says, "that's progress."

"Yeah." They're quiet for a moment—not quite the comfortable silences of their earlier conversations, maybe, but not heavy and awkward and terrible, either. "You're talking," he notes. "You picked up, I mean. You're in between runs now?"

"Finished altogether, actually," she tells him. "At least until Europe."

Jimmy lets out a low whistle. "Well, damn," he says. "Congratulations, superstar. That's some impressive work."

Lacey grins dopily, grateful he can't see her blushing at the compliment. "Thank you," she says primly. "What about you?"

"Oh, I've got, like, fourteen concerts lined up in Japan," he says immediately. "They can't get enough of me in Yokohama."

"Funny."

"I try. Monday off," he tells her, "then a home game Tuesday night."

"Huh," Lacey says, considering that for a moment.

"Huh," Jimmy agrees, and she can tell he's doing the same.

Lacey takes a breath, her chest aching with both the pure narcotic relief of talking to him again and the sharp, hungry awareness that it's nowhere near enough. She missed him globally, yes, but also specifically, all the secrets he murmured in her ear. "What would you do to me?" she asks quietly. "If I was there?"

Jimmy doesn't answer for a long moment, then: "Lacey," he says, and his voice is so quiet. It sounds like he's trying to warn her.

Right away, Lacey's entire body flushes a humiliated, shameful red. "*What?*" she screeches, nearly falling off the lounge chair like a cat shoved off a sill. "Are you seriously going to—since when are you *shy*?"

"I'm not," he says, sounded a little offended. "I'm not. I just—I don't want to talk about this anymore, all right? I don't want to *just* talk about it, I mean. I don't want it to be theoretical with you anymore, Lacey, and I don't know if that's a good idea."

"Why would it not be a good idea?"

"For a lot of reasons."

"Because I'm a distraction?"

"Yes," he says, no hesitation at all. "Because you're a distraction. Because I don't feel casual about you. I don't know if I've got my head on right about this, and I don't—I just want to be sure that you're—look," he tries finally, breaking off and starting again. "I'm at the end of my career. I'm a lot older than you—"

"By, like, five years!" she interrupts, laughing at the absurdity of it. "And also, not to be gauche, but I am already very fucking famous. This isn't, like, *A Star Is Born*, where you're going to hold me back from reaching my potential so you need to hang yourself in the garage—"

"I think he shoots himself."

"All right, well." Lacey laughs. "Don't do that, either."

"I'll try my best."

"Okay," she says. "Well. What are you worried about, then? That I'm going to ruin your shot at the World Series? Because *you* called *me* just now, Jimmy. You're the one who's saying you don't want this to be theoretical. And you're the one who asked what the point of all this was, back when you were so rude to me on the phone, so—"

"About that," he interrupts. "I owe you an apology. I was in a bad mood about other shit, and I was drunk, and I was jealous, and I acted like a schmuck."

Oh, that intrigues her. "What were you jealous of?" she asks.

"Fuck off," he says mildly. "You know what."

Lacey guesses she does, though it truly hadn't occurred to her in the moment. She'd felt stupid about the Toby rumors, stupider still when Jimmy made that crack about not reading the gossip rags. She'd been so busy trying to keep him from figuring out how much their conversations meant to her that it had never actually occurred to her to wonder whether possibly they meant that much to him, too.

Still, "I've had jealous boyfriends before," she tells him now, curling her legs up underneath her. "It's not my style."

"Am I your boyfriend?" It sounds like a challenge.

"I don't know," she says honestly, "and for the record, I don't feel casual about you, either. But we should probably see each other in person before we make any rash decisions, don't you think?"

"Yeah," Jimmy agrees. "We probably should."

Neither one of them says anything for a long moment, both of them waiting, but in the end Lacey's never been good at playing chicken. "Dude," she says finally, "I asked you out once already."

That makes him laugh, the sound of it low and rumbling; Lacey feels it in her ribs and her legs and her spine. "I guess you did," he admits. "Come see me."

"When?"

"As soon as you possibly fucking can."

Lacey breathes in, her stomach flipping with anticipation and hope and desire. She's going to have to tell Maddie, she thinks immediately. She's going to have to tell Claire. She's going to have to admit she's been keeping a secret, going to have to figure out all the hundred thousand ways this is all about to get so much more complicated than it's been so far. But for a second she doesn't care about any of that. For a second all she feels is glad.

"I gotta tell you, pal," Lacey says, as casually as she can possibly manage, "I thought you'd never ask."

CHAPTER TWELVE

JIMMY

JIMMY WAKES UP MONDAY MORNING, AND HE FEELS LIKE HE'S died. His knees are swollen. His hands are killing him. It takes him fifteen minutes to get out of bed. He dry-swallows four ibuprofen and stands in the shower for a long time, alternating the water as hot and cold as he can stand it and trying to figure out how to call this whole thing off in a way that somehow preserves both his dignity and Lacey's. What the fuck was he thinking, suggesting she come here on such short notice? Sure, when they compared their schedules over the phone it became abundantly clear that between the rest of his season and her various celebrity tea parties it needed to be either today or like six weeks from now, but still. Even after weeks and weeks of buildup, all at once this feels way too soon.

He could say a work thing came up, he thinks, scrubbing the shampoo out of his hair. Baseball emergency? Is that convincing? That's not fucking convincing.

When he sits on the mattress in his towel and he picks up the phone, she's already texted. *See you soon! Headed for the airport.*

So. That's that, then. This is happening. Jimmy yanks at his beard, then gets dressed and shuffles downstairs to the fridge. What do people like Lacey Logan even eat? Last night he added three bags of baby carrots and some fizzy water to the grocery app he shares with his housekeeper. Is that sexist? Probably. Jimmy doesn't fucking know. She just seems like the kind of person who probably eats a lot of baby carrots, that's all. She seems like the kind of person who might eat most foods raw.

It's not a small thing, moving a person like Lacey Logan, let alone with so little advance warning. "Want to shoot me your assistant's number?" she asked him yesterday. "That way Claire can reach out to her to talk about logistics."

"Oh." Jimmy hesitated. "Well—"

"You have an assistant, don't you?" Lacey asked, sounding uncertain all of a sudden. "I mean, I just assumed, but if you don't—"

"No, I do." He does, too, a fortysomething blonde named Jennifer who makes sure his bills get paid and dresses almost exclusively in capri pants, but arranging a clandestine hookup is not the kind of thing Jimmy likes to use her for, so instead he got on the phone and talked to Claire himself for almost an hour last night, making dutiful notes on a wrinkled yellow legal pad about security and privacy and accommodations for Lacey's various bodyguards. When they finally hung up Jimmy went outside and stood on the back porch of the farmhouse for a long time, staring out into the darkness, wondering if possibly he was making a mistake.

By the time Lacey turns up a little before one, his body is thankfully approximating basic functionality, though his hands are still aching like all hell. Jimmy shakes them out one more time, hard, then hits the button to open the gate at the front of the property and heads out to the wide front porch, watching the black SUV roll down the long dirt road that leads to the main house. It's early October, and warm, the beeches and black cherries and pop-lars all making a leafy green canopy up above him. Jimmy bought this place mainly because of the trees.

He starts across the driveway as the car slows to a stop, then freezes at the last second, weirdly nervous he's going to get tased if he makes any sudden approaches. Instead he stands there dumbly with his hands in his pockets while her driver gets out and opens the door for her, watching as she hops nimbly down out of the back seat. Her heels kick up a tiny cloud of dust.

"Hey," Jimmy says, lifting a hand in her direction.

"Hey yourself," Lacey calls back, and oh, the fucking *smile* on her. She's wearing jeans and a little red crop top, the smooth, tan strip of her stomach visible in the golden light of the afternoon. Her hair is long and loose down her back. She looks like a one-woman propaganda campaign for the United States of America and all at once it feels insane that Jimmy was ever in his entire life indifferent to her. It feels insane that he almost let her go.

He crosses the lawn then slows down abruptly as he tries to gauge how the fuck to greet her. Do they hug? Do they kiss? It feels deeply negligent on his part not to have considered this be-forehand. He can tell she's trying to figure it out, too.

Fuck it, Jimmy decides. "Hi," he says, and ducks his head to drop a kiss against her smooth, matte cheek. "How was the flight?"

"Fine," she says. "Easy."

"I guess they mostly all are, when you've got your own ride." He offers a hand to first one bodyguard, then the other, shaking in what he hopes is a sufficiently macho and capable way. They're retired marines, both of them, with necks as thick as five-gallon buckets. Jimmy's a big dude, sure, but they look like they could snap him in half.

"Do we want to get these guys set up?" Lacey asks. "Do you have, like, a house manager you want them to huddle with, or——?"

"Oh," Jimmy says, feeling abruptly like he invited Jill Biden to his dorm for a kegger. "It's just me here today, actually." It occurs to him that he should have offered to come to her instead, to swim in her gold-plated swimming pool and eat grapes peeled by her many servants. It was easy to forget, talking to her all these nights, the fact that Lacey Logan changed the economy of every city she visited this summer. It was easy to forget how piddly and small his own life might seem in comparison.

In the end her guys want to scope out the property anyway, presumably to hide infrared cameras in his apple trees and launch drones up over the barn, so Jimmy shows them the small guesthouse where they're going to be staying and sends them on their way, then turns back to Lacey. "Want to drop your stuff?" he asks, shaking his hands out one more time before jamming them into his pockets. "You want some water? Or like . . . juice? I've got juice." He got kombucha, too, like, six different flavors, though personally he's never tried one that didn't taste distinctly like feet.

But Lacey shakes her head, the ghost of a smile appearing just around the very edges of her mouth. "I'm okay."

"Okay." They stand there for another moment, neither one of them saying anything. Briefly, Jimmy wishes he was dead. He doesn't know why it feels so terminally awkward all of a sudden, like he's forgotten everything he ever knew about how to have a conversation. This is *Lacey.* He's spent more time talking to her in the last few weeks than basically anybody else in his life. They once debated the merits of the late-night options at Taco Bell for the better part of an hour while he iced his knees in a hotel bathtub. On top of which, Jimmy is *great* at talking to women. He literally once got approached about doing a podcast called *Fantasy Baseball with Jimmy Hodges,* the conceit of which was that he'd give out romantic advice using sports metaphors.

Finally she lifts her sharp chin in the direction of the backyard. "Show me around?"

Jimmy lets a breath out. "Yeah," he says gratefully, nodding for her to follow. "Sure."

He brings her into the garden first, through the wooden gate and down the wide gravel path: past the rows of raised beds and the melon patches and the berries, the tomato plants that are almost as tall as her. His farm manager Ricky wanted to do honey last year, so there are half a dozen hives lined up along the fence on the orchard side, the low drone of the bees faintly audible in the still of the afternoon. "You take care of this all by yourself?" Lacey asks.

"Oh, yeah, one hundred percent solo," Jimmy says with a laugh. "I'm out here on the plow first thing every morning before practice." Then, when Lacey just looks at him, clearly not realizing he's joking: "No." God, she really does think he's a yokel. "I'm a dilettante. And I'm not here enough. I've got a couple of guys who work for me who do the bulk of it."

"Ah." She nods, flushing a bit. "So you're a gentleman farmer."

"Well," he says, grinning a little lopsidedly, "I don't know that I'd go *that* far."

Lacey doesn't laugh, the silence stretching out like old gum stuck to the bottom of his sneaker. Maybe it was a mistake, Jimmy thinks, all this buildup. Maybe there was no way it was ever going to be as good as it was in his head.

"Show me the horses," she suggests, her voice a little desperate. "You said there are horses, right?"

Jimmy nods. "There are horses," he agrees, and leads her across the back field toward the tall white barn. The barn is Jimmy's favorite place on the whole property: the cool, quiet darkness of it, the sounds of the animals snuffling to each other in their stalls.

"Full disclosure: it, uh, smells like a barn in here," he warns her, touching her arm as they're about to go inside. "Just, like, to let you know ahead of time. In case that's something you're not so cool with."

Lacey laughs. "I've been in a barn before," she assures him.

Jimmy doubts that very much, actually. "When?"

Her eyes narrow. "I don't know," she defends herself. "Times."

"Uh-huh." Jimmy nods. "Okay."

He leads her inside and walks her down the row of stalls, past the goats and the chicken coops to where the three of them are standing patiently side by side. "What are their names?" Lacey wants to know.

"Epitaph," Jimmy says, pointing to a tall, serious-looking palomino. "Valentine. And Paul Revere."

Lacey narrows her eyes. "Why does that sound familiar to me?"

"Dunno," Jimmy says with a grin.

Lacey purses her lips, but she doesn't push him. "Can I pet them?" she asks instead.

"Sure."

It's sweet, the cautious way she does it, standing on her tiptoes to scratch Valentine behind his ears and running her hand over Epitaph's velvety nose, staring into their solemn eyes like she's expecting them to reveal the secrets of the universe. "Hi, friend," she says softly. She reminds Jimmy of a Disney princess, which is not something he has historically looked for in a woman, though he'd be lying if he said it wasn't sort of working for him in this particular moment. "There's carrots in the bag there," he tells her, pointing to the canvas sack Ricky leaves hanging on a nail beside the stalls. "If you want to—"

"I do," she says, and for a moment the sound of the horses' happy chomping fills the barn, Lacey feeding them one after another like she's putting dollars into a vending machine.

"Enough," Jimmy says finally, laughing a little. "You're going to give them the shits."

Lacey rolls her eyes, dropping the last carrot back into the bag. "Charming."

"Well, I'm just saying," he continues, doubling down and not sure why. "You want to clean up after 'em?" He can feel that he's leaning into something here, cosplaying some dopier, more rural version of his own personality. He thinks it's possible he's trying to protect himself, though he's not entirely sure what from.

Lacey notices it, too: "This is very Zac Brown Band of you," she says as they head back toward the door. "This whole setup you've got here."

Jimmy looks at her sideways, smirking a little. "Is that an insult?"

"Maybe a little," she concedes with a smile. "But also, it's an incredibly beautiful farm."

"Thanks."

"Are you going to live out here full time?" she asks. "After . . . ?"

"After I retire?" Jimmy considers that for a moment. He could go anywhere, theoretically, move to Europe or spend a year traveling through Southeast Asia, but he's never really been the kind of guy to do that. It'll be strange, not to have anything keeping him in town. "I guess I haven't really thought about it. Why, is that what you'd do?"

"I don't know," Lacey says thoughtfully. "I'm never going to retire, though, so it's kind of a moot point."

"Fair enough."

"I mean it," she says.

"I do not doubt you for a single second."

Lacey nods and looks away from him, at the light seeping in through the barn door. Jimmy can feel it again, that heavy awkwardness, the feeling of having made an avoidable and costly mistake. He wonders if her plane is still waiting for her over at BWI, fueled up and ready. They could call it, he reasons. They could part respectfully, as pals.

"Do your hands hurt?" Lacey asks, out of nowhere.

Jimmy blinks at her, surprised. *Yeah, sweet cheeks*, he thinks reflexively. *All the fucking time*. "A little," he admits. "Why?"

"You keep—" She mimes what he was just doing without even realizing it, shaking her own hands out like she just touched something scalding. "You were doing it in New York, too."

"Oh," Jimmy says, tucking them into his pockets, deeply self-conscious all of a sudden. He guesses he does it so often he doesn't always notice anymore. "Yeah. I mean. They're fucked, pretty much. Nerve damage, couple old breaks. It's not a big deal."

Lacey looks at him for another moment, then pulls his hands out of his pockets again and laces their fingers together, squeezing gently. "Look," she says, "maybe we ought to just—"

That's when Jimmy kisses her.

Lacey gasps and kisses him back right away, popping up on her tiptoes and vining her arms around his neck, pressing her whole front against him. "Oh, thank *fuck*," she mutters, and Jimmy laughs out loud, the sound of it echoing off the high wooden beams and mixing with the dust motes, disappearing between the shadows and the shafts of sunlight seeping in.

"Thank fuck," he agrees, dizzy with her smell and her smile

and how familiar her kiss feels, like somehow they've done this way more than just the one other time. Jimmy smooths his palms over the soft, bare skin of her waist. He reaches down to squeeze her ass, then walks her backward until her spine bumps up against one of the tall wooden posts holding the barn up, wanting every inch of his body to be touching every inch of hers. "Hello."

"*Hi*," Lacey agrees, dropping her head back to give him access as his mouth wanders down the pale, delicate column of her throat. "Were you worried that night in New York was a total fluke and we actually had, like, zero chemistry in person?"

Jimmy drops his forehead against her shoulder, sucking gently at the crook of her neck. "The thought had occurred to me, yes."

"Not true, though." Lacey arches, grinding her hips against him.

"Nope." He lifts his face again, really looks at her. "Not true."

He kisses her for a long time, dragging her arms up over her head and holding them there for safekeeping, sliding his denim-covered knee between her thighs. They're alone here, Jimmy reminds himself even as she's gasping her quiet encouragement, even as his own heart slams wildly away with adrenaline and need. Alone-ish, anyway. They can take their time.

But fuck, he doesn't want to wait anymore.

He opens his mouth to tell her so, then loses the words altogether as she pulls one hand free and runs her palm over the bulge in his jeans, her short nails scraping against his zipper. Jimmy growls, he can't help it, pressing himself roughly into her touch. *"Lacey."* Just for a second he lets himself imagine it, turning her around and peeling her clothes off right here in the humid darkness, burying himself deep inside her from behind; still, he's only going to get to do this for the first time one time, and he's damn well going to do it right. "Sweetheart. You gotta let me get you on a bed."

Lacey pulls back and nods at him dazedly, her cheeks flushed pink and her chest rising and falling inside her top. She takes his hand and lets him lead her wordlessly out of the barn and back through the early-autumn garden, past the pool and in through the side door of the house. Upstairs they're quiet for a moment in the dim light streaming in through the bedroom windows, watching each other; finally Lacey reaches up and plucks his ballcap off by the brim, setting it down carefully on the dresser beside his wallet and his keys. "No hats in the house," she explains calmly, then puts both hands on his face and kisses him one more time.

CHAPTER THIRTEEN

LACEY

LACEY CRACKS ONE EYE OPEN AS JIMMY'S MOUTH FUSES OVER HER collarbone a few long, hazy minutes later, stealing a glance around his bedroom. It's nothing like she thought it would be, this house. Lacey doesn't know what she was expecting, exactly—Joanna Gaines farm decor? Black-and-white photos of baseball stadiums? Possibly she *was* expecting black-and-white photos of baseball stadiums, actually—but instead it's all wood floors and fireplaces and big leather couches, a place that invites a person to stay. Lacey wants to rummage around his pantry and page through his day planner. She wants to know everything about him there is to know.

For now she squeezes the back of his neck, then pulls away, sitting down on the edge of his neatly made bed and leaning back on her palms. "Take your clothes off," she instructs.

That surprises him, which was the point. "'Scuse me?"

"You heard me."

"I did." Jimmy raises an eyebrow, smirking. "Take *your* clothes off, how about."

"You've already seen me naked," Lacey points out. "Or partly, anyway."

"Not enough."

Lacey doesn't move. "James," she says, honestly impressed by how calm she's managing to sound right now, the way her voice isn't even shaking at all. "Take your clothes off."

Jimmy is quiet for a moment. His gaze is so, so even. "Okay."

He keeps his eyes locked on hers the whole time he's doing it: shrugging off his Henley and flicking open the clasp on his watch, sitting down in the armchair to do his sneakers and socks. He reaches back to tug his undershirt over his head like a little kid, rucking it up over the bulk of his shoulders, stands up to take off his jeans, then hooks his thumbs in the elastic of his boxer briefs and pulls those off, too.

"All right," he says, once he's naked except for a thin gold chain at his neck. "Now what?"

Lacey looks at him, at the hugeness of his body: his cock long and thick against his stomach, his muscular thighs spread just slightly apart. She wants him to fuck her until she forgets her own birthday. She wants to watch him get himself off. "You know," she says thoughtfully, "on second thought, this actually might be too much of a distraction for me. I think maybe I should head back, get a little bit of extra rehearsal time in, maybe schedule an interview or two—"

Jimmy makes a face. "Funny."

"I am funny."

"Not as funny as you think you are."

"Liar." Lacey stands up on two unsteady feet, crossing the carpet and reaching for him. She touches him for a long time, smoothing investigative palms over the warm planes of his chest and his stomach, running a finger down along the sharp cut of his hip. When she rakes her nails lightly over the high, round curve of his ass his entire body shudders, like she plugged in a hidden amp somewhere: "Duly noted," Lacey murmurs, smirking, and does it again.

Jimmy growls, then blushes, the heat creeping visibly up his chest and neck. "Yeah, yeah," he says, but he's smiling, rolling his eyes a little. He has a nice smile, Jimmy Hodges. She forgot that about him, from back in New York. When she reaches out and wraps her hand around his cock he just stands there, almost docile, his only tell the way his pulse is ticking wildly inside the soft skin of his throat.

Lacey strokes him a few times, curious: learning the weight and the curve of him, the faintly heartbreaking warmth of his skin against her palm. There's something kind of hot about it, being fully clothed and so obviously in charge here, like she's tamed some enormous animal. The quiet pleasure of bringing him to heel.

Eventually Jimmy gets bored, though, stripping her out of her jeans and top and sandals, his thick fingers surprisingly nimble as he works the tiny buckles. "This is nice," he observes, nodding at her frilly bra as he reaches back to pop the clasp open. "This for me?"

Lacey shakes her head. "My pilot," she says sweetly. "He likes a high-end undergarment."

Jimmy smirks. "You know what?" he says, scooping her into his arms and dumping her flat on her back onto the mattress. "I deserved that. I did."

"You did," Lacey agrees, stretching her arms up over her head, the tips of her fingers brushing his headboard. She's expecting him to climb up on top of her but instead he just stands there for a minute, staring at her, his plush mouth slightly open. "All right," she says finally, rolling her eyes at him. "Get on with it, will you?"

"Fuck off," Jimmy says easily—still gazing at her, one scarred knee up on the edge of the mattress. "You got to look."

Lacey squirms, but it's not like she's not enjoying herself. She's used to being looked at—hell, she's looked at more or less every second of her life—but there's something different about the way Jimmy Hodges is doing it, like he's making a game strategy in his mind for what he's about to do to her. "I guess I did." Eventually, though, it starts to feel like too much: the anticipation of it, how wound up she is after all these stops and starts. "Jimmy," she says, her voice coming out high and urgent. "Please."

Just for a second, Jimmy's eyes widen. Then he nods, climbing up onto the bed beside her and leaning over to dig around in the nightstand. "All right, princess," he says gruffly. "Hold your horses."

"You hold *your*—give me that," she says, holding her hand out for the condom. Then, off his faintly amused expression: "What?" she asks. "I'm modern."

Jimmy snorts. "You're something," he mutters, but he hands it over, both of them watching with interest as she rips it open and rolls it on with two shaking hands. Jimmy kisses her again once she's finished, bracketing her shoulders with both elbows and dropping down into the cradle of her hips. The weight of his body is almost enough to calm her down but the instant the tip of his cock catches she gasps so hard and so loudly Jimmy pulls back like she's kneed him directly in the nuts. "Sorry," he says, and for a second he sounds more panicked than she's ever heard him. "Fuck, sorry."

"No no no," Lacey says quickly. "Don't stop, just—" Oh god, she's like a cartoon cat riding a ceiling fan, her tail straight up in the air. "Look." She makes herself breathe. "There's just—a lot of preamble here, obviously, so I think we should probably both— you know. Adjust our expectations."

Jimmy nods seriously. "Adjust our expectations," he repeats, his eyes crinkling up just the slightest bit.

Lacey's mouth drops open. "Fuck you!" she says, shoving him gently. "Don't laugh. I'm serious."

"I'm not laughing," he says, and to be fair he doesn't actually seem to be. In fact, the expression on his face is so fond—is so *intimate*—she almost can't make herself breathe. "Lacey," he murmurs, ducking his head and scraping his beard gently along the valley between her breasts, "let me try to do this, okay? Before you decide it's inevitably not going to be as good as you imagined it being?"

Lacey presses her lips together. "Okay."

Jimmy swallows. "Okay," he agrees, and drops his head again, both of them watching as he notches himself inside her. Lacey pulls her legs up to make room. He takes his time about it, the rasp of his beard against her cheek and the slow, relentless way he's filling her, every single nerve ending in her body buzzing with pleasure. "You good?" he asks quietly, pulling back to check in with her, and Lacey starts to say yes but then he reaches down between them and the second his thumb finds her clit she's already coming, the orgasm bursting inside her fast and sudden as the chorus of a song.

"*Oh*," she manages—crying out, grabbing at his shoulders. She doesn't even know if it feels good, necessarily, it's so unexpected. It just *feels*.

For a second Jimmy just stares at her in wonder. Then his whole face explodes into a grin. "How am I doing?" he asks cheerfully, once Lacey can speak again. "Just, in terms of your adjusted expecta—"

"Shut the fuck up," she says—groping for him, pulling his full weight on top of her. "It's not always—I mean, I was just—" She shakes her head. "Come *here*."

"I'm here," Jimmy promises, and kisses her again.

\\\\\\\\

"*GUYS AND DOLLS*!" LACEY ANNOUNCES AN HOUR LATER, FLIP-ping over onto her stomach to look at him in the dimness of the late-afternoon bedroom. "That's where it's from." She puts on her best old-timey New York accent, singing: "I got the horse right here, the name is Paul Revere."

"*Guys and Dolls*," Jimmy agrees, tucking one arm behind his head. They were quiet for a long time once they were finally finished; she thought maybe he'd fallen asleep. Lacey dozed, too, though she's not generally much of a napper, wrung out by the stretch and the satisfaction and how powerful it made her feel to undo him like that, to take him apart with both hands. She shivers at the memory of the sound that tore from his throat as he came deep inside her, so low and ragged and after-dark private that she already knows there's no way she's leaving this house before she gets him to make it again. "'Fugue for Tinhorns.'"

"Are you a Broadway person?"

Jimmy chuckles. "No."

Something about the way he says it intrigues her. "Was your *wife* a Broadway person?"

"She . . ." He shrugs. "She liked musicals, yeah."

"Aha." Lacey props herself up on one elbow, pleased to have solved the mystery. She's about to ask him to say more about her—

tell me about your failed marriage is a weird flex as far as post-sex conversation goes, probably, but she's curious—when her phone starts to ring in her jeans pocket. She leans over the edge of the mattress to pull it out, wincing a little when she sees her mom's name on the screen. "Hold that thought," she says, scrambling up off the bed and scooping Jimmy's undershirt from where it's puddled on the area rug, pulling it over her head as she goes.

"Hi," she says as she shuts the bathroom door behind her, sitting on the lid of the toilet seat and stretching the cotton over her bare knees, breathing in the warm smell of his skin and deodorant. "Everything okay?"

"Where are you?" her mom wants to know.

"Um." Lacey hesitates, looking out the window at Jimmy's teeming garden, the tidy rows of trees beyond the fence. It was strange and a little disconcerting when she got out of the SUV earlier, the quiet, rural seclusion of this place. There's normally at least a house manager at Lacey's: someone making the coffee and cleaning the bathrooms, someone slipping her clean underwear back into her drawers. She's so used to having help that she barely even registers the extra bodies at this point. It's the solitude that catches her off guard. "What do you mean?"

"What do you mean, what do I mean? It's a perfectly normal question. Are you home?"

"Oh," Lacey says, getting up again and easing open the mirror above the sink, peeking inside Jimmy's medicine cabinet: painkillers mostly, plus about a thousand vitamins and supplements. Another box of condoms. A brush. "Um, yeah. Also, you know what I meant to tell you? You were totally right about the choreography for 'Fameland.' I dropped the extra turn and it worked like a charm."

"I told you," her mom says—momentarily distracted, just like Lacey knew she would be, and they chat for another minute before she tells her mom she needs to go.

"I ordered food and it's going to be here in a second," she lies, hoping her mom won't ask what restaurant. "I'll call you later."

Back in the bedroom Jimmy is still prone on the mattress, the tiny gold pendant on the chain he's wearing lying flat at the base of his throat. "Are you Jesus-y?" Lacey asks, crawling back up the bed and picking it up to look at it more closely; it's warm, from the heat of his skin.

Jimmy snorts. "Am I *what*?"

"You heard me." She drops the medal back against his chest and stretches out beside him, propping herself up on her elbow and tapping his sternum with one finger. "That's Jesus, isn't it?"

"It's Saint Michael the Archangel," Jimmy corrects her, "but no. I was raised pretty Catholic, I guess, but I wouldn't describe myself as Jesus-y."

"No judgment." Lacey shrugs. "A lot of my fans are pretty Jesus-y. Also, a lot of my fans are Wiccan."

"You've got a lot of fans."

"I do," Lacey agrees.

Jimmy smirks, looking at her with something like amusement as he smooths one calloused hand down the curve of her side. "Was that Slenderman?" he asks, nodding over her shoulder at her phone on the nightstand. "Who called just now?"

"Wh—*Toby*?" That makes her laugh. "No."

"Just asking." Jimmy lies back and shrugs into the pillows, scratches idly at his broad, bare chest. "Heard you guys might be getting back together."

"He's going to super bummed to hear I just had sex with you, then."

"That's what I was thinking."

Lacey rolls her eyes. "I told you I was never getting back together with Toby," she reminds him, slinging one leg over his hips and settling herself on top of him, rubbing herself idly against his belly. "And if you thought I was, we could have just talked about it."

"We could have," he allows, smiling a little. He keeps looking at her like this, Lacey notices: his face open and easy, like here is a person you could tell weird, secret stuff to and it would probably be fine. He reaches up and curls his hands around her waist, squeezing a little. "Nice shirt."

"Thank you," Lacey says, planting her palms on either side of his body and leaning forward so the neckline gapes open. "I stole it from some guy."

"Poor bastard," Jimmy says, working his palms up underneath the hem and cupping her breasts, swiping his thumbs along the sensitive skin of the undersides. "Probably already knows he's never going to get it back."

"Probably," Lacey agrees—or starts to, anyway, losing the end of the word in a gasp as he pinches her nipples.

"That feel good?"

"Yes," Lacey admits, arching her back until he gets the message and does it again, harder this time. "But also, like. I've had orgasms before, all right? I'm not having, like, some kind of nineteen-seventies Judy Blume novel sexual awakening with you here."

Jimmy nods pleasantly. "Great," he agrees, letting go of her body long enough to pull another condom from the nightstand. "I have no idea what that means."

It's slower this time, Lacey sore and sweetly swollen, Jimmy's mouth on her shoulders and her breasts and her neck. "You're better in bed than Toby was, okay?" she says finally—breathless and laughing, the last dregs of the orgasm still fizzing through her; in the end he grabbed her hand and dragged it down between them to help her along. "Is that what you want to hear?"

Jimmy seems to consider that. "I mean, I wasn't fishing," he says, flipping them so she's back underneath him in one smooth motion, weirdly agile for a person his size. "But sure, a girl likes to get a compliment from time to time."

Lacey pulls her knees up, shifting her hips as he sinks back inside her. "Is that what a girl likes?"

"Yeah," Jimmy says, grinning down at her in the fading twilight. "Yeah, I think it is."

CHAPTER FOURTEEN

JIMMY

JIMMY'S ALONE IN HIS BED WHEN HE WAKES UP THE FOLLOWING morning. He lies there for a moment, watching the sun spill in through the window, taking stock. He's waiting to feel terrible, and he unmistakably does—his hands in particular are killing him, the knuckles swollen and fucked-up looking—but mostly he just feels sort of pleased with himself. Mostly he just feels sort of good. They stayed in bed for a long time last night, him and Lacey, talking and napping and fooling around; around eight thirty they wandered downstairs and he made her dinner, a pasta thing that is one of three meals he reliably knows how to cook, except he usually makes it with sausage and he made it with tomatoes instead. It's better with sausage, frankly, but all things considered Jimmy found he didn't much care.

"Can I ask you a question?" Lacey said, eyeing him across the kitchen—her long hair sex-messy and tangled, the heels of her smooth bare feet banging gently against the cabinets. "Do you make this pasta for every woman who ever stays here?"

Jimmy hesitated. "I mean," he said finally, "not this *exact* pasta."

"Uh-huh."

"I mix it up a little," he defended himself. "And also, for the record, no other women have stayed here since I met you in New York."

Lacey quirked an eyebrow. "Hooked up with any other women in bathrooms?" she asked.

"Nope."

"Well," she said, "me either." Then she grinned. "When I write my song about you it's going to be called 'Hookup Pasta.'"

"Double platinum," Jimmy predicted, stepping between her knees and sliding his palms up the long, tan expanse of her thighs. "Record of the Year."

Now he gets up out of bed and pulls on a pair of sweatpants, padding down the stairs in the early-morning light. He can hear Lacey singing quietly to herself in the kitchen, an old ballad by Sam Cooke or the Platters, something he recognizes but isn't able to name. She has a pretty voice, Lacey—and Jimmy knew that, obviously, but it sounds different here in his house, reminds him of the low, unselfconscious way his mom used to sing to herself in the mornings when he was a kid. *Singing clears the gunk*, she used to say. He tries to remember the last time he heard her sing something, and can't. She got a little hard after Matty died, not that Jimmy blames her. It turned him a little hard, too.

"Morning," he says now, dropping a kiss on Lacey's shoulder. She's wearing his T-shirt again and she looks like one of those old American Apparel ads, tall and gorgeous and half-naked. She smells like his detergent and like sex.

"Morning," she agrees with a smile. "I made coffee. Or I, like, tried to make coffee, anyway. I'm not very good at it."

Jimmy nods sympathetically. "Your many minions usually do that for you, huh?"

"Screw you," Lacey says, but she's smiling. "But yes. In my defense, your machine is a full spaceship." She hands him a mug over her shoulder, then turns to face him, fingertips curling around the edge of the counter. "Can I ask you something?" she says, her expression full of consternation. "Why does one human person need so many bags of baby carrots?"

Jimmy throws his head back and laughs.

They drink their coffee in the pool, floating on their backs in the deep end, the sparrows chatting up in the trees and a playlist from Lacey's phone drifting quietly out across the yard.

"I like this song," Jimmy says, lifting his chin at the speaker. "Is this you?"

"What? No!" Lacey laughs. "You think I'd put myself on a playlist and just casually play it for you, all smooth-like, hoping you'd be into it?"

"I kind of think that, yes."

Lacey rolls her eyes. "If I'm fishing for compliments, Big Man, you'll know it," she promises. "Anyway, no. It's Henrietta Lang."

Jimmy nods, listening for another moment: the contralto voice and the vaguely creepy lyrics, what he thinks might be a tenor guitar. "Are you guys pals?"

"Nah," Lacey says, looking a little bashful. "We don't really run in the same kinds of circles. I love her, though. I think she's brilliant. I was maybe going to go see her in New York the night I met you, actually, but I chickened out at the last minute."

"Why?"

"I told you," Lacey says, her shrug just visible underneath the water. "I can't just pop into other people's shows like that. It would have been a total clusterfuck."

"Really?" Jimmy has his doubts. He doesn't want to, like, mansplain her own life to her or whatever, but it does kind of feel to him like maybe not everything needs to be quite as complicated as she's making it. She's famous, yeah, but it's not like people are actually watching her every second. "Are you sure about that?"

"I am sure about that," Lacey says firmly. "Anyway, I don't want to talk about me anymore. Let's talk about something else instead. Let's talk about baseball."

That makes him laugh. "Just generally?"

"I actually know some stuff about it generally," she confesses, trailing one hand through the bleachy blue water. "I watched the Ken Burns documentary, back when you and I first started texting."

Oh, Jimmy is in trouble with this girl. "Did you really?" he asks, surprised and charmed in equal measure. "Isn't it, like, ten parts?"

"Eleven," Lacey corrects him. "I like to be informed."

"I know that about you." Jimmy smiles. "Well. We made the Wild Card Series," he reports, a little embarrassed by the pride and excitement he can hear in his own voice as he tells her. "Did you and Ken cover what that is, or—?"

"Let's pretend we didn't."

"It's the opening round of the playoffs, basically," Jimmy says, trying not to sound like a pedant as he gives her a quick and dirty primer. "We're the number six seed—which is, to be clear, the worst you can be and still make it into the series—so Seattle, who's third, is going to host us. Whoever wins those games goes to the Division Series, and then the League Championship after that."

"And then the World Series and Disney World?"

"And then the World Series and Disney World."

"You ever made it that far?"

"Not Disney World," he confesses. "The other thing, once."

Lacey nods. "I knew that, too, actually," she admits, looking at him a little guiltily over the tops of her designer sunglasses. "I googled it."

He smiles again, though only for a second. It wasn't exactly a high point of Jimmy's career. "You did, huh?"

"Six years ago, right? You got close."

"I—" Jimmy opens his mouth, closes it again. "Yeah," he says finally. "We got close." Jimmy's never played a season like that in his entire life, is the truth: the pieces clicking neatly into place from the very beginning, a crew of guys he loved like kin. Jimmy wasn't surprised when they made it to the Series—none of them were—and he wasn't surprised when they won the first three games against Miami, either. It felt inevitable that they were going to win it. It felt predestined that it was theirs to reach out and take.

They flew down to Florida for Game 4, Jonesy hitting bombs and Tito zipping all over the outfield and Tuck pitching some of the most beautiful innings of baseball Jimmy had ever seen, sending hitters chasing after pitches hooked just outside the strike zone and catching them looking as his slider dipped across the plate. Two outs at the bottom of the fourth, Jimmy remembers, the O's up by three and a rookie second baseman from the Marlins up at bat. The kid was new as a freshly minted penny, a mid-season call-up eager to make a name for himself, and as his swing connected neatly with Tuck's fastball Jimmy thought for a moment there was a chance he was going to. He remembers the scream of the crowd as the kid dropped his bat and took off around the bases, rounding second as the Birds struggled to get their acts together and crossing third by the time they finally put hands on the ball. Jimmy made the catch just as the kid dove for home plate, desperate and wild—

And took a flying leap into Jimmy's left side.

Jimmy's not deluded enough to think that him tearing his shoulder is the reason the Marlins came from behind and won that night, let alone the reason they swept the next three games and won the Series. Still, he thinks about it sometimes, what might have happened. He thinks about how it all might have felt.

"Anyway," he says now, clearing his throat, "wasn't meant to be."

"That's very stoic of you."

"I'm a stoic guy."

"A regular Marcus Aurelius."

"That's what they call me." He can tell that she knows he's full of shit and he wants to distract her into forgetting, so he backs her up against the edge of the pool and kisses her, sliding his hands up her rib cage and tracing the cheerful white piping on her bathing suit top. "You could take this off, you know."

Lacey smirks. "I could, huh?"

"Just saying." He works the tip of one finger underneath the edge of the spandex, rubbing gently around the very edge of her nipple and feeling it harden up underneath his touch. "There's no-body here."

"My bodyguards are in the pool house, dumbass."

"They're not watching."

"Somebody's always watching," she counters with an ease that nearly takes his breath away. "Always." Then, wrinkling her nose: "Sorry. Is that a total boner-killer?"

"Nah," Jimmy lies, kissing her one more time before pulling away and sitting down on the steps in the shallow end. "Just kind of makes me wonder if I should start waxing my chest."

"Don't you dare."

"Does it get tiring?" he asks, stretching his legs out in front of him. He's supposed to do PT in this pool, theoretically, but in practice he hardly ever does. "Being the entirety of the American zeitgeist?"

Lacey shrugs. "I don't really think about it that way," she says. "I chose this, and there are certain things that come with it. And certain accommodations or calculations that I have to make because of that."

"No topless sunbathing," he says sadly.

"Tits away," she deadpans, and Jimmy guffaws.

Back in the house he makes them a couple of green juices, which is the single healthy habit he held on to from his marriage. "You want to go to breakfast?" he calls over the whir of the juicer as she sits down on the sofa in the great room. "There's a place in town that's got good eggs."

"Oh!" Lacey hesitates, turning around to look at him over the back of the sofa. "Um."

All at once, Jimmy gets it. It's like a record scratch, the moment he figures it out. "Okay," he says slowly, handing her a glass of health the color of ectoplasm and sitting down on the couch beside her, cracking his knuckles and hoping vainly for a little bit of relief. "So this is gonna be a secret, huh?"

Lacey looks sheepish. "It's not that I *want* it to be a secret," she says, not quite looking at him. "It just gets complicated once it's not."

"Calculations," Jimmy says, nodding slowly. "Accommodations."

"Don't be mad."

"I'm not mad," he says, and he's not, truly; in fact, he's closer to hurt than angry, but fuck him if he's ever going to admit that out loud. "I mean, that's fine. But for the record, I think I could probably handle it. The complications, or whatever." He takes a sip of his grass-tasting juice. "I mean, if you're embarrassed about it, then that's another story—"

"I'm not *embarrassed*." Lacey's temper flares; he can see it.

"Okay." Jimmy shrugs. "Well, then. I guess I just don't love the idea of sneaking around like some teenager who doesn't want his dad to catch him breaking curfew, that's all."

"Oh, because historically you've been the king of romantic integrity?"

Jimmy feels his jaw twitch. "I've never tried to hide it when I cared about someone."

"Clearly, which is why the whole world knew when you gave chlamydia to Kit Benedetto."

"To be clear," Jimmy defends himself, "Kit Benedetto gave chlamydia to me."

"Apologies." Lacey rolls her eyes. "There was already a blind item on the Sinclair," she reports.

"I don't know what that is."

"A blind item is when—"

"No, I know what a blind item is." For fuck's sake. "The other thing you said."

"It's a gossip site," she says, and it clicks for him then, the hot pink web page the guys were looking at back in the locker room that day. "And sure, it was vague—the blind item, I mean—but not so vague that my fans aren't going to be able to sniff it out in half a second, so I just want to be sure we're ready. For, like. Whatever happens." She chugs the juice in one long gulp, setting her empty glass on the coffee table and letting out a tiny, ladylike burp. "Excuse me," she says primly. Then: "It might be worth it for you to talk to Maddie. My publicist. About how we'd want to handle it if it did get out."

Oh, Jimmy does not want to do that. "I've been a starting player in the MLB for thirteen years, Lacey. I know how to handle the press."

"My press is different from your press."

"Okay," he says, knowing he sounds sullen and not being able to do a hell of a lot to stop it. Fuck, his hands are killing him. They feel like they're on fire. He shakes them out one more time, fighting the urge to get up and go into the kitchen, open the door to the freezer, and jam them inside. "If you say so."

"I say so." She looks at him for a moment, appraising. "Come here," she says quietly. "Give me your hands."

Jimmy shakes his head. "It's fine."

"I know," she agrees calmly. "You're a big strong sports hero. I said come here."

Jimmy sighs, but he does it, shifting closer on the sofa until he's close enough to smell the sunscreen and chlorine smell of her. He feels annoyed in every direction: at his body for being old and creaky, at Lacey for thinking he's too stupid to handle reporters. At himself for caring either way.

Lacey picks up his right hand and examines it for a moment, turning his wrist this way and that before pressing gently, then with more pressure, digging her thumbs into the meat of his palm. "That okay?" she asks, raising an eyebrow.

"Yeah." Jimmy huffs a sheepish laugh. "That's okay."

Lacey nods and reaches for his left hand this time, pressing at the webbing between his thumb and index finger. Jimmy drops his head back against the sofa, his eyes closing almost involuntarily as she tugs gently on each of his fingers. He's been half-hard since basically the first second she touched him, but it's not until she slides his index finger into her mouth, scraping her sharp white teeth gently over the pad of his fingertip, that he realizes exactly what she's after. "La-cey," he says, cracking one eye open.

"What?" she asks. She's grinning, looking deeply pleased with herself. "What the fuck did you think I was going to do, miraculously heal all your various injuries? I'm not a fucking sports medicine doctor."

"Uh-huh." Jimmy reaches for her, pulling her into his lap and tugging at the ties on her still-damp bathing suit. "Come here."

But Lacey wriggles away. "I'm busy," she informs him, and drops to her knees in front of the couch.

Jimmy lets out a quiet, disbelieving swear. He doesn't want her to feel like—just because they sort of argued—Jesus fucking *Christ*, he cannot put a thought together at all. "Okay," he manages finally. "Okay, you definitely don't have to—"

"I know I don't have to, thanks," Lacey says, looking up at him with open amusement. She ghosts her nails down his thighs in a way that makes him shiver, then hooks her fingers in the waistband of his swim trunks and snaps it back against his skin. "Do you want me to or not?"

Jimmy hesitates. Of course he fucking wants her to. He wants all kinds of shit he has no business wanting: to get inside her and stay there for the foreseeable future, to hold her down and get her off and be the best she's ever had. "Lacey," he tries again, but she's already working his shorts down over his hips and wrapping her hand around him, swiping her thumb over the liquid at the tip. "Sweetheart—"

"You gotta tell me," Lacey decides, resting her sharp chin on his knee and *grinning* at him, this hugely tickled, hugely dirty expression on her face. "You want me to do it, you gotta say."

Jimmy growls, he can't help it—how hard he is and how badly he wants her, how shy he suddenly feels. "Please."

"Please what?"

For fuck's sake. "You know what."

Lacey rolls her eyes. "Prude," she teases, then tucks her dark hair daintily behind her ears and ducks her head.

Jimmy groans. He closes his eyes like a reflex, then opens them again, equal parts desperate to watch her and afraid the sight of it is going to end him way too fast. Her mouth is obscenely, heartbreakingly warm. He never brought this up as a possibility, all those nights they talked on the phone together. Never even let himself think about it. Jimmy threads his fingers through her hair as she does her thing, rubbing gently at the back of her neck. He feels scraped raw and helpless, like she could well and truly wreck him without ever meaning to. Like she leaves a trail of destruction in her wake. Lacey watches him from her spot on the floor, no tension or distrust in her face at all as she takes him deeper, sucking fast and sloppy like all she wants is—

"Okay," Jimmy announces finally, reaching down and hauling her to her feet, pulling her into his lap so she's straddling his thighs. "Come up here."

"Oh, sorry," she says, wiping the corner of her mouth with one red fingernail. Her lipstick is, somehow, still immaculate. "Were you not having fun?"

"Fuck off," he says, dropping her bathing suit top on the floor and getting his mouth on her—sucking and biting, rougher than he's been with her so far. "Too much fun."

"No such thing."

"Wrong." Jimmy tugs her bottoms to the side, opening her up with two fingers and groaning quietly when he feels how wet she is. "Oh, I see how it is," he says. "You were having fun, too, huh?"

Lacey drops her head back in pleasure, grinding herself against his hand. "I may have been."

"Good." Jimmy lets her use his fingers for a moment longer, then pulls back and fits himself inside her, holding as still as he can manage while she works herself down onto his cock. She's beautiful like this, her chest flushed pink and eyes narrowed in concentration, wet bottom lip caught between her teeth. Jimmy drops his face into the crook of her neck, momentarily overwhelmed by her; the last thing he registers before she rolls her hips and his brain stops working entirely is her quiet gasp of pleasure, the press of her hand in his hair.

CHAPTER FIFTEEN

LACEY

LACEY'S PLANE BACK TO LA TAKES OFF ON TIME, BUT BARELY. She's late to the airport following a protracted goodbye at Jimmy's, his big hands creeping up inside her hoodie as she leaned against the door: "You want to be my girlfriend?" he muttered in between kisses, his deep voice muffled against her mouth. Lacey pulled away, laughing at the high school earnestness of it; still, her heart was a dollar-store helium balloon taped to a locker, bright and shiny and straining to get free.

"Yeah," she admitted, a little breathlessly. "I kind of want to be your girlfriend."

Jimmy grinned. "Okay," he said, like it was just that easy. For a moment it felt that easy to Lacey, too. "You're my girlfriend."

Claire is waiting for her on the tarmac, iPad in hand. "Welcome back," she chirps. "How was it?"

"It was great," Lacey says carefully. She didn't talk to Claire while she was in Baltimore, which wasn't *unusual*, exactly, though the first time she went away with Toby the two of them texted more or less constantly. She knows Claire is angry with her—that

Maddie is, too, though of course neither one of them would ever say so. She knows she caught them both by surprise. "I'm sorry," she said to Claire the other night, once Lacey had explained what was going on and that she needed a flight to BWI on short notice. "I shouldn't have lied to you."

"No, I mean." Claire cleared her throat, not quite making eye contact. "It's fine. You're allowed to keep your private life private, obviously. You're my boss."

Lacey felt, briefly, as if Claire had slapped her. "Claire," she said. Claire had been the one to collect her stuff from Toby's apartment after the breakup; she'd held Lacey's dress while she's peed at six years' worth of Grammy Awards. Lacey was lying when she told Jimmy she didn't have an active-duty best friend. Paid or not, what was Claire if not her closest of wartime consiglieri? "Come on."

"No, it's fine." Claire shook her head. "I don't know why I'm having this reaction, honestly. I should be apologizing. It's inappropriate."

"It's not," Lacey said, though she supposed it was, technically. Or maybe it wasn't? At the very least, she felt like they probably ought to talk about it more, but there had been travel to organize and packing to do, and now here they are on the other side of it, just the slightest bit unfamiliar with each other. It's strange, feeling like there's a piece of her professional life Lacey doesn't know how to navigate. It's unsettling to feel like she doesn't have it neatly, 100 percent under control.

She climbs into the back seat and slips off her sunglasses, the SUV crawling back toward Malibu while Claire connects with Maddie on FaceTime. "I've got good news and bad news," Maddie announces, sitting at her desk with her hair in a tidy knot on the top of her head. "The good news is, I solved the Toby mystery. The bad news is he did twenty minutes at Largo last night, workshopping some new stuff for what I'm hearing is going to be a Netflix special." She makes a face. "He's calling it *Problematic Fave*."

Lacey presses her lips together, swallowing down a quiet flare of panic. She barely thought about Toby at all while she was with Jimmy. She barely thought about anything public-facing or career-related, actually; she let herself get lost in the moment, let herself get lazy, and now—"Cool," she says, her voice sharp with sarcasm and a little bit of mania. "Do we know what it's about?"

"Mostly about his entire personal brand being that he's a piece of shit," Maddie tells her. "Fatherhood, whatever. But there's also a not-insignificant chunk of it that's about you."

Lacey nods slowly, absorbing that information. "Is there video?"

"There is."

"Okay," she says, ignoring the faint taste of bile at the back of her mouth. "Well, let's, you know. Go to the tape."

"It's already backfiring," Maddie assures her, which is how Lacey knows it must be really bad. "The coverage is terrible."

"It's fine," Lacey assures her, managing with some effort to keep her voice light. This is her superpower, she reminds herself firmly: her insatiable hunger for every crumb of meanness anyone has ever flung in her direction, the knowledge that there is nothing anyone can say about her, no matter how cutting or poisonous or untrue, that she doesn't want to hear. All of it is data, and data is power. Data, Lacey has always been able to use. "I'll just watch."

So Maddie sends her the link, staying on the line while Lacey watches the grainy footage: Toby in black jeans and a trim crewneck Comme des Garçons sweatshirt Lacey bought for him in Tokyo two years ago, stalking back and forth across the tiny stage.

The portion about Lacey lasts just over six minutes, and it's . . . not great. There's the usual low-hanging fruit, of course, digs at the pedestrian quality of Lacey's music and her creepy symbiotic relationship with her fans. But there's a lot of private stuff, too, stuff Toby only knows about her because they were living together, like a botched laser hair removal from a couple of years ago after which she needed to put burn cream all along her bikini line every day for six full weeks. *My ex*, he keeps calling her, trusting everyone to know who he's talking about and also, presumably, trying to shield himself from a lawsuit by never actually using her name. *My ex. My ex.*

Lacey keeps her face very, very blank, rubbing compulsively at an errant cuticle and telling herself there's no reason to feel like she's about to burst into tears. It's not that she didn't know he was capable of this kind of sharpness in his comedy, obviously. And it's not that she can't take a joke at her own expense. It's just that it's *Toby*, who used to drive across LA to get her coffee from her favorite place in Silver Lake when they were first dating and who is so afraid of spiders he once jumped into the pool fully clothed to make his escape from a daddy longlegs strolling up a drainpipe at her place in Nashville. It's Toby, whose mom used to send him seasonally appropriate boxes of breakfast cereal for every holiday, even though he was thirty-five years old. Being leveraged this way by people she once trusted is part of the price she pays for being who she is; Lacey knows this. Still, just for a fraction of a second, she feels sadder than she ever did when they broke up.

She's aware of Claire and Maddie watching her carefully, waiting to gauge her reaction. Lacey bites her tongue hard enough to taste salt. The sum total of everything going on has her feeling out of control and exposed all of a sudden: Toby's set, everything happening with Jimmy. Even the weirdness with Claire. It feels like too *much*, like too many variables to manage. It feels like too many things to keep under control.

"I mean," she says when it's finished, careful to keep her voice cheerful, "I suppose it's fair to say he wasn't deterred by my great plan to sing 'Laugh Lines' in Montreal as a way of letting him know not to fuck with me."

"No," Maddie says, "I guess he wasn't."

Claire puts a hand on her arm and squeezes. "Are you okay?"

Lacey shrugs her off before she can quiet the impulse, wincing when she sees Claire flinch. "I'm fine," she assures them, trying to soften her tone while simultaneously sounding as if she's got it all together. "I think we should ignore it, don't you? Like you said, it's already backfiring. He wants to hang himself out to dry, that's his business."

"Okay," Maddie says. "Well, if you're sure, then, we should talk about a PR rollout for you and Jimmy Hodges."

Lacey hesitates. It's not like she didn't know this was coming; it's not that she doesn't know they need a plan. Still, she finds she doesn't want to talk about it right this second, to turn it into one more thing she needs to manage and strategize about. It's overwhelming. She feels overwhelmed. "I don't think we need to cross that bridge yet."

"Really?" Maddie looks surprised. Lacey is not at all a person who buries her head in the sand. "Because I do have some concerns that after the blind item on the Sinclair, and you flying down there—"

"No, I know, but we discussed it," Lacey says, "and we decided we're going to keep it private for a little bit."

"And if it leaks?"

Lacey smiles. "We can move on."

Maddie eyes her a moment longer, visibly nonplussed. "Sure," she says finally. "Of course."

That was a pretty good hang, Jimmy texts her, just as the car pulls into the driveway. *We should do it again sometime.*

Lacey blinks, surprised by the tiny zip of anxiety that ricochets through her at the sight of his name on the screen, the sinking suspicion that there may be a cost to whatever it is they're doing here that she didn't adequately anticipate—then tells herself not to be ridiculous. Who gives a shit about Toby and his comedy set? She's the one in control of the narrative. She's the one in charge. Some stupid stunt by Toby doesn't change that.

It was, she agrees. *We should.*

\\\\\\\\

THE WILD CARD SERIES IS SHORT, JUST THREE GAMES OVER three nights in Seattle: the Orioles win the first, but they lose to the Mariners in the second, forcing a tiebreaker Tuesday night. "Washington's basically Northern California, on the off chance you're in the mood to take in some playoff baseball," Jimmy says when she calls him that morning to say good luck. "I can leave a funny nose and glasses for you at the gate."

"Tempting." Lacey bites her lip, letting herself imagine it for a moment, being there to watch him on a night as important as this one. Cheering him on while he does what he loves. Then she thinks of Toby workshopping his set back across town at Largo and reminds herself it's better to keep this whole thing under wraps for at least a little while longer. "I'm going to be wearing my Hodges jersey and cheering you on from my mayoral residence," she promises. "Don't fuck it up."

"I'll do my best," Jimmy tells her. Then, just before he hangs up: "Hey. You doing okay, about that video?"

Lacey winces. It's been everywhere the last few days, clips of it playing on the morning shows and on late night, the subject of a million think pieces about misogyny in stand-up and who owns whose stories. She and Maddie both agreed it was better not to comment this time, but none of it shows any signs of letting up and she's starting to wonder if maybe that's a mistake, too. She feels off her game, foggy headed. *Distracted*, to borrow Jimmy's word.

"Totally," she says. "I'm doing fine."

Lacey's never watched the entirety of a baseball game before, and she makes a little one-woman party of it in her screening room later that night, with a bowl of chocolate-covered almonds and a new flavor of kombucha. She's always thought of baseball as a deeply boring sport, but it turns out she sort of likes it when she's got some skin in the game, remembering stories Jimmy's told her about his teammates, watching for a quick glimpse of him behind the plate. His friend Tuck is pitching, the one who's been on the Orioles almost as long as he has. She spies a few guys she recognizes from that very first night at the club.

The Orioles are behind the first three innings, then tied for the better part of the middle of the game. Briefly ahead. Behind again. Jimmy strikes out in the seventh—"Shit," Lacey says out loud, gnawing her thumbnail before she can catch herself—then redeems himself with a three-run homer at the top of the ninth, and then all at once it's over. All at once, he's won.

"Fuck yeah!" Lacey exclaims before she can stop herself, then claps a hand over her mouth even though there's nobody around to hear her. She feels like she's the one who's going to the Division Series. She feels like there's a hot air balloon inside her chest. She watches as the guys rush the field and pile onto each other like puppies, the joy palpable, Jimmy ripping his mask off and dropping it into the dirt as he goes.

She picks her phone up to text him, ignoring a couple of missed calls from Claire from earlier tonight, even though she knows his phone is back in the locker room. She doesn't want to talk about her own stuff right now. She wants to be happy for her boyfriend, who's going to—she knows it in her gut—win a World Series after all this time. *I'm so fucking proud of you*, she types, thumbs flying over the keyboard. *I can't wait to show you in person how much.*

She tucks her phone into the pocket of her hoodie and walks around the house for a bit, the excitement inside her turning to restlessness. She wants to stretch her legs, to go until she runs out of road. Lacey gets this feeling sometimes, even though she knows it's silly: like she's stuck in a cage of her own construction. Like she's trapped. All at once she wishes she'd gone to the game after all, that she was there to celebrate with him, to run her fingers through his champagne-soaked hair. Who cares if people know they're together? she thinks wildly. She *wants* people to know. She wants to be there for him. She's going to go to the next one, she decides. When is the next one, even? She'll find out.

Upstairs in her bedroom she flicks over to ESPN to watch the postgame press conference while she washes her face and puts on her night cream. She's never watched one of these before, either, but she wants to keep looking at him, to see the flush of pleasure on his handsome face. She liked watching Toby perform, obviously; she thought his jokes were reasonably funny. But this feels different.

"Hey, Jimmy," a reporter says, first question out of the gate, "any truth to the rumors you're dating Lacey Logan?"

Lacey whirls around as if someone has stabbed her, watching as Jimmy freezes, like there's a glitch in the cable feed. The panic is naked on his face. Even if she didn't know anything about it, she'd know the reporter was right.

There's a brief, horrible silence, nothing but the sound of the cameras clicking like a plague of cicadas. Lacey can hear her own breath in her ears. She waits for someone to jump in and end the press conference, to hustle Jimmy back to the locker room. That's what Maddie would have done. Lacey would have been in the car by now. Lacey would be in Burkina fucking Faso.

"I'll tell you one thing for sure," Jimmy says, the words coming out all in a rush. "If I *was* dating her, I sure as shit wouldn't write a corny fucking comedy routine about it."

Lacey drops the jar of night cream all over the floor.

CHAPTER SIXTEEN

JIMMY

He calls her as soon as the press conference is finally over, weaving through the cavernous hallways until he finds an empty equipment room to duck into. She sends him to voicemail after one ring, a text popping up a moment later: *I saw it,* she reports curtly; then, in rapid succession:

I'm on the phone with Maddie

Making a plan

Please don't say anything to anyone else yet

Jimmy swears under his breath. *I'm so sorry,* he tells her honestly, his whole body buzzing with adrenaline and shame. He feels like he took his dick out and rubbed it all over the fucking microphones when he wasn't paying attention. *I got rattled.*

Clearly.

Jimmy winces, shoving his phone back into his pocket and shuffling into the locker room, where the entire team immediately bursts into rowdy applause, Hugo shimmying his hips lasciviously and Jonesy chanting his name like something out of an old episode of *Jerry Springer.* Jimmy honestly can't tell what the rest of them are more excited about, the fact that they just made it to the fucking Division Series or the idea of him embarrassing himself in front of a dozen national media outlets on the biggest night of his career in the last five years.

"You're a sly dog," Tuck says, slinging a sweaty arm around Jimmy's shoulders, clutching a bottle of champagne by the neck with his free hand. "I gotta say, Hodges, you're a sly fuckin' dog."

"We're going out!" Tito announces, wrapping his arms around Jimmy's waist from behind and attempting to lift him off his feet. "You coming?"

"Of course he's not coming," Jonesy puts in, yanking his jersey over his head and tossing it onto the floor. "He's gotta go home and call his famous girlfriend."

"Fuck you," Jimmy mumbles—rolling his eyes and shaking his head a little, shrugging out of Tito's grip and trying to maintain a shred of fucking dignity. Across the benches Ray is looking at him with an expression he doesn't like—a little bit of meanness, like maybe he thinks Jimmy stole his girlfriend, like he took something that didn't belong to him. He's going to need to handle that, Jimmy realizes dully, adding it to the ticker tape of action items accumulating rapid-fire inside his brain. He's going to need to handle a lot of things.

In the end he Venmos Tuck some cash to buy a round and sends the rest of them off to a speakeasy at the top of the Smith Tower, then takes a car back to the Grand Hyatt. There's an accident right outside the entrance to the hotel—at least, Jimmy *thinks* it's an accident in the moment before he realizes it's actually half a dozen photographers with their SUVs parked haphazardly up on the sidewalk, their cameras drawn like guns.

"Oh, fuck me," he says out loud, briefly feeling like all his internal organs are about to fall out his asshole. He hasn't had main-stream media wait for him outside a venue in years, not since way before he was married, and definitely never this many of them at once. Lacey was right, he realizes dully. Her press *is* different from his press. He cannot believe he just fucked this up as hard as he did.

He yanks his ballcap down over his eyes—which, *Why?* he thinks, even as he's doing it; after all, it's not like he's fooling anyone—and tumbles from the back seat of the SUV before the driver has even really stopped all the way. He keeps his head ducked as he hurries through the sliding doors and crosses the lobby, ignor-ing the cheerful catcalls echoing in his wake: "How long have you and Lacey been together, Jimmy?" the photographers want to know, and "How did you two kids even meet?" For a second he's afraid one of them is going to try and follow him into the elevator, that he's entered some horrifying new Princess Diana level of pursuit by the paparazzi, but in the end he taps his key card and jams the button for his floor without incident, leaning his head back against the wall of the car as the doors slide shut. There's another guest in there already, a woman with a dog in one of those little vented carrying cases.

"Are you anybody?" she asks as the elevator whooshes up-ward, peering at him curiously through her tortoiseshell glasses.

"Definitely not," Jimmy says.

Upstairs he collapses onto his bed for a minute, staring up at the ceiling and trying to empty his clamoring mind. He should be happy—they made the fucking Division Series tonight, did they not? The season isn't over yet; his *career* isn't over yet—but instead he's filled with weird but unmistakable dread, the knowledge that he's just set into motion a chain of events, not just for himself but for his entire team, that he's going to be utterly powerless to con-trol. All at once it doesn't feel like this whole thing was such a good idea to begin with. All at once it feels like he should have put it off until the season was done.

He's still lying there when he feels his phone start to buzz in his pocket. When he fishes it out he sees it's Lacey's name on the screen. Jimmy flinches before he can stop himself, queasily reminded of the way he felt when Rachel would call way back at the end of their marriage. The knowledge that he had failed, spectacularly, and that it was about to be elucidated to him in great detail exactly how.

"I'm so sorry," he says, when he hits the button to answer.

"It's fine," Lacey chirps, her voice clipped and tidy. "We'll figure it out. I mean, for the record, it would have been nice if you hadn't sounded *quite* so condescending when you told me you knew how to handle the media—"

"Yup," Jimmy agrees, squeezing his eyes shut. "That would have been the move, I can agree." He sighs. "Do you want me to say I made it up?"

"What?" she says, a little shrilly. "No. No! That makes you look insane. And frankly it makes me look insane by association, so—"

"I don't understand how they knew," he says, his voice pleading. It feels important that she doesn't think he leaked it. It feels important that she doesn't think he told.

"My fans figured it out a few days ago," she says. "They knew I was in Baltimore, which, combined with the blind item, was enough for them to—"

"Wait," Jimmy says, confused. "How did they know you were in Baltimore? We didn't go anywhere."

"Flight plans are public record."

Jimmy sits up so fast he gets lightheaded. "They track your *plane?*"

"Of course they track my plane, Jimmy." She says it like it's normal. "Anyway, like I was saying, that combined with the Sinclair thing—"

"Is still just total conjecture."

"Not for them," she says. "And not in reality, clearly." She sighs. "Maddie says we need to debut as soon as we possibly can."

"We need to what now?"

"Debut," Lacey repeats—a little impatiently, like she thinks he's being stupid on purpose. "Take control of the story. Go out together. Give them a narrative."

"Give who a narrative?"

"Everyone! The media. My fans. Every baseball jabroni who's already on Reddit complaining about me besmirching the sacred and pristine arena of professional sports with my rhinestones and vagina. Either we give them something to talk about, and fast, or they come up with something on their own. And please believe me when I say the first thing is always better."

Jimmy rests his elbows on his knees for a moment, leaning forward and scrubbing his free hand over the back of his head. "Can I ask you something?" he says finally. "Did you ever think that all this weird fucking lore exists around you because you're the one who's actively creating it? That people are like this about you because you expect them to be?"

"Wow, no," Lacey says, her voice perfectly even. "The notion had never occurred to me."

Jimmy winces. "Okay," he amends, "I didn't mean—"

"No, really. Thank you for teaching me this important and heretofore unknown truth about myself."

"Lacey—"

"I have built this career with my brain and my voice and my

two fucking hands, James. If I tell you my fans are going to need something from me, it's not because I'm divining it from the phases of the moon or some random Twitter user. It's because, contrary to what people like to tell themselves, doing what I do at the level that I do it takes a lot of strategy and intelligence. I need you to trust me about that."

Jimmy thinks about that for a moment—or tries to think about it, anyway, but he's distracted by the uninterrupted buzzing of his phone at his ear. The thing hasn't stopped vibrating since the press conference: messages and notifications stacking up on top of each other like the cards at the end of the old Microsoft version of solitaire, filling the entire screen. He's going to need to put it on Do Not Disturb. Fuck, he's going to need to throw it into the Potomac. It feels insane now, the idea that he was the one who gave her shit about not wanting to casually go out to breakfast the other morning. *I've been dealing with the press for thirteen years.* He might as well have told her he could do open-heart surgery because he used to watch reruns of *Grey's Anatomy* on cable at the gym in the mornings. He wants to beg for her fucking forgiveness. He wants to stand outside Camden in a sandwich board that says *I'm a dumb schmuck.*

He also—just a little bit—wants to call this whole thing off before it gets any more out of control and go back to concentrating on baseball.

"Okay," he says instead, holding a hand up even though she can't see him. He's in this now, he tells himself. He's committed. And he'll be damned if he isn't going to take it all the way. "I'm sorry. Tell me what we need to do."

CHAPTER SEVENTEEN
LACEY

"I CAN'T BELIEVE I HAD TO HEAR ABOUT THIS ON TELEVISION," her mother huffs on the phone a few days later, her consonants the slightest bit mushy but her indignation still razor-sharp. "I mean, talk about humiliating. I'm surprised at you, Lacey; I raised you better than that. It's not like you to sneak around."

"I wasn't *sneaking*," Lacey says, raking a hand through her hair as she curls up on the couch in the living room of her place in Cincinnati. It's the smallest of her properties, four bedrooms in a gated community in Grove Park that she keeps in equal parts because she's sentimental about Ohio and because she finds it's best not to stay at her mom's house if she can help it. "It's just . . . new."

"Seems like sneaking to me," her mom counters. "When is he coming in? Are you at least going to bring him by the house to say hello?"

Lacey grimaces at the thought of it. "He's only going to be in town for, like, twelve hours," she hedges. "It's just a quick in-and-out, a publicity thing. On top of which, it's not that serious, Mom. There's no reason for you to meet him yet."

"Well. That's not what they're saying on *Access Hollywood*." Her mother sniffs. "You never wanted me to be around Toby, either."

"That's not true," Lacey protests, though in fact it is extremely fucking true. Toby and her mom met exactly twice in all the time he and Lacey were together, once at one of Lacey's LA shows and once at a Mother's Day brunch at Nobu during which Toby looked on in horror as her mom calmly drank two entire bottles of pinot grigio and suggested they order another—which, now that Lacey is reflecting on it, was a lot of overwrought moral outrage from a person who turned out to be a literal cocaine addict. Still: not an experience she's eager to repeat. "Next time for sure, okay?"

"Am I even going to see *you* while you're here?" her mom presses, the sound of what might or might not be a wineglass clinking against the countertop faintly audible in the background. "Or are you in and out too fast for that, too?"

Lacey squeezes her eyes shut so hard that colors briefly explode behind her eyelids. "Of course you'll see me," she promises. "When have I ever come into town without you seeing me? Let me just chat with Claire about the schedule and we'll set something up."

"God forbid we make a plan without involving your assistant," her mom shoots back, which Lacey knows from experience means she's about to really get cooking in terms of her various maternal grievances. "Tell Claire she can come without you if you're too busy, how about. I'll make her all your favorite foods."

They hang up a few minutes later, though not before her mom asks Lacey for the contact information of the designer who did her Nashville house; not one to make the same mistake twice, Lacey has just texted her Jenny's office number when they're interrupted by a call from Maddie.

"Hey there," Maddie chirps, once Lacey has said her goodbyes and switched the line over. "I just wanted to go over logistics for tomorrow."

"Sure," Lacey says, grateful for a concrete plan to follow. The idea is to play it as an old-fashioned all-American romance: dinner and drinks in Lacey's hometown, apple pie and homecoming court. "Cute," Jimmy said, when she explained it to him over the phone a couple of nights ago. "Can I ask you something, though? Did you even actually go to real high school?"

"In fact I did," Lacey retorted, then grudgingly amended: "For, like, two years."

That made him laugh, the sound of it reassuring and familiar; for the first time since his disastrous press conference, Lacey felt herself relax. She knows he isn't crazy about this idea, the staged, theatrical quality of it, and she also knows he feels like he can't complain about it since he's more or less the entire reason they're in this situation to begin with. "Are you sure this was an accident?" Maddie asked when Lacey called her to strategize. "You don't think there's any part of him that saw an opportunity—"

"I don't," Lacey said honestly, although of course since the moment Maddie mentioned it she hasn't been able to get the possibility out of her head.

"Because I'm just saying, he has more to gain than you do," Maddie continued bluntly. "It's the end of his sports career, he's looking for a way to stay relevant—"

"Wow," Lacey said. "Thanks a lot."

"Well, it's my job to game out all the possibilities," Maddie reminded her, not unkindly. Lacey knows this. They had a plan for if Toby overdosed in the first few months after they broke up. They have a plan, though they have never explicitly talked about it, for if Lacey's mom shows up drunk somewhere in public and goes entirely off the rails. Lacey can recognize, intellectually, that they need a plan for the scenario in which Jimmy is using her to stay in the spotlight after he retires. Still, the idea of it doesn't exactly make her feel great.

Jimmy flies in late the following afternoon, the Orioles' first game of the Division Series leaving them only a narrow window of time to make this happen. They could have just done it in Baltimore, but Maddie wanted their first public outing to be on Lacey's turf. "Is that a huge pain in the balls for you?" Lacey asked him, when they were all on the conference call hashing out the details. "What with the timing and all?"

"I mean," Jimmy said mildly, and Lacey could hear the shrug in his voice clear across the country. "Does it matter?"

Now she swings her front door open, her stomach swooping at the sight of him standing there on the other side of it. This happened when she got out of the car at the farm, too: the way she was momentarily caught off guard by the size of him, the disarming hugeness of his shoulders and chest. "Hi," she says, feeling herself blush.

"Hi," Jimmy says, then drops his duffel bag on the hardwood floor and ducks his head to kiss her.

Lacey makes a quiet sound as he kicks the door shut behind him, her whole body humming underneath the warm authority of his touch. How is it possible this is only the third time they've been together in person? How is it possible they haven't been doing this their entire adult lives? She lets herself sink into it for a moment— his hands spanning her rib cage, his mouth moving slowly down her neck—then taps her fingers gently against his biceps. "Before this goes any further," she murmurs against his jaw, already wincing a little, "I should tell you I've got a house full of various assistants right now."

Jimmy hums into her skin, his palms skating down over the curve of her ass. "I mean," he says slowly, "group sex has never really been my thing, but if you think it'd be rude not to invite them to join—"

"Cute."

"Thank you." Jimmy straightens up, tucking his hands obediently back into his pockets. "Well, in that case. Nice to see you. Looking forward to our business dinner."

"Likewise." They stare at each other for a minute, grinning goofily. Lacey feels something in her stomach uncoil. She wishes they could send the team away and stay in tonight, just the two of them, and she imagines it before she can stop herself: sprawling sacked-out on the couch playing Scrabble or watching something on cable, a candle flickering on the coffee table and dinner simmering away on the stove. Normal-people shit.

Jimmy's thinking it, too: "You want to, like, go for a walk or something?" he asks, sounding almost bashful. "Before we have to do . . . all this? Is that allowed, for you and me to just—I mean. Are we allowed to do that?"

Lacey's heart sinks, just a bit. "We're allowed to do that," she says, "and I'd love to. But I don't actually think we've got time."

"Really?" Jimmy frowns, looking down at his watch. "I thought dinner wasn't until eight."

"It's not," she says, "but I've got to sit for hair and makeup. They wanted me already, actually, but I wanted to see you when you got here."

"Ah." Jimmy nods. "Got it."

"It won't take that long," she promises quickly, which is of course a lie. She thinks again of his ex-wife, with her low-key ponytails and Madewell denim, and feels self-conscious about being so ostentatiously high-maintenance. But what exactly is Lacey supposed to do, on a night as important as this one? She's not about to slap on some Maybelline and call it good. "And then the stylists have some stuff they pulled for you, too."

Jimmy laughs at that, then abruptly stops laughing. "Wait," he says, "really?"

"Yeah," Lacey admits with a wince. "Somebody was supposed to talk to you about that." She guesses *she* should have talked to him about that, actually, but she knew he was going to get this exact look on his face and start grumbling about wearing a costume for his mainstage community theater debut, and she wanted to put that off as long as possible. "They've got some stuff for you to pick from."

"Chicken suit?" he deadpans immediately. "*Beavis and Butt-Head* T-shirt? Lady Gaga's meat dress?"

"You don't have to wear anything you don't want to, obviously." Lacey wraps her arms around his neck one more time. "Maddie just thought that maybe—"

"Without professional guidance I might show up to dinner in gym shorts and a pair of cleats?"

"I think they were more envisioning a backward baseball cap and sunglasses with Croakies."

"Croakies are very practical," Jimmy fires back, then shrugs. "Whatever," he concedes. "I'm a man of the twenty-first century. I can appreciate a bespoke designer ensemble."

Lacey exhales. "Okay," she says. "Thank you."

In the end they put him in a pale blue suit with a subtle check pattern and a pair of spanking white high-tops, his hair brushed back off his forehead and a Breitling gleaming quietly on one wrist.

"Um, wow," Lacey says, finding him in the living room once the hair and makeup team finally takes off, the house suddenly quiet. "You look hot."

That makes him smile. "Really?" he asks. "Because I think I look like Ross and Chandler in the episodes of *Friends* where they're in college and Courteney Cox is wearing the fat suit." He tilts his head to the side, wrapping a hand around her waist and pulling her closer. "*You*, on the other hand, look hot."

Lacey grins back, a dark thrill zipping through her. She meant what she told him back at the farm—it's not like she was wandering alone in some barren orgasm desert waiting for him to come along and rescue her—but the truth is she's never felt as deeply, naturally *sexy* as she does with Jimmy. She's never liked her own body quite so much. She uses her chest to nudge him backward until the backs of his knees hit the sofa and he sits down, then hikes her dress up and settles herself in his lap with one knee on either side of his thighs.

Jimmy tips his handsome face toward her, then hesitates at the last second. "Am I going to fuck this whole"—he gestures at her general person—"situation up if I kiss you?"

"Depends how hard you commit, I guess." Lacey raises an eyebrow.

Jimmy smirks. "I'm pretty fucking committed," he murmurs, then presses his mouth against hers.

It escalates more or less immediately, his big hands wandering down her body, reaching up underneath her dress. Fuck dinner, Lacey thinks with surprising clarity, pressing herself against the warm, broad expanse of him, grinding herself against the bulge in his pants. Fuck the entire elaborate production. Instead they can just go upstairs and get directly into bed, and then tomorrow—

"Uh." Claire clears her throat from the doorway; Lacey springs to her feet before the sound is even all the way out, smoothing her dress down and wiping the edge of her lip. "Sorry," Claire says, not quite looking at either one of them. "I didn't know you were—I wouldn't have—the car's here, whenever you're ready."

"Oh, no worries," Lacey says, composing herself as quickly as possible. It's not like Claire hasn't seen worse, obviously; still, all at once she's blushing clear up to the roots of her hair. "You guys have talked on the phone, yeah? Jimmy, this is my assistant Claire." Her smile is ferocious, she can feel it. "Claire, Jimmy."

Jimmy puts a hand out—but does not, Lacey can't help but notice, make any move to stand upright quite yet. "Nice to meet you," he says as they shake. "Sorry for the, ah, inconvenience. Of . . . myself."

He's joking, Lacey can tell, but Claire doesn't laugh. "Not at all," she says, her tone friendly but businesslike. "Glad to have you on Lacey's team."

"Glad to . . . be on it," Jimmy says, a little uncertainly. He does stand up then, his knees cracking audibly, and reaches for Lacey's hand. "Let's do this thing, huh?"

Lacey nods, still smiling. "Yup," she says. "Let's do it."

〰〰〰〰

CLAIRE BOOKED THEM A TABLE AT SCOTTI'S, A HUNDRED-YEAR-old red-sauce Italian place with candles stuck into wine bottles on top of the checkered tablecloths. Lacey watches as Jimmy looks around, taking in the vehement unfanciness of the dining room, clocking the fact that Lacey purposely didn't ask for any kind of privacy. "I see what you all did here," he says quietly, taking a sip of his Peroni as a middle-aged woman two tables over snaps the world's least subtle iPhone photo. "This was very clever."

"Apple pie and homecoming," Lacey murmurs back, motioning over a wide-eyed tween so that they can take a selfie together. "Once you really get to know me, I think you'll find I'm a very normal Midwestern girl."

The waiter comes by three different times to ask if they're ready to order while Jimmy scrutinizes the menu like he thinks there's going to be a test of his reading comprehension after dessert. "Do you not like Italian food?" Lacey finally asks. "Sorry, I probably should have asked you that before now."

Jimmy shakes his head. "I like Italian food fine," he says. "I just feel like the internet is going to conduct a symposium on the semiotics of whatever I order right now, so I want to be sure I'm, you know. Doing my part to contribute to your team."

Ugh, Lacey *knew* that comment had rubbed him the wrong way as soon as it came out of Claire's mouth earlier. "I can think of some ways for you to contribute," she shoots back—trying to make a joke of it, nudging her ankle against his underneath the table. "If you're looking for ideas."

Jimmy smiles at that, though Lacey isn't sure if she's imagining that it doesn't quite reach his eyes. He hasn't smiled much since they got here, actually; their conversation feels stilted and fake, like they're two actors in a high school play who haven't entirely memorized their lines. "You excited for the series?" she asks once he's finally decided on the lasagna, aware that she sounds a little desperate. *Act like you're having fun,* she wants to tell him, but she's afraid someone will be able to read her lips.

"You could say that," Jimmy allows—and now he's smiling for real, just a little, presumably amused by her increasingly sweaty attempts to move them along. *Help me, then*, she thinks, trying to send the message telepathically across the table. *The whole point is to make it look like you're having fun.*

Well, no, Lacey amends to herself, glancing at Jimmy a little guiltily. The point is to actually *have* fun, obviously. It just so happens to be fun they're having in front of an audience, for public relations purposes.

It feels like they sit there forever, dutifully eating the kind of heavy, cheesy, salty dinner Lacey already knows is going to make her workout tomorrow morning feel impossible, wondering why she ever thought this was a good idea. It was a mistake, she sees now, to push him to do this; it was the latest in a long string of strategic errors she can't quite seem to stop making ever since he came along. Already Lacey is dreading their walk out to the car, when the photographers who have gathered outside the restaurant will inevitably take a million pictures to be promptly analyzed by a legion of amateur body language experts who'll declare their relationship a disingenuous, farcical PR stunt before they ever even make it back to her house. Maybe she *should* have just had him deny it altogether, she thinks wildly. Maybe they weren't ready for this after all.

Jimmy surprises her, though, slinging his arm around her once he's signed his name to the credit card receipt and helped her into her jacket. Just like that he's Handsome Everyman Jimmy Hodges again, feigning good-natured surprise as they step out onto the sidewalk and flashbulbs explode in every direction. "Hey, guys," he says, nodding with a lopsided grin at the scrum of photographers outside the entrance to the restaurant. "Who are you waiting for?" He cranes his neck. "Listen, you're never going to believe this, but I think I saw Lacey Logan in there with some dopey-looking asshole from the Orioles."

Oh, they like that, the laughter sincere and good-natured. Lacey couldn't have coached him better herself. "How was dinner?" one of them calls, still snapping busily away.

"It was incredible," Jimmy says easily, angling his body in a way that suggests they have his full attention even as he's guiding Lacey into their waiting SUV. "You guys should get in there, order some tiramisu. Tell them to send me the bill."

Lacey turns to look at him with some amazement once the door is closed behind them. "Nicely done," she admits.

Jimmy clears his throat. "Learned from the best," is all he says. It doesn't necessarily sound like a compliment.

They're quiet on the car ride back to her place, neither of them saying anything as he follows her up the front walk, as she keys the code into the pad beside the door and turns to wave good night to Javi. He'll stay on until midnight, parked in the SUV in the driveway until someone else from the team arrives to replace him. She's got twenty-four-hour coverage, even at home.

Once they're inside Lacey walks from room to room flicking the lights on—putting Henrietta Lang on the sound system, getting them each a glass of water—before finally running out of small, plausibly necessary tasks and sitting down hard on the edge of the sofa. She was stalling, that's all. She was buying time.

"Do you want to talk about it?" she asks quietly.

Jimmy plays dumb. "Talk about what?" he asks, shaking out his hands before tucking them back into his pockets.

"You know what." Lacey rolls her eyes, irritated all of a sudden. *Stop being such a fucking baby*, she wants to tell him. *This wasn't the playoffs. This was barely a Wednesday.*

"No, I mean—I don't know." Jimmy shrugs. "It was just a weird night, that's all. Performing it, like that. I knew you brought me here to put on a show, obviously. I guess I just didn't realize it was going to be so—so—"

"So what, exactly?" Lacey asks. "Since when are you uncomfortable in the spotlight?"

"I'm not uncomfortable in the spotlight," he counters, sounding a little offended. "I am extremely fucking comfortable in the spotlight."

"Okay," Lacey says, "then what? Is it that thing that Claire said, is that the problem? Is it because I'm more famous than you?"

Jimmy guffaws. "Are you serious right now?"

"I'm just asking!" she protests, though there's a part of her that knows she's being snotty on purpose, that's leaning into her own ego a little bit. "It's a valid feeling."

"It's not my valid feeling," he insists. "I don't care about that."

Lacey throws her hands up. "Well then, what?"

"Lacey—"

"Because not to keep beating this drum or whatever, but you're the one who made this whole thing public to begin with, so—"

"I know that, thanks." Jimmy's eyes flash. "Believe me, you and your team of lady avengers have made abundantly sure that I know that. But apparently that also means I'm not entitled to feel any kind of way about this whole thing—"

"Any kind of way about the two of us being public?" Lacey interrupts him. "Or any kind of way about me?"

Jimmy doesn't answer for a moment—perching uncomfortably on a media console at the other end of the living room, visibly too big for this space. Lacey closes her eyes, leaning her head back against the sofa. "Look," she says finally. "If you don't feel like the lift is worth it here, or you're thinking maybe you made a mistake, then by all means—"

"That's not what this is," Jimmy says immediately. When she opens her eyes he's himself again, his expression hot. "Are you kidding me? I—Lacey. Yeah. That's not what this is."

"Then what?" she asks—or starts to, anyway, but is cut off by the sound of her phone ringing, the screen lighting up with Javi's name.

"Sorry to bother," he says, when Lacey answers. "But the guard at the booth just called me. There's somebody asking for you at the gate."

\\\\\\\\\

"Mom," Lacey says four endless minutes later, watching from the doorway as her mother wobbles up the front walk. "Hi."

"Hi, sweet pea," her mother says, then turns to Jimmy—looking him up and down, openly appraising. "Well, I will say this much about you, cutie: they certainly weren't kidding about you being tall."

"Jimmy," Lacey says before he can answer, trying to keep her voice from shaking. Her mom has never done this before, just waltzed right in with no warning; it's true she doesn't generally require an explicit invitation, but normally she at least calls before she arrives. "This is my mom."

"Janine," her mom says, holding a manicured hand out before turning to Lacey. "I had dinner with some gal pals," she reports, which Lacey immediately knows is a lie. Much like her only daughter, Janine Hall Logan has very few friends. "So I was in the neighborhood, and I thought—"

"Did you *drive* here?" Lacey interrupts, horrified by the thought of it.

"Of course I drove here," her mother says, like Lacey is the one who's being unreasonable. "Not all of us have twenty-four-hour chauffeurs."

"You know I would get you a driver if you wanted," Lacey protests. In fact, she would love it if her mom would accept her offer of a driver, if only so that Lacey could stop worrying about her drunkenly crashing her fucking car into a family of four out for a celebratory dinner at Culver's. "We can set that up whenever you want."

Her mom ignores her, turning back to Jimmy. She smells like white wine and perfume, her hair in a perfect updo and her lipstick just the tiniest bit smudged. "My daughter has been trying to keep us hidden away from each other," she confides with a conspiratorial grin. "Which one of us do you think she was more embarrassed of, you or me?"

"Me, definitely," Jimmy says without missing a trick. "My table manners are abysmal. And I almost wore Croakies on our date."

"Oh, come on now," Lacey's mom says, giggling girlishly. "I doubt that very much."

"I'm going to get you some water," Lacey announces.

"You don't have a bottle of wine open, do you?" her mom asks, sitting down on the sofa and making herself comfortable. "I would love a glass of sauvignon blanc."

"Nope," Lacey calls tightly over her shoulder. "I sure don't."

Jimmy hesitates for a moment before following Lacey into the kitchen, watching in silence as she yanks a cabinet door open and reaches for a glass. "Just don't, okay?" she snaps, slamming it against the water dispenser so hard she's lucky it doesn't shatter to pieces. "I mean—I don't want to—just. Don't."

Jimmy takes a step back. "I'm not," he promises quietly. "I'm not."

She digs some cheese from the fridge and a box of crackers from the cupboard, peels a clementine and puts it all on a plate. By the time they get back into the living room, though, her mom is curled up fast asleep on the couch, open-mouthed and snoring softly. Lacey swears under her breath. "Mom," she says, setting the plate and the glass on the coffee table and laying a hand on her mom's warm, bony shoulder. "Mom, come on, wake up." Her voice is trembling; she can hear it. Jimmy is watching silently from across the room. "Mom, please." Then, when her mom still doesn't stir: "*Mom.*"

"I think she's out, Lacey." His voice is so, so gentle.

"I know that," Lacey retorts, then feels her whole body sag, the weight of the last few hours—the weight of the last few months— hitting her all at once. "I don't want to just leave her here," she confesses, sitting down hard on the arm of the sofa. "Passed out drunk on my couch? That's so bleak."

Jimmy nods. "Okay," he says, coming closer, looking to her for permission; Lacey motions for him to go ahead and he bends to scoop her mom off the cushions, lifting her into his arms like a child. "Where to?"

Lacey sighs. "Guesthouse," she says.

Jimmy nods. "Lead the way."

He trails her out the back door and across the patio, along the edge of the pool. Her mom doesn't stir once the whole time. He lays her down on the mattress in one of the bedrooms, standing in the doorway as Lacey tucks her in and turns off the light.

"Well," she says once she's led him back out to the yard, sitting down on one of the enormous double loungers that ring the bean-shaped pool. Someone has already taken care of draining and closing it for the season, though the truth is she isn't sure who. "Now you know."

Jimmy stops walking. "Okay," he says, sitting down beside her. She can hear his knees crack in the quiet night. "Is that supposed to put me off?"

"I don't know." Lacey shrugs. "Maybe. It's objectively off-putting."

"You realize I have a little bit of experience with this kind of thing."

It's the first time he's even alluded to the circumstances of his brother's death, and her first instinct is to act like she has no idea what he's talking about. Her second instinct, shamefully, is to say *My mom is nothing like your drug addict brother* but that's horrible, that's awful, and anyway it's not even true. Her mom is *exactly* like his drug addict brother.

"Yeah," she agrees finally. "I know you do." She digs the heels of her hands into her eyes for a moment, waiting to see if she's going to cry or not, then finally decides not and drops them back into her lap. "What was he like?" she asks. "Matthew, right? Matt?"

Jimmy nods. "Matty," he corrects softly. "We called him Matty. And he was, like. The best person in the world."

"Oh yeah?" Lacey smiles. "Say more."

Jimmy reaches up and rubs at his shoulder, not quite looking at her. "He could do anything, you know? He wasn't afraid of anything." He tilts his head to the side. "He was a great fucking ballplayer, I'll tell you that much. That's how I got into it to begin with, actually—because I wanted to be like my brother."

Lacey holds her breath, but to her surprise he keeps going,

telling her all sorts of things: How Matty got a full scholarship to college. How Matty played baseball for Notre Dame. How Matty blew out his knee his first semester of college and some stupid, irresponsible fucking doctor gave him a prescription for oxycodone, and that was the end of Jimmy having a brother, pretty much. It's the most earnest, the most unguarded she's heard him sound about anything since the very first night they met, like how a little kid would talk about a superhero. The sum total of it breaks Lacey's heart.

"Anyway," Jimmy finishes with a shrug, "he died of a heroin overdose a few weeks before I got called up, so." He clears his throat. "While I'm sure this situation with your mom creates a lot of logistical and emotional issues for a person in your particular position, if you're looking for me to be squeamish about it, you're going to have to find another guy."

Lacey is quiet for a moment, gazing at him in the darkness. "Thank you," she says eventually.

"For what?"

"For telling me that," she says. "For trusting me with it. And for the rest of it, too—for helping me with my mom, for coming out here and doing all this to begin with. For the whole dog and pony show."

"Yeah, well." Jimmy's lips twist. "The whole dog and pony show isn't so bad." He leans back against the lounger, crossing his ankles. "Come here," he says, opening his arms to her. Lacey scooches back and stretches her legs out, leans her head against his chest. She can hear his heart beating like this, the steady tap of it settling. It feels like something she can imagine doing for a long time, over many years. Over a lifetime, Lacey's never thought that much about having kids—it's always felt like something she might do someday, like starting her own label or going into space—but all of a sudden she's thinking about it in bright, vivid Technicolor, Jimmy Hodges as a dad. You could carry a daughter on those shoulders. You could hold a baby son in those arms. All at once she's wishing for a pen, for something to write with. She wants to capture this feeling before it disappears.

"What?" Jimmy asks, peering down at her.

"What what?"

"You have a face of, like. Consternation."

"Oh. No." *I was imagining you putting a hundred babies in me, or at the very least I'm thinking of writing a song about it* does not feel like something she ought to say to him on this particular evening, so she slides one hand up under his shirt to distract him: rubbing a hand over his stomach, raking her nails gently over the hair on his chest. Jimmy grumbles his quiet approval, so she keeps doing it, scratching lightly, feeling the muscles of his stomach jump under her touch. Her hand wanders down over the fly of his jeans, over the zipper where he's already hard through the denim. Jimmy groans and reaches for her, hauling her up on top of him. Lacey gasps. "I wanted to do this all night long," he murmurs, reaching up to tuck her hair behind her ears.

Lacey raises an eyebrow. "You mean when you weren't thinking about how fast you could possibly get the fuck away from this entire situation?"

She's joking—at least, she's sort of joking—but Jimmy doesn't laugh. "That wasn't what I was thinking," he says immediately, hands stilling on her body. "Hey. Lacey. Look at me. That wasn't what I was thinking."

Lacey can't help but notice that he doesn't tell her what he *was* thinking, either. "Touch me," she says, instead of pressing him for details. Jimmy does it, pulling the zipper on the back of her dress down and working the clasp on her bra open. Catching her nipple between his teeth.

Lacey sits up long enough to work his fly open, lets him push her skirt up over her hips. "I don't have a condom," he warns her when she wraps her hand around him, stroking gently.

"At all?"

"I mean, no, in the house I do." He thrusts up into her hand, looking faintly helpless. "Want to go in?"

Lacey considers that. His skin is so, so warm. "Do you still have chlamydia?" she asks.

Jimmy smirks. "No, darling," he says. "I think I'd be dead by now if I still had chlamydia."

"Does chlamydia kill you?"

"Didn't feel like something I wanted to find out."

Lacey nods, considering. "Do you have anything else? Like, illness-wise?"

"No."

"Are you sure?"

"Yes."

"Okay."

Jimmy's eyes widen. "Okay?" he asks, gaze searching hers with urgency, like he's afraid he isn't understanding correctly. "Okay, like—?"

"Okay, like I have an IUD," she says, which is true. She's thinking about what his kids might look like, sure, but she's not insane. "You're good, go."

So. Jimmy goes, groaning so loudly she's glad she's got so much land around here, glad Javi is parked safely on the other side of the house and her mom will be passed out until at least lunchtime tomorrow. Lacey laughs, she can't help it, muffling the sound of it into his skin. "Good?" she asks, shifting around until she gets comfortable.

"Yeah," he says, rubbing at her hips, her back, up and down her spine. "That's good."

It's good for her, too, the way he's touching her, the night air cool on her bare skin and the sound of the crickets calling to each other in the trees. Lacey closes her eyes, giving herself over to the moment. Holding on tight to the here and now.

CHAPTER EIGHTEEN

JIMMY

HE FLIES HOME EARLY THE NEXT MORNING, LANDING JUST IN time to make it to practice at Camden. The Division Series starts tomorrow, the team flying up to Boston for Game 1. The air is colder, not quite feeling like fall yet—it takes time for autumn to come in Baltimore—but not quite summer anymore, either, the leaves turning to flame overhead. There's a scrum of reporters waiting for him outside the clubhouse when he arrives, plus a cluster of teenage girls who don't exactly fit Jimmy's usual fan demographic. "How was Cincinnati?" one of the journalists calls—at least, Jimmy thinks that's the question. The girls are all screaming like they just saw a Jonas Brother, and honestly it's kind of hard to hear.

"It was good," Jimmy reports as blandly as humanly possible. "I'm glad to be back here, though. Ready to play."

He repeats some variation on that sentiment two dozen times in the next twenty-four hours, to his coffee guy and his barber and to Moira, the team doctor, as she shoots cortisone into his swollen knees; to his assistant Jennifer, who after three years of courteous, professional efficiency has suddenly developed more than what one might call a passing interest in the minutiae of his personal life. It's all anyone wants to talk about, it seems, Jimmy and Lacey Logan. It's all anyone wants to hear. Dimly, he's aware that he couldn't have picked a worse time for this to happen, an awareness that sharpens into stark, unforgiving focus when they lose the first game of the ALDS at Fenway Park, 5–3. BAD LUCK CHARM? reads the front page of the *Sun*.

They pull it back in Game 2, thank fuck, beating the Sox 7–6, though Jimmy strikes out twice and Hugo winds up on the injured list following a bad landing on his right wrist; still, all anyone wants to talk about at the presser later that night is whether Lacey Logan is going to be coming to Camden anytime soon.

"Didn't realize your girlfriend had gotten called up to the majors," Tito says once it's over, all of them back in the away-team locker room, the stink of sweat and foot spray heavy in the air. He's teasing—at least, Jimmy thinks he's teasing—but Jimmy cringes anyway. This is exactly what he didn't want to happen: the way it's pulling everyone's focus, the way it's singling him out in the exact moment they need to be operating as a unit. This is exactly what he was trying to avoid.

Two things happen the afternoon before the third game of the series. The first is that Toby announces his Netflix special, *Problematic Dickhead* or whatever the fuck it's called, which for some reason a significant number of national media outlets seem to believe Jimmy might have an opinion regarding. The second is that Lacey calls him as he's driving over to Camden. "So here's a question," she says, the connection crackling through the Bluetooth. "What do you think about me maybe coming to see you play some baseball?"

"Seriously?" Jimmy laughs at that, then realizes all at once she isn't joking. "Do you *want* to come see me play baseball?"

"I'm thinking about it," she admits. "I might."

"When?"

"I don't know," she says. "Game 4? I think it sounds like fun."

"*You* think it sounds fun?" he asks before he can stop himself. Game 4 is tomorrow fucking night. "Or Maddie thinks it sounds fun?"

"Rude!" she says, laughing a little. "We both think it's a good idea."

"Because of Toby's comedy thing?"

"Because you're my *boyfriend*, Jimmy!" Lacey sounds stung. "And I'm proud of you, and I'm excited you're in the playoffs, and I just—whatever. If you don't want me to, I won't."

Right away, Jimmy feels like a massive douchebag. "It's not that I don't want you to," he says quickly, though he's not actually sure that's the truth. He tries to imagine it, just as a thought experiment, Lacey up in one of the boxes with all the other WAGs: Jonesy's wife, who he's always in a fight with, Tito's longtime girlfriend and their three quiet, polite kids. Rachel used to come sometimes, though she always liked to sit in the cheap seats instead of upstairs in the suites eating Sysco chicken tenders from catering. She used to bring a book of crossword puzzles, her sneakered feet propped up in front of her while she worked through the clues. "Of course I want you to."

"Okay," Lacey says, still sulking a little. "Well then?"

Jimmy hesitates, paused at a red light not far from the stadium. His instinct is to tell her no. The stakes are too high, and already he knows what it's going to be like, the way she has of bringing the circus to town everywhere she goes: the press, the fans, the general hysteria. They're talking about the playoffs here, not some sleepy afternoon game in the middle of June that doesn't matter. He should tell her it isn't a good idea.

Then he thinks of kissing her bright red mouth in the middle of the field, confetti raining down all around them. Flashbulbs exploding like stars.

"Absolutely," Jimmy says, hitting the gas as the light turns green up above him. "Let's make it happen."

\\\\\\\\

THE FRONT OFFICE LOVES THE IDEA, OBVIOUSLY. THEY'RE PRACtically salivating, counting their coins like predatory cartoon forest animals in a 1970s Disney movie. "You think she'd want to do a promo spot?" one of them asks when they call him in later that afternoon to talk logistics.

"To promote . . . the fact that she's attending the game?" Jimmy asks, shaking his head a little. "I think maybe we want to preserve the element of surprise there, boys, don't you?"

The guys are, understandably, significantly less enthused. "I thought we were supposed to be playing professional sports here," Jonesy grumbles when word gets out around the locker room after the game that night. They won, which puts them ahead 2–1 in the series; Jimmy had hoped the lead would soften the ground for him a little bit, though it doesn't seem to have worked that way. "Not hosting the Jimmy Hodges Dating Experience."

"Pretty serious talk from a guy who mooned reporters from the bus last season," Jimmy chides, but it's not like he doesn't understand what Jonesy is getting at. He's supposed to be the captain of this team and instead he knows this is going to make things objectively more difficult for his guys, who he's supposed to be looking out for. His guys, who he honestly loves.

"Oh, pull it together, you mooks," Tuck says. "You guys are just worried you're going to embarrass yourselves in front of a pretty girl."

"Thanks," Jimmy says once they're alone. "For the assist back there, I mean."

He's fully expecting some well-deserved ribbing in return, but Tuck doesn't so much as smile. "I didn't do it for you," he says. "I did it for them. Somebody needs to be thinking about morale out there, and it's sure as shit not you."

"Seriously?" Jimmy blinks, surprised by the suddenness of it. They've barely talked about Lacey at all. They've barely talked about much of anything lately, Jimmy realizes, now that he's stopping to think about it; he guesses he's been—well. Distracted. "What the fuck, dude?"

"You what the fuck!" Tuck shoots back. "I'm supposed to be your best friend, Jimmy. You didn't think a heads-up would have been appropriate?"

"Is that what this is about?" Jimmy asks. "You're salty you didn't get the celebrity gossip ahead of time? Buy you a little social capital with Rose?"

"Oh, fuck you," Tuck says. "You know I don't give a shit about that kind of thing. What I *do* give a shit about is you throwing a curveball like this into the most important game we've had so far this season." He shakes his head. "You really think it's a good idea for her to just, like, casually drop in?"

"People come to our games all the time," Jimmy says as coolly as he can manage. "I generally try not to pay them too much mind either way."

"Bullshit," Tuck says immediately. "You know this isn't the same." He blows out a noisy breath. "I'm not trying to be a dick to you, bro. But we have worked too fucking hard, and we have gotten too fucking lucky for you to be throwing it away now on a piece of—"

"Don't say it," Jimmy interrupts him. "I mean it. Don't say it. That's not what this is."

"Of course that's what this is!" Tuck explodes. "What are you trying to tell me, that you're in love with her? That she's your soul mate? No, of course not. She is very fucking beautiful, and she is very fucking famous, but is whatever is happening here worth throwing away your last chance to win a World Series? I'm your best friend, dude. I've been your best friend for a lot of years, and I don't want you to do that. Not for you, not for me, and not for the rest of this team."

"You don't know what you're talking about," Jimmy says stubbornly. He's out on a limb, he knows he is; all at once, it feels very, very important that he doesn't look down. "I am the leader of this team—"

"Then fucking lead it!" Tuck explodes.

"Thanks for the tip," Jimmy tells him, then turns and stalks out of the room.

〰〰〰〰

HE'S STILL STEWING AN HOUR LATER WHEN LACEY TEXTS HIM A mirror selfie of her wearing high-waisted jeans and a number 14 Hodges jersey. *Is this right for a baseball game?* she wants to know.

She's flying in tomorrow morning, with the idea that someone from her camp will tip off the press while she's in the air. *Asking for a friend.*

Jimmy grits his teeth, flopping backward onto his mattress. He doesn't care what she wears to the baseball game, truthfully, and he knows she really doesn't care what he thinks, either. She's got a team of eleven people who are going to make sure she breaks the internet. She is never, at any time, without a plan. *Looks great,* he types, then tosses his phone on the nightstand and switches the lamp off. He doesn't fall asleep for a long time.

\\\\\\\\

THE PLAN IS FOR HER TO HEAD TO HIS PLACE FROM THE AIRPORT so they can spend some time together before Jimmy needs to be at the stadium, but there's bad weather out in the middle of the country that means she's still in the air come midafternoon. *Be there in plenty of time for the first pitch,* she promises breezily, but in the end she's still on the plane when Jimmy gets up on the bench in the locker room to give the guys his pregame speech.

"Just one more," he promises them, his heart red and wet and thrumming; the ALDS is a best-of-five series, which means if they win tonight they'll leave the field as Division champs. "Just one more; that's all we need."

They're going to take it, too. The beginning of the game is a breeze, three quick runs in the bottom of the second inning. Tuck's grin is beatific in the stadium lights. This is it, Jimmy thinks to himself, not bothering to tamp down his excitement. They're going to go all the fucking way.

He's just turning to Tuck to say so when the roars start up all around the stadium; Jonesy almost drops the ball onto the grass.

When Jimmy lifts his head there's Lacey up on the Jumbotron, all dark hair and winning smile and oversized Hodges jersey. For a second there, he'd honestly forgotten she was on her way.

"Ladies and gentlemen," the announcer intones, the sound of it barely audible over the screaming, "please welcome a very special guest to Camden Yards!"

And that's when the game starts to turn.

Jimmy strikes out in the third and sixth and seventh. Tuck strikes out in the eighth. The Sox smash bomb after bomb into the outfield, the Orioles scrambling and slow. It feels like Jimmy is watching a car crash: the board at 5–3 Boston, 6–3 Boston, 7–3 Boston. It's 11–3 Boston at the top of the ninth. It's excruciating. Jimmy knows part of what's *making* it so excruciating is his ego, that he doesn't want his team to lose in front of his girlfriend. But also: he doesn't want his team to lose in front of Lacey Logan, international superstar.

It happens anyway.

It's 12–3 in the end; Sox take it. Jimmy stalks off the field, spitting once into the cool red clay and looking at nothing. Looking at nobody at all.

CHAPTER NINETEEN

LACEY

IT OCCURS TO LACEY, AS THEY RIDE SILENTLY UPSTAIRS IN THE elevator of his building in Fells Point an hour later, that she doesn't actually like Jimmy's condo very much at all.

It's not even just that it's sterile and anonymous—although it is both of those things, she thinks sullenly, as the doors slide open and they step into the tall, cold foyer, a stereotype of a rich bro's bachelor pad. It's that it feels like it belongs to someone else entirely than the person who owns the farm. It makes Lacey uneasy, the idea that Jimmy could be equally at home in both of these places. It makes her wonder how many versions of him there might possibly be.

She drops her purse on the leather sofa and sits down, watching as he stalks over to the bar and pours himself a sizable drink. "Would *you* like anything, Lacey?" she asks, her voice loud and theatrical. She knows she sounds snotty, and she doesn't care. "A lemonade, perhaps? An Arnold Palmer?"

Jimmy downs the bourbon in one long gulp, sets the glass down hard on the counter. "Can you not?" he asks. He didn't shower after the game and he smells like sweat and ballpark dust, the sharp iron tang of shame and defeat. "I mean, can you just give me a minute to be—" He breaks off.

"Sorry," she says, a little abashed. A person didn't need to be a baseball expert to know it was an ugly loss. "Yeah, of course." Lacey shifts her weight, trying to get settled on his stupidly large, stupidly low-to-the-ground leather couch. "You want to talk about it?"

Jimmy shakes his head once. "Not especially."

"Okay," Lacey says, only then they're just quiet again, both of them sulking, the silence getting bigger and denser and heavier like a cloud she wants to reach up and burst with one finger. She rubs her hands over her knees. This couch is ridiculous, truly, far too big for anyone to comfortably sit on; she's tall for a woman, and still if she were to sit all the way back on it her feet would stick out like a child's. She *feels* like a child, here in this tense, silent apartment, like the person she was before she became Lacey Logan: out of her depth and guileless, the kind of girl who still played with Barbies until seventh grade without realizing that was embarrassing. The kind of girl who didn't understand the rules.

Lacey glances across the room at the bunch of Jimmy's shoulders, the muscle ticking like a bomb inside his jaw. It was terrible, sitting in that suite making small talk with all those other women, watching it all fall apart on the field and not being able to do a single thing about it. How vulnerable it made her feel on his behalf. She knew full well the cameras were on her as much as they were on Jimmy, watching every single purse of her lips and twitch of her eyebrows, capturing her every wince and tell. *I'm proud of him!* she wanted to shout, though of course she knew the worst thing to do would be to draw any more attention to herself than she already had just by virtue of coming here. *I'm still very much intending to have sex with him tonight!*

She had been, too—had been looking forward to comforting him, actually, to distracting both of them into believing this wasn't a big deal—but when she got down to the locker room she could see right away that he was closed for business: his jaw set and his eyes hard, his body unyielding when she wrapped her arms around him. The rest of his team looked at her like she was a plague. "I'm sorry," Lacey murmured into his chest, but either he didn't hear her or he pretended not to. He didn't say anything the entire ride home, staring out the window of the SUV at the city rolling darkly by.

"Look," Lacey tries now, twisting her fingers into knots in her lap. It's strange, feeling like she doesn't have the first notion of how to handle him like this. It's strange to feel suddenly like she might not know him very well at all. "It was one bad game, right?"

That's the wrong thing to say. Right away Jimmy whirls on her. "Are you serious right now?" he asks, his dark eyes wild. "You of all people are going to stand here and have the balls to tell me it was one bad game?"

"The series isn't over!" she points out, struggling upright off the couch—wanting to make herself larger, to even the playing field somehow. "You guys can go back to Boston and—"

"I don't want to hear the series isn't over, Lacey!" Jimmy shakes his head. "I don't want to hear that it's one bad game. I can't *have* one bad game. This matters to me. This *matters* to me—"

"I know that!" she interrupts. "Of course I know that."

"Do you?" Jimmy asks, sounding sincerely curious. "Because for a person who's so deeply and pathologically obsessed with her own career, sometimes it's like you can't quite metabolize the fact that somebody else might care about theirs. What did you think was going to happen tonight, huh? Like, when you were picturing this whole thing, what exactly were you imagining?"

Lacey throws up her hands. "I thought you were going to win your game and we'd go out for ice cream sundaes, Jimmy, what do you want me to say? Like, I'm sorry your team had a bad night—"

"Why do you think we had a bad night, exactly?"

All at once, Lacey hears the drumbeat of danger coming closer. "Don't," she warns him.

"Don't what?"

"You know what!" Lacey insists. "Uh-uh, Jimmy. No way. Like, by all means, go ahead and throw a tantrum if you need to, walk it off, but I'll be damned if I'm going to stand here and let you make noise about how any of this was somehow my fault for showing up to your game when you're the one—"

"I said it at the very beginning, didn't I?" Jimmy shakes his head. "I told you I was worried this was going to be a distraction for both of us, and we can't afford to have any distractions right now."

"*You* can't."

"I can't!" Jimmy bursts out. "I'm literally trying to win the World fucking Series! I don't get how you of all people don't understand that!"

"Yeah, well." Lacey throws her hands up. "It wouldn't have become a distraction in the first place if you could have kept your fucking mouth shut like I asked you to."

That blow lands: Jimmy sputters for a moment, shrugging violently. "Well, I'm sorry I'm not a criminal mastermind like you," he says, a flash of embarrassment visible through the dark scrim of his anger. "I don't have perfect media training, I guess. I don't talk to the world in fucking riddles and assume everyone will drop everything to figure out what I'm trying to tell them because they're all so deeply obsessed with me."

"I have never, not once, talked in riddles with you!" Lacey explodes, stung by the deep unfairness of it. "I have been direct and I have been forthright and if you didn't want me to come to your damn baseball game to support you, then you should have done the same thing and told me so! This wasn't a surprise pop-in, Jimmy. You had plenty of time to put a stop to it if you wanted to, and you didn't, so now—"

"Oh, please," he protests. "You know as well as I do that you weren't asking for permission, Lacey. On top of which, you didn't come to support me! You came because your fucking publicist told you it would be a good thing to do to distract the people who write the articles on the Sinclair from the fact that your ex was making shitty jokes at your expense."

This is, it must be said, a little bit true, and Jimmy must see it in her expression before she can figure out how to spin it, because his own face turns rock-solid. "Yeah," he says. "That's what I thought."

Lacey considers that for a moment, looking around at his tacky chrome floor lamp, his dopey concrete floors. She does not want to be here, she thinks clearly. This is no longer a place she wants to be. "Okay," she says. "You know what, Jimmy? You win. I don't want to fight about this anymore tonight. We can cool off and talk about it more later, okay? In the meantime, I'm going to go back to my hotel."

"Wait." Jimmy blinks at that, visibly startled by the idea of it. "You booked a hotel room?"

"Of course I booked a fucking hotel room!" God, there is so much he doesn't understand about the way her life works. There is so much he still doesn't get. "You think I am a person who ever, under any circumstances, comes to a city without booking a hotel room? I booked three different blocks of hotel rooms, at three different hotels, just like I do literally every time I travel."

"I just—" Jimmy frowns. He looks so surprised, just for a second. He looks so enormously, bizarrely *hurt*. "I thought you were staying here."

"Well." Lacey quirks an eyebrow. "I guess it's a good thing I had a backup plan, huh."

Jimmy's eyes narrow then, like this information confirms some mean suspicion about her that he's been quietly harboring. Like this was a trap and she just walked right into it. "Of course you did," he says, nodding slowly. "You always do, right? You're always three steps ahead of everyone else."

"What does that even mean?" Lacey demands. "Do you even *want* me to stay here right now? Because you're certainly not acting like a person who—"

Jimmy shakes his head. "This is too much for me," he announces. "All of this is too much for me. The machine of it, the Lacey Logan industrial complex. You sneeze and it changes the Nasdaq. It's too much for me."

"You mean *I'm* too much for you."

She's expecting him to contradict her, but Jimmy only shrugs. "Yeah, Lacey," he admits quietly. "Sometimes, yeah."

Lacey absorbs that blow in silence. Up until right this moment she thought this was just a regular argument that they were having but she can see now that it's more than that, that it's serious—that Jimmy is the kind of person to go nuclear, that he could end this right now and be fine with it. He could have been fine never talking to her again after that night in New York City; he could have been fine never talking to her again after the last time they fought. All at once it's glaringly obvious that Lacey herself has been the one pushing this relationship forward the entire time, that she has been the one pursuing him since the moment she asked him to leave that club weeks and weeks ago, and the fact that she somehow deluded herself into thinking otherwise feels like a grave and strategic misstep on her part. She doesn't know what's wrong with her lately. She's never felt so out of control in her entire life. "Well, okay," she says, throwing her shoulders back and affecting carelessness as best as she possibly can. "That's instructive. Thank you for your honesty. We're done, then."

"Wha—hang on a second." Jimmy holds a hand up, panic flaring in his eyes. "I'm not saying done forever. I'm saying let's take some time to cool off, same as you said, until—"

"Until what, until your career is officially over and you need someone to glom on to in order to stay relevant?"

Jimmy looks stung. "Wow," he says. "Screw you, Lacey."

"Screw you," she shoots back, keeping her voice very even. She's not going to let him see her fall apart. He wants to think she's a robot, that she has a computer for a brain, let him think it. She's Lacey fucking Logan, and she doesn't give a damn. "I'm going now."

"Yeah," Jimmy says, "I think that's probably for the best."

It takes Lacey a moment to gather her things and her person, to snatch her jacket off the abominable sofa and shove her purse underneath her arm. She feels unsteady in her shoes as she makes her way back toward the foyer. They were all wrong for a baseball game, she sees now. Everything she did was all wrong.

Jimmy scrubs a hand over his face, yanking ineffectually at his beard. "Lacey," he says, and for a second she thinks he's going to be himself again, tell her he's sorry, he's being ridiculous, he's falling in love with her. That they can get through this together. That they can be a team.

"You need to leave through the garage," he reminds her quietly. "There's press outside."

Lacey laughs out loud, sharp and ringing. "No shit, Jimmy." Both of them stand in silence as she waits for the elevator, her heels echoing as she steps inside. She waits until the doors whoosh shut behind her before she crouches on the floor, makes herself as small as humanly possible, and lets herself start to cry.

CHAPTER TWENTY

JIMMY

JIMMY SITS ON THE COUCH FOR A LONG TIME AFTER LACEY LEAVES, staring blankly out the window at the city. He wants another drink, badly. He wants another drink, or he wants his brother, or he wants to hit something over and over until his knuckles are shredded and bloody. Instead he gets up and runs seven miles on the treadmill even though it's twelve thirty a.m. and he just caught nine innings, even though he just pounded two fingers of Basil Hayden. It hurts like all hell, which is what he was after. The pain feels like something he deserves.

When he's finished he collapses into bed and sleeps for four hours, then gets up and drives over to the clubhouse, the sun dripping up orange and pink and yellow in the rearview as he cruises through the city toward the park. They don't need to catch the bus to the airport for another couple of hours, but Jimmy likes being the only one here in the morning: the bleachy, mineral smell of the tunnels, the grounds team and the maintenance guys all going about their days. It's peaceful—or it usually is, anyway. This morning when he gets into the locker room he finds Tuck is already waiting for him, sitting in a rolling chair with his ankles crossed on one of the benches and an enormous Starbucks cup in each hand.

"Thought you might show," he says, reaching forward and handing one over. "You all right?"

"I'm fine," Jimmy promises him gratefully, tossing his bag in his locker before sitting down and taking a sip. It's still hot enough to burn through some of the hangover fog in his brain. "I'm good."

"Bullshit." Tuck raises an eyebrow. "You look like a fucking untoasted bagel. You want to go play catch?"

Jimmy barks a laugh, then reconsiders, looking at Tuck for a moment. "Yeah," he says. "That would be good."

So they go outside and drink their coffee and toss the ball back and forth for a while, not saying much, just breathing in the fresh clean air and the smell of the grass and watching the sky turn full morning. Jimmy's head has almost stopped throbbing by the time Jonesy shows up. "If you guys were looking for someplace to be alone to practice French kissing, you could have picked a more private venue," he calls, strolling out of the tunnel with his sunglasses perched on the brim of his ballcap.

"We were waiting for you to give us some tips, actually," Tuck shoots back. "Hodges keeps coming in too hot with his tongue."

Hugo turns up before Jonesy can answer, the rest of the guys trickling out onto the field one after another, all of them in their practice uniforms, quietly warming up. They're all early, Jimmy realizes—they must have planned it—and for a second he loves them all so fucking much and so fucking deeply he almost needs to turn around and walk off the field so he doesn't fall down.

He clears his throat instead, swallowing down the strange lump that's settled there, swiping as surreptitiously as he can at his cheekbone behind his sunglasses. "What?" he says, when he catches Ray looking at him. "I got something on my face?"

"Little bit of jizz, yeah," Jonesy pipes up helpfully, motioning to the side of his own mouth.

Jimmy snorts. "Fuck you," he says, but he's laughing, which he knows was the point.

But Ray shakes his head. "I was just, uh. Waiting for your speech, is all."

Jimmy rubs a hand over his chin and looks back at him for a moment, at this kid whose entire career in the majors is still in front of him like a carpet, like the fucking yellow brick road. Then he takes a breath and gets to work.

"Some of you guys know I got into baseball in the first place because of my brother," he begins, jamming his hands into his pockets and rocking back on the heels of his cleats. "He was older than me, and he was my hero, and he loved this game more than anything. And I stood around and watched while the world crept in and took that from him and stole his focus and made him less than what could have been. Less than what he was." Jimmy clears his throat. "Anyway," he continues, "I promised myself that for his sake I was never going to let that happen to me, and you know what? I mostly haven't. No matter what shit was going on in my personal life, no matter what the media was saying about me—about us—I always tried to check it at the door. The last couple weeks, though . . ." He shakes his head. "Look, you fucks have been here the last couple weeks. You know what it's been like. And I owe you all an apology for that."

"Aw, Cap," Jonesy says, "it hasn't been so bad."

"Are you kidding?" Hugo cuffs him gently on the side of the head. "You've been complaining louder than anyone, you grouchy little pissant."

"No, he's been right to complain," Jimmy says. "It's been a shit-show, and we can't afford it. But in the end there's nothing more important to me than baseball, and I'm not about to let anything fuck it up. So let's go to Boston and let's play our fucking faces off, and let's bring this thing back to Baltimore, all right?"

Tuck claps first, God love him. The rest of them join in a moment later until the sound of it is almost loud enough to fill the chasm in Jimmy's chest. And if it still feels a little like the fucking wind is whistling through his ribs in there every time he thinks about what happened with Lacey, well, this is for the best, Jimmy reminds himself firmly. He's exactly where he's supposed to be.

"Come on," he says, slinging his arm around Ray's shoulders and steering the kid back across the ballfield, the sun high and bright in the sky. "Let's get out of here, huh? We've got a fuckin' flight to catch."

\\\\\\\\\

THEY PULL IT TOGETHER, THANK FUCK. THEY MORE THAN PULL IT together, actually: they win Game 5 against Boston and they win the first three games against the Astros in the League Championship Series the following week, the Texas air thick and hot and still. They lose two in a row after that, but they don't even feel like losses, exactly; they feel like stopovers, like breaks before they win again. They make mistakes and fix them. They identify their problems and they correct. And sure, the press keeps right on asking him about Lacey at every available opportunity, but Jimmy's got no problem telling them he's got nothing to say about that, because he does in fact have nothing to say about it. He wanted to concentrate, and he's concentrating. He wanted to win, and here they are.

The problem, of course, is that he feels like absolute shit.

It's not that he's lonely, exactly. After all, he's never fucking alone. He's either playing baseball, preparing to play baseball, or sleeping, calling pitches all through his dreams. Still, he wakes up every morning with a stiffness in his joints and a heaviness in his shoulders, a gnawing uneasiness he can't shake. He remembers this from after his divorce, the feeling of having perpetually just misplaced something. He tells himself, sternly, that it will pass.

It . . . does not so much seem to be passing.

Still, one thing about Jimmy is that he's a goddamn Hall of Famer when it comes to ignoring pain and discomfort, so he grits his teeth and pushes through it as much as humanly possible. He takes his fucking fish oil. He ices his swollen knees. This is it, he reminds himself every single morning in the mirror. This is the moment he's been waiting for his entire fucking career.

Ike calls from New York the morning of Game 6 against the Astros. "You all right?" he asks gruffly, the city clanging away in the background. "You need help?"

"Yeah," Jimmy jokes, "that'd be great, actually. You want to come down to the clubhouse, give me some pointers on my swing?"

"Cute."

"We're playing pretty well, actually," Jimmy teases. "We're in the ALCS. Dunno if you've seen on the news."

"I'll wait 'til you're finished," Ike says, then keeps talking anyway. "I don't mean with the baseball, dumbass. I mean with the . . . romantic shenanigans."

That makes Jimmy laugh. "I'm all right," he says, which isn't untrue, strictly speaking. "I can handle the romantic shenanigans on my own." He rubs a hand over his beard. "Anyway, I gotta tell you, I appreciate the offer, but you're a little late. That's over, anyway."

"Is it?" Ike asks. "That's too bad. She was very definitely out of your league."

"Thanks for that."

"Just saying. You doing all right?"

Jimmy shrugs even though Ike can't see him. "I'll live."

"I'm sure you will," Ike says agreeably. "So what's next, then?"

"Well, I've got the World Series coming up, hopefully. So that'll probably eat the next couple of weeks."

"Oh, you're on fire today." Ike snorts. "I'm talking about after the Series."

"Oh." Jimmy considers. "I don't know. A vacation, I guess. Double knee replacement. A brand partnership with a company that manufactures glucosamine."

This time Ike doesn't even bother to tell him he's not funny. "I mean it," he says instead. "You have something planned for yourself? Are you getting a dog? I've known you since you were a kid, Jimmy. You are not the kind of guy who is going to go gracefully into retirement."

Jimmy scowls. "I have a dog," he protests grouchily, though it's not like he doesn't know what Ike is getting at. It's been staring at him, the future, open-mouthed and hungry. He's not entirely sure it won't eat him alive. "Two, actually. At the farm."

"Good for you." Ike is unmoved. "I mean it. It's hard for a lot of guys after, especially if you're, you know. Unattached."

"I hear you." Jimmy grits his teeth. He doesn't want to talk about feelings with Ike. He doesn't want to talk about feelings with anyone, actually. It's a thing that happened, him and Lacey. It's over now. It's fine. He's not about to fall apart over it.

"All right," Ike says finally, still sounding less than convinced. "I'll see you out there."

"See you out there," Jimmy promises, and hangs up. He keeps the phone in his hand, though—turning it over and over like a worry stone, feeling the smooth, warm weight of it in his palm. At last he opens his contacts and scrolls to Rachel's name. He stares at the screen for a long time, his thumb hovering over the button to dial. Then shoves the thing back into his pocket altogether and takes the elevator downstairs to his car.

\\\\\\\\

RACHEL LIVES WAY OUT IN A POSTWAR DEVELOPMENT IN Towson, blocks and blocks of tidy raised ranches all in a row. The house is small, maybe half the size of the new-build McMansion she and Jimmy lived in when they were first married, with a Radio Flyer trike in the driveway and red geraniums in the window boxes. A trio of pumpkins sit crookedly on the front steps.

Jimmy parks on the street, then heads up the front walk to ring the doorbell, looking uneasily over his shoulder as he goes. It feels abruptly like a donkey move on his part to have come out here in broad daylight, knowing anyone could have followed him. Knowing anyone could have seen. There haven't been a ton of photographers outside his house the last few days—Lacey's fans know she's back in LA, and none of them, it turns out, are particularly interested in Jimmy for Jimmy's sake—but still. That's all he fucking needs, a headline breathlessly announcing he's throwing Lacey Logan over for his ex-wife right before Game 6 of the ALCS.

Assuming his ex-wife even answers her door. Jimmy stands on the stoop for a long moment, hands shoved into his pockets, rocking back on his heels. He's just about to give up and tell himself he did his best when the lock snicks open.

"*Jimmy?*" Rachel squints at him through the screen. "Oh my god."

"Uh." Jimmy holds his empty hands up. It occurs to him, belatedly, that he should have brought her something, a plant or a box of bakery muffins. A list of all the reasons he knows he's a piece of shit. "Hi."

"*Hi.*" She looks past him—she's checking for reporters, too, he realizes, and feels the back of his neck get warm. "Are you okay? Is something wrong?"

Jimmy shakes his head. "Nothing's wrong," he says, feeling awkward and deeply selfish. Fuck, he should have called before he came. He thought—he guesses he thought—

That's the problem with you, Jimmy, Rachel said to him once, right before their divorce was final. *You never think.* "I didn't mean to get the jump on you."

"Didn't you?" Rachel's lips twist. She's wearing her teaching clothes, jeans and a cotton sweater with little polka dots that he recognizes from way back when they were married. They haven't seen each other in four years. She's lost a lot of weight in a way he thinks is a shame, though he knows it's none of his fucking business. She's done something different with her hair.

"No, I just—" Jimmy blows a breath out. "Can I come in?"

Rachel hesitates. "Sure," she says finally, and opens the screen door so he can step inside. He brushes his cheek against hers by way of greeting, quick and polite, and the smell of her perfume makes him time travel.

The house is clean and quiet inside, with one of those big wooden signs that says HOME hanging on the wall in the foyer. Through the door of the den he briefly sees the profile of a toddler sitting on the carpet in front of the TV, something with blue cartoon dogs flickering jauntily across the screen. It turned out it wasn't that she didn't want to have kids, Rachel. She just didn't want to have them with him. Jimmy guesses he doesn't blame her for that.

"Can I get you anything?" she asks, once he's followed her into the kitchen. "A beer?"

"No," he says. "No, I'm not going to stay, I won't keep you." He tried to time this so her husband wouldn't be here; Jimmy doesn't particularly want the guy to walk in while he's standing here trying to do whatever he's trying to do here, and he can tell by the look on Rachel's face that she doesn't particularly want that, either.

"Okay." She stands on the other side of the breakfast bar, flattening her hands against the granite. "So what's up?"

Jimmy takes a deep breath. He had the whole ride over here to figure out what he was going to say to her. Fuck, he had four full years to figure out what he was going to say to her, but now— "How are you?"

Rachel quirks an eyebrow. "I'm good, thanks," she says slowly. "I'm really good."

"Good," he agrees. "I mean. I figured you were, I just—" He breaks off. "I'm sorry," he tries. "It's just I—I mean—" He blows out a breath. "I met someone."

"Yeah," Rachel says—and she's smirking at him openly now, though not unkindly. "I think I might have heard something about that." She straightens up. "Did you come all the way out here to let me down easy? Because I gotta tell you, buddy, it's a little late for—"

"No," he interrupts. "No, of course not." He laughs. "I guess I just—I met someone, and then I turned around and immediately fucked it up, which won't be super surprising to you, I'm sure, but the point is, it made me remember that I owed you an apology for fucking our thing up that I had never actually gotten around to delivering, so. I wanted to finally nut up and do that." He clears his throat. "I'm really sorry about all of it, Rach."

Rachel is quiet for a long moment, looking at him across the breakfast bar. Sometimes Jimmy used to think she could see the bones underneath his skin. "How'd you fuck it up?" she asks finally, tilting her head to the side with an expression on her face like she's expecting this to be amusing. "With your, ah. New someone."

Jimmy laughs again, yanking at his beard a little. "I don't know," he says, glancing past her. "By being myself, probably."

Right away, Rachel shakes her head. "Uh-uh," she says flatly. "That's a bullshit answer."

"It's—" Jimmy startles. "What?"

"It's a bullshit answer," she repeats, "on top of which it begs a kind of blanket absolution I have to tell you I'm not necessarily inclined to provide."

Oh, this very well may have been a big mistake. "Rach—"

"Don't *Rach* me, Jimmy." Rachel's voice is perfectly even. "You drop in out of the blue after literal years and tell me you ruined your new thing by being yourself; I tell you *no*, yourself was never that bad, at which point we hug it out and you go on your merry way feeling confident that whatever actually happened between you and that woman not only couldn't have been your fault but also couldn't have possibly been prevented? Is that what you were picturing when you came over here?"

"I—" Jimmy snaps his mouth shut. It kind of *was* what he was picturing, if he's being completely honest with himself, but hearing it out loud makes him feel like a psychopath. "I—"

"Well?" Rachel raises an eyebrow.

Jimmy swallows hard. "On second thought," he tells her sheepishly, "I think I actually will take that beer."

That makes her smile, just a little. "I only have the douchey kind."

"The douchey kind is great."

Rachel pulls a bottle from the fridge and holds it out in his direction, but when he moves to take it from her hand she holds on an extra second. "I chased you our entire marriage, Jimmy," she says quietly. "I was *desperate* for you to come to me, do you understand that? To trust me, to tell me things, to show me you loved me as much as you loved baseball. *That's* the thing I want you to apologize for. Not for all of it; not for your whole personality. I want you to apologize for never chasing me back."

Jimmy takes the beer and sets it down on the counter without opening it—absorbing her words in silence, looking at her here in her lovely new life. "I can see that," he tells her truthfully. "I'm so sorry, Rach."

Rachel holds his gaze for another moment, then shrugs and clears her throat. "Well," she says. "For the record: yourself was never that bad."

"Okay." Jimmy feels himself smiling at her: her slightly exasperated expression, her hair falling in her face. Rachel was the first woman he ever loved, and standing here he can feel a satisfying ache in his chest, a longing not for the past he might have had but for the future that might still be in front of him, one full of adventure and high drama and the sound of someone singing old rock and roll songs on weekend mornings. He feels abruptly certain of what he wants, here in this kitchen. He feels suddenly sure.

"Mommy!" comes a small voice just then, drifting in from down the hallway. "Can I watch another one?"

"You may not," Rachel calls back. "I'll be there in one second." She looks at Jimmy. "I should probably—"

"Yeah," he says quickly, "yeah, I'll leave you to it. Thank you, for this. For talking to me."

"Of course," she replies. "You too. And hey, good luck out there tonight."

Outside the autumn light is toasty, the air still decently warm if you stand directly in the sun. Jimmy detours by the farm instead of going directly back to the city, leaving the Tahoe running in the driveway and wandering around the back of the house. It's been a couple of weeks since he's been out here and he was expecting the garden to be mostly buttoned up for the year, but as the dogs trot gamely along behind him down the gravel path he realizes with a jolt of surprise that everything is still busy growing: The bees are still buzzing lazily around the flowers. The tomatoes are still red on the vines. Jimmy's lived in Maryland for a decade and a half now, but still he manages to forget this every single year: back in Utica the grass on his mother's front yard will have frosted over, but here the growing season doesn't finish until damn near Christmas. In a lot of ways, this is actually the best part.

"How about that, huh?" Jimmy says, reaching down to scratch the dogs underneath their soft, graying muzzles. "Turns out it's not over yet."

CHAPTER TWENTY-ONE

LACEY

HE DOESN'T CALL, OBVIOUSLY.

Not that Lacey thought he was going to, but.

She hoped.

She flies back to LA the morning after their horrible fight in his apartment. After all, what else is she going to do, spend the rest of her life alone in a suite at the Ritz-Carlton in Baltimore wearing her stupid Jimmy Hodges jersey? Not like she's never been dumped before, she consoles herself. She still has the playlist on her phone from last time, so. That's convenient. It's called *Like a Fish Needs a Bicycle*, which Lacey thought was very clever seven months ago but now just kind of makes her want to barf.

Javi picks her up and they take the service elevator downstairs beside a maintenance guy clutching an industrial vacuum cleaner and not even bothering to pretend he isn't staring at her. "Tough break last night," he says sympathetically as they whoosh toward the parking garage. "How's your boy Hodges doing?"

Lacey musters her most beguiling smile, hoping her face isn't noticeably puffy, that this stranger isn't going to think too hard about why apparently she slept here last night and not at Jimmy's condo in Fells Point. "Oh, he's fine," she promises airily. "He'll be okay."

She knows he will, too, the way he's wired. That's the worst part.

The problem with the tour being over is there's nothing to do to distract herself. Back in Malibu she wanders the house feeling restless and edgy and out of sorts: picking things up and putting them down again, walking into rooms before abruptly realizing she has no idea what she's there for. She picks a low-hanging fight with a Republican sports columnist from the *Wall Street Journal*. She calls her real estate agent and asks him to put together some listings in the Hollywood Hills. She writes a moody piano ballad, the chorus of which is an extended metaphor about Miss Havisham from *Great Expectations*, then rips it out of her notebook and throws it into the garbage.

"What do you think about me doing some surprise dates while I'm here?" she asks Maddie, the two of them and Claire eating superfood-packed grain salads from Erewhon in Lacey's backyard as a pair of hummingbirds zip though the jasmine that rings the pool.

"Here?" Maddie asks, sounding surprised. "Like, in LA?"

"Yeah!" Lacey says, briefly buoyed by the idea. She learned her lesson about lying, though she hasn't told the two of them the whole truth, either, just mentioning as casually as possible after her trip to Baltimore that she and Jimmy had decided to lie low while he focused on the playoffs. "At the Greek or someplace, maybe? Something intimate, just real fans. We could run a contest for tickets."

Maddie's gaze flicks for half a second over to Claire. "We could," she hedges, "but the logistics of that might get complicated on such short notice."

"Well, sure," Lacey says, "but not so complicated that we couldn't make it happen, right? I mean, we've certainly done harder things."

"We certainly have," Maddie agrees carefully. "I do think, though, that in light of the headlines, there might be some danger of overexposure."

"Oh," Lacey says, feeling abruptly foolish. The press coverage has been . . . bad, pages and pages of commentary about how Lacey is directly responsible for the collapse of Jimmy's career, the Baltimore Orioles, and major league sports in general. It's not that she didn't expect that—of *course* she expected that—but she's surprised by how true it feels even though it's objectively not, even though his team just took the League Championship and the prevailing wisdom seems to be that they've got a pretty good shot at winning the World Series, too. Of course, Lacey is out of his life now, so. Maybe everyone else knew what they were talking about after all. "Right. Totally."

"Could be better to let people miss you for a few weeks," Maddie continues, spearing an artichoke heart on her fork.

"Besides," Claire jumps in, "you've been going a million miles an hour for months now. No shame in taking a break before the European leg."

"Of course," Lacey agrees. "I should rest."

She . . . doesn't rest. She can barely even sleep, just lying there all night, every night tangled in the sheets, rehashing that last argument with Jimmy over and over in her mind. She doesn't know why this feels so much worse than it did with Toby, why it feels like some kind of yawning hole has opened up where her heart and lungs used to be. She and Jimmy barely knew each other, she reminds herself. Whatever happened between them was, unequivocally, a rebound fling. He'll go off and play in the World Series and she'll go to Europe on tour and they'll be funny, slightly wistful anecdotes in each other's memoirs one day, and if, in the meantime, she keeps thinking about his stupid farm and his stupid horses and his stupid good face, the tiny crow's feet around his eyes when he smiles, well, that's nobody's business but Lacey's own.

She googles *Jimmy Hodges + postseason*.

She googles *Jimmy Hodges + breakup*.

She throws her phone across the room.

\\\\\\\\

DAYS PASS. LACEY WALLOWS. SHE SPENDS LONG NIGHTS IN HER leggings with her laptop warm on her lap and her phone in her hand, reading through Tumblr posts and Twitter threads, clicking over to the Explore tab on Instagram. She taught the algorithm a long time ago to feed her basically only posts about herself, which used to feel satisfying but now just feels a little bit sick, like she's an ouroboros consuming her own content in an endless, queasy loop. She needs to get a hobby. Hell, she needs to get a *life*.

There is one post that catches her eye, though, a cheeky selfie of Henrietta Lang in front of a cluster of palm trees: *Los Angeles,* the caption reads, *I am in you! Come see us tonite at the El Rey Theatre.* The photo is time-stamped from this morning, which means the show doesn't start for—Lacey clicks over to Henrietta's website to confirm—a little over six hours.

Which is, she thinks, a smile spreading over her face alone here in her bedroom, plenty of time to decide what to wear.

Powered up by a sudden burst of energy, Lacey throws off her covers and scampers toward the bathroom for a long-overdue shower—then stops in the middle of the rug and feels her shoulders drop, reflexively beginning the long and laborious process of talking herself out of the idea. She thinks of every talking head on ESPN accusing her of turning the Division Series into a circus. She thinks of Maddie's warning her she's already overexposed. Still, Lacey thinks, it wouldn't necessarily have to be a huge deal, would it? Maybe Jimmy was right, that people are only weird about her because she expects them to be, because she invites it. Maybe it's possible to fly under the radar after all.

Lacey picks up her phone, starts a new text to Javi. *Hi!* she begins, her heart thrumming with the disproportionate thrill of doing something brave and spontaneous. Something that's just for her. *I'm going to go see Henrietta Lang at the El Rey tonight and would like to travel light.*

Sure, Javi texts back. *Though I think a team of three would be more appropriate for a venue of that size.*

Lacey bites her lip. She knows this is as close as Javi will likely get to telling her he thinks it's a bad idea, and normally it would be enough to cow her, but instead she sets her jaw. *I think it'll be fine,* she insists, hoping she sounds more confident than she's necessarily feeling. *I'll sneak in late and leave early.*

Claire texts her fifteen minutes later, predictably. *Hey there!* she begins. *Javi told me you're planning to go to the Henrietta Lang show tonight. So cool! I did just want to share that I reached out to the venue and they can provide a seat in a private area up on the second level but won't have any extra security available. I know Javi mentioned you wanted to travel light so I did just want to be sure we were okay with that!*

Lacey chews her lip for a moment, briefly losing her courage. Probably after everything the smart move would be to just stay in tonight. She could invite Claire over to watch a movie and order

ramen; they could get ice cream sandwiches from Van Leeuwen,
try some of the million high-end beauty products Lacey's always
getting sent in the mail. She's almost decided to scuttle the whole
endeavor entirely when all at once she shakes her head, remembering how disappointed she was with herself when she chickened
out and missed Henrietta's show back in New York. Maybe she
doesn't have to submit her every decision to focus-group testing.
Why shouldn't she just do what she wants to do?

Yup! That's fine! she types, hitting send and marching herself
up to her closet to pick an outfit.

〰〰〰

LACEY HAS NEVER PERFORMED AT THE EL REY—SHE GOT HER
start on the festival circuit, state fairs and opening gigs for boy
bands, then quickly leapfrogged to headlining arena shows of her
own—but she's always loved the look of it: the enormous chande-
liers and the art deco sensibility, the brilliant neon lights of the mar-
quee. She sneaks in just as Henrietta's opening band is finishing up
later that night, smiling her thanks to a gawking attendant and following Javi across the lush red carpet of the lobby. What she really
would have liked to do is disappear into the crowd down in general
admission—she used to love to do that when she was younger, to
stand crushed shoulder to shoulder in a thick, anonymous sea of
bodies, her arms thrust into the air with wild abandon—but she
knows that's ridiculous, so she trails Javi obediently up a narrow
flight of stairs to the box reserved for her up in the mezzanine,
sitting down in one of the two folding chairs lined up side by side.
Lacey glances at the empty seat for a second, trying not to think
about anyone who might or might not be sitting here beside her
in an alternate universe, but before she can start to feel too sorry

for herself the lights are going down and the crowd is whooping and clapping and cheering, Henrietta is stepping onto the stage in wide-leg jeans and an oversized blazer, slinging the strap of her guitar over her head.

Lacey leans forward and rests her chin on the railing, unable to keep a slow, reflexive smile from spreading across her face. This is what she loves about music, the way it engages her brain and her heart and her body. The way it calms the endless churn of her mind. For a moment it doesn't matter that Toby's spreading garbage about their breakup or that she besmirched Jimmy Hodges's precious postseason. All that matters is the sound of Henrietta's voice ringing out in the darkness. All that matters is the beat of the drums. Lacey loses herself completely to the melody and the lyrics, and later it will occur to her that that's why she doesn't notice when the energy in the room starts to change.

It's whispers at first, a general restlessness—at least, she thinks it is; by the time she registers the sound it's turned into a murmur, some commotion at the back of the lower level near the doors. Lacey sits back in her seat, glancing over her shoulder for Javi and trying to ignore the creeping instinct for approaching danger she's honed over a dozen years in the spotlight, but when she turns back around and chances a look down at the crowd, she realizes with a start that Henrietta has all but lost them. Almost nobody down there is even facing the stage anymore, all of them craning their necks and peering curiously up into the mezzanine.

Almost everyone is looking for her.

That's the moment when a hand drops onto her shoulder; when Lacey turns around to look at him, Javi's face is grave. "Hey," he says, and she can tell by how preternaturally calm he sounds that this is about to be a total shitshow. "We've got a little bit of a situation."

\\\\\\\\

WORD IS OUT, JAVI TELLS HER. SOMEBODY POSTED A PICTURE OF her on Instagram; there's a group of fans outside the venue, trying to push their way into the building. They need to get out of here, and they need to get out of here now.

"Okay," Lacey says—nodding obediently, already getting to her feet. The crowd in the mezzanine has grown by at least half since she got here, she realizes suddenly; there are people on the stairs now, the venue's security trying unsuccessfully to clear them out. "Let's go."

Javi takes her arm as they head quickly toward the staircase, doing his best to clear the path in front of them, to shove the grasping limbs out of their way. "There she is!" someone shouts, and Lacey feels herself flinch. She moves as best and as quickly as she can, ducking as people grab at her, touching her hair and her clothes and her hands. She trips on the last couple of stairs, stumbling for one terrifying second before Javi pulls her roughly to her feet.

"I'm sorry," she says, but he doesn't reply so she repeats herself once, then again and again until it's just a chant she's muttering over and over as he steers her along. This has happened twice before—once at a concert in Singapore, and another time at a radio festival in Nashville—but both of those times she had the whole team with her, a phalanx of protection to get her safely into the car. *I think it will be fine!* she told him this afternoon, like some kind of idiot. She's never felt like such an amateur in her entire life.

"Keep your head down," Javi advises, raising his voice so she can hear him over the screaming. Dimly she can hear that Henrietta has stopped playing; faintly she's aware of her asking everyone to please be cool. "Let's just get into the car."

"Should we—"

"Into the *car*, Lacey." It's the most sharply he's ever spoken to her in all the years they've known each other, and it's not until that moment that Lacey is really and truly afraid.

The air changes after what feels like an eternity, the smell of the night and the pavement all around her, and Lacey realizes all at once she's been squeezing her eyes shut; when she opens them again Javi is shoving her into the back seat of the SUV. Her driver in LA is usually a guy named Kevin, but Kevin is on vacation and so it's someone else tonight, Steven or Stephen. Normally Lacey is much better about getting names. Shit, she's really rattled. This was such an enormously bad idea. "What the *fuck*," Steven/Stephen says as Javi climbs into the passenger seat, slamming the door behind him. He's bleeding a little, Lacey sees with a gasp, right at the side of his mouth.

"Just drive," Javi orders.

"Yeah, I'm trying!" the driver snaps, leaning on the horn, the sound of it enough to make Lacey cover her ears. The crowd is too thick: they're pounding on the roof, on the windows, the sound of it like a hailstorm. Like bombs falling. Like the end of the world. "I'm going to fucking kill someone."

"I'm sorry," Lacey says over and over. "I'm sorry, I'm sorry."

Javi ignores her. "Is one of them on the—one of them is on the fucking car."

It's more than one of them, Lacey realizes with horror. It's three and then four of them like something out of a zombie movie, all of them banging on the windows, all of them screaming her name. It occurs to her, not for the first time, that her fans may love her deeply, but also if given the opportunity they might tear the flesh right off her bones.

At last they break free from the crowd and pull off down the street, Lacey going limp in the back seat with sudden safety, with the feeling of a near miss. "Fucking insane kids," the driver mumbles.

"I'm so sorry," Lacey says again. Already she's planning how she's going to handle this with him and with Javi, with a bonus or vacation time or a Rolex. She'll send something to the staff at the venue. She'll smooth it over with Henrietta.

But Javi isn't listening, craning his neck to look out the window. "We're not done," he says grimly. "On your left."

Lacey's heart sinks at the sight of the black SUV creeping up behind them. Still, "It's fine," she insists. She can recognize photographers when she sees them. "The windows are tinted. They're not going to get anything."

"Maybe," Javi says, pulling out his cell phone. "But I'm not taking any more chances tonight, are you? I'm calling the cops."

"Don't bother," the driver says, stepping on the gas. "I can shake 'em off."

He can't, though; Lacey watches in horror as the second car pulls up alongside them—way too close, incessant. "They're going to run us off the fucking road," Javi says, then turns his attention to whoever has picked up on the other end of the line. "Hello? My name is Javier Mendoza. I'm head of security for the entertainer Lacey Logan. We're headed south on—" He cranes his neck. "Where the fuck are we?" he asks, or starts to, and the last thing that Lacey remembers is the shriek of the tires on the pavement. The jolt of the crash in her bones.

CHAPTER TWENTY-TWO

JIMMY

TUCK CALLS AND WAKES HIM UP AT SIX THIRTY, THE LIGHT JUST leaking through the bedroom windows and the last of the birds barely waking up outside the glass. "Yo," he says when Jimmy mumbles a groggy hello, "is Lacey okay? Did you fly out there?"

"What?" Jimmy struggles upright, rubbing a dazed, sleepy hand over his face. Tuck doesn't know they broke up. Nobody knows they broke up, really; Jimmy hasn't said anything to anyone, assuming Lacey would at some point send him further instructions via carrier pigeon or a chip she had secretly implanted in his brain while he slept. She hasn't, though, and the last week or so the thought has occurred to Jimmy that it's possible she'll leave him hanging indefinitely as a final fuck you, fielding questions about her at every media appearance he makes for the short remainder of his career and into whatever he winds up doing next until one day it suddenly comes to light that she's been married to the son of an oligarch from Monaco for eleven years. "Um. No, why?"

"What do you mean, why?" Tuck sounds incredulous. "You didn't talk to her?"

"Not this morning," Jimmy admits, which isn't a lie. "Why, what's going on?"

"Dude," Tuck says, "she got got by some huge, crazy mob of fans in LA last night. I think she's in the hospital." A pause. "She really didn't call you? Everything okay with you guys?"

"Everything's fine," Jimmy manages. "Everything is great."

He hangs up without saying goodbye, opening the browser on his phone and searching. Sure enough, two seconds later: *Megastar Lacey Logan Hospitalized Following Crowd Incident in LA.*

Jimmy's vision starts to swim as his eyes flick over the headlines, the panicky taste of iron hot at the back of his mouth. He thinks of his mom calling to tell him about Matty, about how soft and sorry her voice was. This isn't that, he scolds himself almost immediately, scanning the article; this is nothing like that.

Still, though. Still.

He chugs the glass of water on his nightstand, forces himself to read more carefully: A concert, a car accident. *Security at the venue was quickly overwhelmed.* A never-ending cascade of hot takes:

Looking for attention just like always

This is why we can't have nice things!!!!

Police are investigating the cause of the accident, which according to sources familiar with the incident occurred when the SUV in which Logan was riding was pursued by a second vehicle as she attempted to leave the venue.

Making everything about her.

It's Lacey Logan's world, including at other people's concerts, apparently.

Logan was treated for what her publicist described as "minor injuries" at Cedars-Sinai and released.

Jimmy scans three more pages of Google results trying to figure out how hurt she was, exactly, then realizes he's being an enormous fucking chump and calls her instead. *Are you okay?* he texts, when she doesn't answer. *You don't have to talk to me if you don't want to. I get it if you don't want to talk to me. I just want to make sure you're okay.*

Her reply comes through a moment later: *It's four in the fucking morning here, James.*

Then, before he has time to be properly abashed: *I miss you.*

Jimmy's whole body goes briefly boneless; he flops backward onto the mattress, scrubbing a hand over his beard. He thinks of what Rachel said to him back in her kitchen. He thinks of what Lacey said to him the last time they fought.

He has to report to Camden for Game 1 of the World Series in a little over twenty-six hours.

He doesn't have time for distractions.

He needs to make a choice.

"Fuck me," Jimmy mumbles out loud in the empty apartment, then gets up off his bed to go pack.

\\\\\\\\\

HE FLIES COMMERCIAL, OBVIOUSLY, LIKE A SCHMUCK, THOUGH HE has his assistant call a black car to meet him at LAX. "Mr. Hodges," the driver says, when he comes down the elevator at baggage claim. "Do you have luggage?"

"Nope," Jimmy says, holding up the same battered Nike backpack he's been carrying since he was a rookie. "There's actually a not-insignificant chance we're going to wind up coming directly back to the airport in an hour."

The driver's thick eyebrows twitch, but he doesn't comment.

Jimmy follows him through the crowded airport and into the parking garage; they cruise in silence down the 405 toward Malibu, the palm trees rolling by outside the tinted windows of the SUV. More people could stand to have this guy's discretion, in Jimmy's opinion, though he guesses it's also entirely possible he has the woman who runs the Sinclair on speed dial and this whole dumbass gambit will be all over the internet before he even gets a chance to do what he came all the way out here to do. It's always a possibility, when it comes to Lacey Logan. Turns out, it's a risk Jimmy's willing to take.

"You can just pull over up here," he says finally, when according to his phone they're half a mile from her complex. "I've got to, uh—make a call."

Jimmy grits his teeth, the full idiocy of this particular endeavor hitting him all at once as he scrolls to her number in his contacts. He didn't tell her he was coming here. She isn't expecting him, and it's not like he can stroll up to her porch and ring the doorbell; just watch her tell him to go fuck himself and leave him standing out there in front of who the fuck knows how many dozens of cameras while she holes up with her ex. A few hours ago, this felt not just romantic but like something he was committed to do, like the only path forward. Now, all at once, he feels like an enormous swinging dick.

He takes a deep breath, dials her number. "I really am okay," she says, when she picks up. "This isn't something where you have to feel sorry for me and—"

"I'm not calling because I feel sorry for you," Jimmy interrupts her. "I'm calling because I'm outside."

Lacey barks a laugh at that, sharp and a tiny bit hysterical-sounding. "Shut up," she instructs, her voice wobbling a little. "No you're not."

"Well, no," Jimmy admits. "I'm not right outside, technically. But I'm, you know. Close. If you have time to hang out for a little bit."

"Has anybody seen you?"

"Not yet," he says. "Why, you want me to hop out and go say hello?"

But Lacey doesn't answer. "Wait a second," she says instead. "How are you—don't you have—I mean. Doesn't the World Series start, like. Tomorrow?"

That makes him smile, he can't help it. "You're a person who pays attention to when the World Series starts now, huh?"

"Shut up," Lacey tells him again. "Yes. Answer me."

Jimmy glances up at the driver, still assiduously pretending not to listen. "Yeah," he admits. "Starts tomorrow."

"And you came here."

"Yeah, Lacey. I came here."

"Okay," Lacey says softly. "Well. I'll have Claire open the gate."

\\\\\\\\

SHE'S NOT WEARING ANY MAKEUP, IS THE FIRST THING JIMMY NO-tices. It makes her look younger, more vulnerable than he thinks of her as being. Her mouth is pale and thin. "Hi," he says, tucking his hands safely into his pockets so he doesn't reach for her, then pulls one out again to offer a wave to Claire. "Good to see you again."

Claire nods like, frankly, she could take him or leave him. He's going to have to work on that, Jimmy thinks. "Lacey," Claire says, "if you're okay here, I'll—" She motions toward the door.

"Yeah," Lacey says. "Yes, of course. Thank you."

They're alone then, the house huge and quiet all around them. Lacey sits down on the couch. "I need to fix things with her," she says, nodding in the direction of the driveway. She's wearing a fancy gray sweatsuit and slippers, her dark hair in a braid down her back. "Claire, I mean. Although let's be real, I need to fix things with everybody."

Jimmy frowns. "Everybody like who?" he asks, but Lacey doesn't answer.

"You really didn't have to come out here," she tells him instead. "I didn't mean to make you worry, especially if you've got your whole—" She shakes her head, pulling one knee up to her chest. "I'm fine."

"Oh, yeah," Jimmy tells her, sitting down on the enormous tufted ottoman across from her and stretching his legs out, his ankle just barely knocking hers. "You look great."

"Fuck you," she says, but she's smiling a little. She's got her wrist wrapped in an Ace bandage. "It's not a big deal," she says, when she catches him looking. "It's not even broken. I'll be fine for the next leg of the tour." She waggles her fingers in jazz hands to illustrate, then she stops halfway through and abruptly starts to cry.

Jimmy startles. He's never seen her cry before and before he knows what he's doing he crosses the space between them, sitting back on the couch beside her and pulling her gently into his lap. He holds her for a long time while her body shakes, these huge sobs that feel like they're coming from her marrow. "I'm so embarrassed," she says into his chest, her tears leaving wet spots on his T-shirt. "I fucked up."

"How did you fuck up?"

"Something could have happened to those kids. Something could have happened to Javi—"

"Javi was doing his job."

"I told him I didn't want more security!" Lacey wails. "He suggested more—everyone suggested more; everyone *more* than suggested it—and I told him I wanted to travel light."

Jimmy shrugs. "It's Javi's job to put his foot down," he argues. "It's his job to make sure what you're doing is safe."

But Lacey shakes her head. "Nobody ever puts their foot down with me," she reminds him. "And I knew that, and I took advantage of it." She pulls back to look at him, her face red and blotchy and beautiful. "I like being who I am," she says. "I *love* being who I am, but I just, after everything—I wanted to be somebody else for a minute, you know? And I thought maybe I could just . . . take a break really quick. Blend in, be like everybody else." She shrugs. "But I couldn't."

"I get it," Jimmy murmurs, twisting the end of her braid around two fingers. "I do."

Lacey sighs, sitting back and clearing her throat a little, smoothing her good hand over the wet spots on his shirt. "I'm sorry I ruined your game," she announces.

Right away, Jimmy shakes his head. "You didn't ruin my game."

"Everyone thinks I did," Lacey counters. "*You* thought I did."

"Yeah, well, I was being an asshole," Jimmy declares with a shrug, "and fuck everybody else. I'm a grown-ass man and a professional fucking athlete. I can ruin my own games." He pulls her closer again, leaning back so her head rests against his chest. "Anyway, it turned out fine. We're going to the World Series."

"I saw," she says with a watery smile. "I pay attention to that stuff now. Congrats."

"Thanks," Jimmy tells her, then feels himself hedge. "I mean, we'll see how it goes."

But Lacey shakes her head. "You're going to win," she says, and Jimmy nods.

"Yeah," he agrees, and feels himself grin with the truth of it. "I'm going to win." He's done dicking around and half-assing. He's done trying to protect himself by acting like he isn't desperate for all the things he wants.

"I know you think I should say I'm sorry," she tells him. "For being a distraction, or whatever. For showing up and thunder-stealing. For being as big as I am."

Jimmy stares at her. "That's not what I want you to say."

"Isn't it?"

"Of course it's not what I want you to say," he says, a little offended. "Why would I ever want you to say that? It would be bullshit, first of all."

"Well, yeah," she agrees with a slightly phlegmy laugh. "It would be."

Jimmy sighs, yanking at his beard in frustration. "Look," he tells her finally. "I knew what I was getting into the second I left that club with you in New York City. Maybe not the details," he says, anticipating her protest, "but the general outline. I knew who you were, Lacey. I knew what your situation was. And you asked me if I wanted to leave with you, and I said yes." He shakes his head. "How much fucking space you take up is one of my favorite things about you. What I'm sorry about is that I didn't have the balls to be as honest about who I am and what I wanted as you are. As you always have been."

She lifts an eyebrow. "Oh yeah?"

Jimmy nods. "I should have said I didn't feel ready for that whole big night out in Cincinnati. And I should have been honest about not being sure it was a good idea for you to come to the game. And, like"—he holds a hand up—"I know I was the one who wanted to go out to breakfast that day, and I know I was the one who was like, *What's the big deal about being public*—"

"You were," Lacey agrees quietly. "And when I tried to tell you what it was actually going to be like—"

"I was an idiot," Jimmy agrees with a shrug, "and I didn't listen. I talked a big game, but I was ultimately full of shit and underprepared, and I took it out on you. I'm really sorry, Lacey. I really do apologize."

Lacey is quiet for a moment once he's finished, then sits upright. Jimmy thinks she's about to climb out of his lap altogether but in the end she just shifts around to look at him, legs on either side of his thighs and the two of them face-to-face. "Wow," she says. "Can I ask you something? Are you sure you failed at couples therapy?"

Jimmy snorts, tipping his head back against the cushions. "I emphatically failed at couples therapy, yes."

"Well." She shrugs. "Sounds like you learned something."

"Not on purpose."

"Osmosis, then," Lacey decides, reaching up to worry a loose thread in the seam at his shoulder. "I'm sorry, too," she says eventually, "for knowing the whole press situation was kind of eating you alive and not doing anything to stop it. And for accusing you of wanting to be with me to stay relevant."

Jimmy shrugs. She's perched back on his knees, enough space between them for plausible deniability. He stops himself from pulling her closer, but barely. "It's a valid worry. I would worry about it, if I were you."

"I'm *not* worried about it," Lacey says hotly. "I said it specifically to hurt you. I've been around people who are using me, Jimmy. I can smell it on them. That's not what this is."

"No," Jimmy agrees, looking at her evenly. "That's not what this is."

"What is it, then?"

"I don't know, Lacey," he tells her honestly. "I don't know. I want to win this fucking Series. I want it like I've never wanted anything else. But then it's going to be over, and I know I *don't* want to go back to my condo with my ring and be proud of myself *by* myself and never talk to you again and feel weird every time one of your songs comes on the radio until finally I drop dead in a puddle of my own drool. I want you to be there when it's finished. I want something with you that's going to last." Jimmy takes a breath. His heart is pounding like he just ran suicides up and down the bleachers for an hour, knocking wildly around in his chest. "I'm serious about you, Lacey. I think I could be really fucking serious."

Lacey kisses him.

Right away Jimmy kisses her back, the pure, unadulterated relief of it like a hot shower after extra innings. The feeling is replaced a moment later with something darker, his head swimming, all the blood in his body rushing to his dick. *Easy*, he thinks as he nudges her mouth open, *be careful*, only it's not easy or careful, it's like somebody slammed open a fire door inside him and everything he's barely managed to hold back for the last couple of weeks, everything he told himself he wasn't really feeling, is raging out of him all at once in an uncontrollable blaze. He *missed* her, he realizes, hooking his hands behind her knees and pulling her toward him until their chests are fused together. He missed her tall, pretty body. He missed her expensive-perfume smell. "Where are you hurt?" he mutters into the crook of her neck, running careful hands over her ribs and stomach. He wants to strip her down and check her for damage. He wants to stand guard outside her door for the rest of his natural life.

"I'm okay," Lacey promises between kisses, wrapping her arms around his neck and scratching gentle fingers through the hair at the back of his neck. "You're good. Just touch me."

Jimmy does, tugging off her hoodie and peeling off the tank she's got on underneath it, unable to keep from wincing at the constellation of blue and purple bruises around her ribs and arms and shoulders. There's a mark in the shape of a hand where someone grabbed her through her clothes. "I'm sorry," he tells her, tracing a finger along the lace of her bra strap. "I should have been there."

Lacey laughs at that, full-throated. "Bro," she reminds him, "Javi spent fifteen years in the United States Marine Corps. I love you, but I gotta say I don't think you were the thing standing between me and—" She breaks off, blanching, both of them registering the confession at the same time. "Um." Lacey clears her throat. "Sorry. I just meant—"

"It's okay," he says. "I get it."

Lacey wrinkles her nose. "Sorry," she repeats, leaning forward and bumping their foreheads together. "Did I just make it weird?"

Jimmy shakes his head. "No," he promises, and kisses her again to show her he means it. He boosts her gently off his lap and peels the rest of her clothes off—taking his time about it, mindful of the bruised places. He kneels down in front of the sofa and tugs her gently toward the edge of it, then lifts her long, warm thighs up over his shoulders and sets about apologizing to her for real.

It takes some time, her hips shifting against the cushions, the muscles in her calves flexing and relaxing against his back. "Don't stop," she gasps, reaching down to thread her fingers through his hair, tugging a little. "Oh my god, Jimmy, please don't stop."

"Not stopping," he promises. Holy shit, is Jimmy not ever stopping, his whole world narrowing to her smell and her taste and the urgent way she's moving, her quiet, half-desperate sounds. He'll stay here while the rest of the team plays the Series without him, he thinks vaguely, working two gentle fingers inside her. He'll stay here until the day he dies.

"Come up here," she gasps when he's finally wrung it all out of her—her hands scrabbling for the hem of his thermal and yanking it up over his head, pulling at his shoulders so he'll come close and kiss her without bothering to peel his arms out of the sleeves. "I mean it, I want you to—"

"Yeah." Jimmy nods dazedly and nudges her back onto the cushions, but Lacey shakes her head. "Not here," she says, wrapping her arms around him. "In my bed."

So Jimmy scoops her up and carries her up the wide, curving staircase, down the long hallway to her room. The thermal's cutting at a weird angle across his neck, but he doesn't care. He sets her down on her bed, then gets up there beside her and lets her strip off his jeans and his boxers, running her hands across his stomach and chest like she's refamiliarizing herself with the topography of his body. Like she's checking to make sure he's really here.

"I love you, too," Jimmy says right before he pushes himself inside her, and as soon as it's out of his mouth he knows it's the truth. He loves her like the first day of pitchers and catchers reporting. He loves her like the bottom of the ninth. What's happening between them isn't a distraction. What's happening between them is the main event. "Hey. Lacey. I love you, too."

When it's over they lie there for a long time, the quiet of her house all around him. Jimmy uses one finger to trace ghost patterns over the skin of her back. "I'm going to Europe," she murmurs finally, her sleepy voice muffled against his chest.

Jimmy lifts his head to look at her. "Today?"

Lacey smiles. "After Christmas," she reminds him. "For the tour." She's quiet for a moment then, pushing herself up on her elbows. "I'm just, you know, putting it out there. On the off chance you're looking for something to do after you retire."

Jimmy laughs at that. "Sure," he says, letting himself picture it for a moment: waking up beside her in a hotel bed in Paris, waiting for her backstage in Berlin. "Europe sounds nice." He presses a kiss against her shoulder. "I got a couple of things I gotta do before then, though."

Lacey smiles, her dark eyes shining. "Just a couple of errands."

"Quick stop back home," he agrees. He raises an eyebrow. "Speaking of which: you, uh. Wanna come to a baseball game tomorrow night?"

"What?" Lacey shakes her head—she shakes her whole *body*—so hard she almost falls off the bed. "No!"

That surprises him. "Really?" he asks, propping himself up on one arm. "You don't?"

"No!" she insists again, sitting up and resting her chin on one bare knee. "Are you demented? You literally just said you were sorry you didn't tell me not to come the last time."

Jimmy makes a noncommittal sound, reaching out to tuck a loose strand of hair back behind her ear before flopping down onto the bed one more time. "Horse is out of the barn at this point, wouldn't you say?"

"Listen to you, with the farm metaphors." Lacey rolls her eyes. "Also, not for nothing, I don't seem to be what one might call a good luck charm."

"Yeah, well." Jimmy shrugs into her pillows. He likes how her sheets smell, like fresh air and lavender and whatever expensive shampoo she uses. Like Lacey herself. "Luck's for losers."

Lacey huffs out a noisy breath, but she's laughing, and that's how he knows he's got her. "Jimmy—"

"Look," he says, pulling her back down so she's lying sprawled across him, her sharp chin digging into his chest. He doesn't want to stop touching her. He never wants to stop touching her ever again. "I will be the first to admit that our last public outing left something to be desired. And if I'm not a good enough baseball player to win the Series with you there, then so be it. But I don't actually think that's true, do you?"

Lacey considers that for a moment. "No," she says. "I think you're exactly that good."

Jimmy smiles. "Yeah," he says, and ducks his head to kiss her. "I think I am, too."

\\\\\\\\

THE NEXT NIGHT, JIMMY STANDS IN THE LOCKER ROOM AT Camden, breathing in the familiar smell of bleach and sweat and listening to the sound of forty-five thousand baseball fans humming in the seats. His heart is a fist inside his chest. "You ready?" he asks, looking around at his guys. "Because this is it."

"Born ready," Tuck promises. "Let's do this, Cap."

Jimmy nods. "Let's do this," he echoes. He takes a deep breath and walks up the ramp through the tunnel, toward the field where the lights are shining brilliantly overhead. Jimmy glances up at the stands as he goes, at the place where he knows his future is waiting. Then he turns and crouches behind the plate.

ACKNOWLEDGMENTS

As a former theater kid turned professional writer there is no greater creative joy than throwing something out into the universe and having someone else say, "*Yes,*" and thank you to everyone who was so excited about the idea for this book when I mentioned it, mostly joking, on Instagram. Turns out I was serious, I guess??

Whenever anyone asks how I like my agent I tell them I would die for her, and I am not actually being facetious. Elizabeth Bewley, thank you for your steady hand and killer instincts and for patiently explaining rudimentary publishing things I 100 percent ought to know by now. I trust you completely and I am so glad we finally found each other after being ships in the night for so long.

HarperCollins has been my home for many years, and I am lucky to have a truly excellent team there. Thank you to Millicent Bennett for your keen and sophisticated eye, Liz Velez for literally everything, and Heather Drucker, Rachel Molland, Megan Looney, and Lisa Erickson for all you do to get my books into readers' hands. Thank you also to Michael Fierro and Jamie Kerner; extra thanks to Olivia McGiff for all your hard work on the cover, which is truly just perfect for this book.

A special thank-you to Suzette Lam and Susan Schwartz for the heroic last-minute assist.

Thank you to Sarah Enni and Zan Romanoff for their smart, engaging podcast *On the Bleachers*, which was hugely helpful to me as I tried to understand literally anything about professional sports. Mistakes are mine, which will not surprise anyone who ever knew me in gym.

Thank you to Lucy Keating for Jimmy Hodges's gold chain.

Cristina Lyons and Sara Sicilian, thank you for lunch club and for all the rest of it. What a treat when two of your new favorite characters show up halfway through the book.

Tom Colleran, thank you for this incredibly beautiful life of ours. I really just love you so enormously fucking much.

ABOUT THE AUTHOR

KATIE COTUGNO IS THE *NEW YORK TIMES* BESTSELLING AUTHOR of *Birds of California* and *Meet the Benedettos* as well as eight novels for young adults. She is also the coauthor (with Candace Bushnell) of *Rules for Being a Girl*. She lives in Boston with her family.

READ MORE FROM
Katie Cotugno

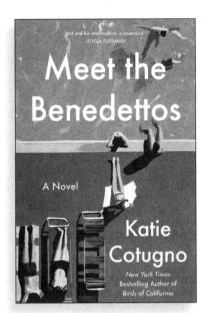

"A smart, sharp, sisterly take on *Pride and Prejudice*. Katie Cotugno writes with such precision, giving each character a chance to shine, while still giving readers what they want—smoldering, unshakable chemistry between Elisabetta and Darcy. It's hot and fun and modern, a must-read."

—ELISSA SUSSMAN, bestselling author of *Funny You Should Ask*

"Exquisite and delicious. . . . Cotugno has made a name for herself rendering messy, honest, tangled love stories. But with *Birds of California*, she has outdone herself."

—TAYLOR JENKINS REID, author of *Daisy Jones & The Six* and *Malibu Rising*